SEVEN MOON CIRCUS

The First Trilogy

SEVEN MOON CIRCUS

The First Trilogy

ESCAPE FROM VERDANTA
THE RINGS OF BARABOO
THE BATTLE OF CRESTIVAL

RANDY MORRISON

Ringleader Books, San Diego

Copyright © 2013 Randal R. Morrison. All rights reserved. Published by Ringleader Books, PO Box 531518, San Diego CA 92153-1518, USA. No part of this publication may be reproduced, stored in a retrieval system, or transmitted in any form or by any means, without written permission of the publisher.

Publisher's Cataloging-In-Publication Data
(Prepared by The Donohue Group, Inc.)

Morrison, Randy.
Seven moon circus. First trilogy / Randy Morrison ; [with illustrations by SC Watson].

p. : ill. ; cm. -- (7 moon circus ; [bks. 1-3])

"The adventures of a wild boy in a space traveling circus."--Cover.
Interest age level: 009-014.
Includes bibliographical references.
Contents: Bk. one. Escape from Verdanta -- bk. two. Rings of Baraboo -- bk. three. Battle of Crestival.

ISBN: 978-0-9892310-1-5

1. Feral children--Juvenile fiction. 2. Space travelers--Juvenile fiction. 3. Circus--Juvenile fiction. 4. Feral children--Fiction. 5. Travelers--Fiction. 6. Circus--Fiction. 7. Adventure stories. 8. Science fiction. I. Watson, S. C. II. Title. III. Title: 7 moon circus. IV. Title: Escape from Verdanta. V. Title: Rings of Baraboo. VI. Title: Battle of Crestival.

PZ7.M677 Sev 2013
[Fic]

This is a work of fiction. Any similarity of characters to real persons, living or deceased, is purely coincidental.

Printed in the United States of America

For Sherry, Piaolien Tai-Tai

With grateful appreciation to Alexander Patrick, Eli Mitchell, Inga, Shana, Karen and Deborah.

PLAYBILL

BOOK ONE: **ESCAPE FROM VERDANTA**

PROLOG 3

Chapter 1   WILD 5
Chapter 2   BLUEMIST. 22
Chapter 3   MAI-KELLINA 32
Chapter 4   QUAGGA 43
Chapter 5   DONOVAN 56
Chapter 6   HURRICANE 65
Chapter 7   CAVES 76
Chapter 8   CONVERTICOPTER 87
Chapter 9   LOOPER 93
Chapter 10 REUNION 98

♪ ♪ ♪ ♪ ♪ ♪ PLAYBILL

BOOK TWO: **THE RINGS OF BARABOO**

Chapter 1   CANNONBALL 109
Chapter 2   MANDRETTA 120
Chapter 3   FREE 126
Chapter 4   CUSTODY 138
Chapter 5   TRICKA 143
Chapter 6   AROMA 155
Chapter 7   FARTHING 160
Chapter 8   REVENGE 168
Chapter 9   EEFANANNY 178
Chapter 10 GLIDERBIRDS 189

BOOK THREE: **THE BATTLE OF CRESTIVAL**

Chapter 1   CARILLONS 201
Chapter 2   TAMBORA 210
Chapter 3   SMOKE 219
Chapter 4   PARADE 229
Chapter 5   CIRCUS 242
Chapter 6   SPECTACLE 251
Chapter 7   CROWN 259
Chapter 8   ORACLE 271
Chapter 9   PROCO 281

EPILOG 293
GLOSSARY 299
FURTHER READING AND EXPLORING 305
SPECIAL THANKS 307
ABOUT THE AUTHOR & THE ILLUSTRATOR 309

BOOK ONE

ESCAPE FROM LUNA VERDANTA

PROLOG

The lunar governor unfastened the miniature dagger from her necklace. Using her painted, pointed fingernails as tweezers, she twisted the crimson gem in the dagger handle one quarter turn. She closed her eyes, clutched the dagger to her heart, and chanted. "Proco, are you there?"

The Quicksilver Messenger crackled. A deep male voice, echoing as if speaking from the bottom of a well, drifted out of the QM. "I am here. Did you meet them?"

"I did."

"Is it him?"

She took a deep breath. "Could be. Can't be sure, yet."

"Who else could it be?"

"The forest attracts many desperate people with dangerous secrets."

She placed the QM on her desk and opened the projection screen. The shadowy image of a man in windswept dark glasses appeared. "How'd they get in?"

"King Donovan gave them permission. I could understand a

scientific expedition, but a circus family looking for a new trick pony? Lunacy."

"Donovan's a fool. Worse than his father. A whole family of lunatics."

"I already sent the boy to Yerkoza."

"Good. They will test him. Hard. When we're sure we have the right one, then I want to take him out while everyone in the empire is watching."

Chapter 1 ☽ ☽ ☽ ☽ ☽ ☽ ☽

WILD

The hot air balloon Jefferson Spitfire sailed into the mist, gliding high above the choppy waters of the Sea of Karoo, the deepest ocean on the green moon. Perched at the edge of the dragonhead basket, Elizabelle peered through her spyglass and scanned the horizon, hoping to spot their destination: the Cloud Forest. She felt lucky just to have the chance to see it, since no human had been allowed to enter the forest since her grandfather was a young boy.

Far below, a thick fog swirled on the surface; it seemed to be struggling to take shape. In Elizabelle's imagination, the fog formed into a huge whale drifting with the surface breeze. She wondered if the whale was trying to escape its natural birthplace in the watery depths so it could explore the solid world of dirt, stone, and tree.

The chilly air current nudged both the balloon and the whale-cloud toward the land. Elizabelle kept her gaze fixed on the whale as it floated to the shore and then crept up the mountainside. As it reached the summit and peeked over the ridge, it lost connection with the tailwind. Suddenly powerless, it broke apart, crumbling as it fell off the cliff and tumbled down into the forest.

ESCAPE FROM LUNA VERDANTA

That whale tried to escape its natural home, Elizabelle thought. *Now it's nothing.*

A whisper of wetness licked Elizabelle's cheek, snapping her out of her fantasy. She stared down into the rolling veils of fog entangling the trees below. Mysterious, hairy creatures moved through the moss-covered branches, swinging their way through dangling vines and enormous bright flowers. Then suddenly something completely unexpected caught her eye. She took a quick breath and squinted through the binoculars, trying to see clearly. She wanted to be sure it was not just another mirage.

Feeling confident, she rose onto her tiptoes, pointed and shouted, "Look down there! It's a kid in the trees!"

"Yeah, sure thing, Dizz." Her younger brother Ripley smirked. "Maybe in the fog in your head. Nothin' down there but wild and weird animals." He leaned over the basket railing and spat through the gap in his teeth.

Elizabelle scowled. "Can you possibly be more gross?"

"Sure! My pleasure."

"Hey, kids, cool it," their mom warned.

"That tall one's a kid. I can tell." Moisture settled on Elizabelle's frizzy hair, making her head glow like a bush frosted with morning dew. "It almost looks like some kind of monkey, but . . . it's a kid. I can tell."

Her mom gently shook her head. "It couldn't be a human child. Not here."

Elizabelle understood. It had been eighty-four years since King Arkenstone II issued his famous Cloud Forest Decree. Without special permission from the king, no human was allowed to enter the

Forest. The royal order protected the Cloud Forest from all intruders and set it apart as an isolated nature preserve, a wild place to test how the plants and animals from the first human world, Ol'Terra, could adapt to living with the native life forms.

Elizabelle had read about the forest and dreamed about visiting it for most of her thirteen years. And now, at last! she and her family were floating right above it. But they were not just sightseers or even explorers. Not today. They had a mission: to find an unusual animal to become the new star of their circus.

Seven Moon Circus was nearly broke. If the circus failed, Elizabelle's parents would lose their jobs training and caring for the circus animals. She would lose all her beloved animal friends. No more goofing around with the crazy clowns. Goodbye to banging on the drums in the circus band. Farewell to her dreams of becoming a horseback ballerina. No more flying to distant moons, putting on spectacular shows. Her whole family would lose their vagabond circus home and become just more ordinary townies, plodding along in some colorless, flat, boring place.

She thought back on the strange events that had brought them here. It was King Donovan, grandson of Arkenstone II, who gave them their golden chance. He invited 7MC to give a royal command performance at the upcoming Crestival, the grand festival of the seven crescent moons. Elizabelle's dad took her to meet with King Donovan, and she made the suggestion herself. "We need a new star of the circus. Some kind of beautiful, amazing animal no one has ever seen. The Cloud Forest is the best place to look for an animal like that."

Charmed by her eagerness, King Donovan signed the letter giving them permission to enter the Cloud Forest, and added, "You'll need my Spitfire, too. It's the best way to get there. Probably the only way. But remember, you must report to the lunar governor first."

Their meeting with Lady Mai-Kellina, the governor of Luna Verdanta, had not gone well. She just glanced at the king's letter, then tossed it aside with a sneer and lectured Elizabelle's parents. "The Cloud Forest is far too dangerous for children. It is home to poisonous plants, bugs, toads, and snakes. The rivers are full of vicious crocodiles. The spit of a gomerana lizard can blind you. Never forget, I run this moon. King Donovan's letter gives you permission to enter the forest, but that's all. Here is my order: you will leave nothing behind, you will harm no living thing, and you will take no living thing out of the Forest. And here is my warning: go at your own risk. If you get in trouble, you are on your own. I will send no rescue."

As the Spitfire balloon drifted toward the surface, the lady governor's harsh words kept ringing in Elizabelle's memory, wrapping her enthusiasm in worry. *Even if we can find a new animal star for the circus, how can we get it out without getting in trouble with Governor Mai-Kellina?*

The creaking sound of trees bending in the breeze jolted Elizabelle back into the present. In the forest, far below their balloon, the bright green leaves seemed to glow in the mist, signaling hope that somehow they might find their precious beast, their new star performer who would bring the Crestival crowd to their feet, chanting and cheering. Maybe the king's invitation and her crazy plan just might succeed. Seven Moon Circus might be saved.

A flicker of movement in the trees caught her eye. "There it is again!"

"Show me, Belle," her mother said.

"Right there!" Elizabelle's arm shot out, pointing straight to the spot.

Her mother aimed the binocs. "Hmm. Something there, all right." Her mother winked and smiled at her. "Maybe it's not just your imagination this time. That one's different. A little taller."

"That's because it's a kid!" Elizabelle blurted.

"Let's find out." Her dad's voice was firm, but warm. "Stand aside, kids!" He yanked on the control lines connected to the parachute valve at the top of the balloon. It burped a bit of hot air, jostling their passenger basket. When he shut off the main burner, the balloon began slowly drifting down toward the forest, whispering softly in the nippy clouds.

Finally her dad announced: "Yeah, I do see something strange. What could it be?"

Ripley piped up. "It's a monkey. A freak monkey. Great! We can use a freak monkey."

"It's not a monkey!" Elizabelle firmly insisted, her eyes glaring at her brother.

"It is a monkey, if ever—"

"Kids, please," their dad interrupted. "I asked your mother."

"Can't tell yet." As the veterinarian in Seven Moon Circus, Elizabelle's mom was rarely stumped about animals. "Long, straight legs. It's standing too tall to be monkey, or an ape or a chimp. Not moving like any kind of monkey. Skin seems splotchy. It could have some skin disease, or . . ." She turned to her husband and raised her eyebrows. "Perhaps it's another Yerkoza experiment? Like the liger?"

Elizabelle sadly recalled the day they had to bury the liger cub. He was a lion-tiger mix, cute and sickly. The Yerkoza bio-engineers had given them the liger for nursing. She still felt sad that they could not save him.

She had heard many stories about the Yerkoza Research and Training Center. Most of their experiments failed. It was not easy to create a completely new kind of animal. Rumors said that many of their failures got buried at sea or, if they were still alive, dumped at the edge of the Cloud Forest, and turned loose to fend for themselves. After that, no one really knew what happened to them.

"Prepare for landing." Her dad flipped kinks out of the ropes dangling from the sides of the basket. Elizabelle and Ripley tightened their landing vests.

Their mom hurriedly sealed up boxes of food, clothes, and tools. After strapping the last belt tight, she peered through her binocs again. "I see six or seven primates, unknown species. The one in the center is probably a mother. A runt, a couple of adolescents, no alpha male. And the one who is a bit taller."

"That's the kid." Elizabelle nodded. "I'm sure. It's not just my imagination!"

"Please, Belle, let's not jump to crazy conclusions." Her mom rubbed the mist off the lenses of her binocs. "A human child in this place would soon be a predator's dinner. Even if it survived, it'd have to live on bugs, and roots, and leaves, and berries."

"Yeah, and slimy worms, too." Ripley hummed and licked his lips. "It'd have the runs all the time!"

Elizabelle ignored her brother's grossness and looked down on the scene below, trying to focus on things she had only seen before as blurry images taken from King Donovan's orbiting spy-eye. Even now, as they prepared to land, the spy-eye orbited high above them, recording everything that was visible through the clouds.

The Spitfire balloon continued drifting downward, quivering with each little gust. A peephole opened in the haze, revealing a spot where a gurgling river turned and sprayed out a sandy beach on one side. Several boulders rested on the edge of the stream. On the other side, the dense forest crowded right up to the water's edge. The trees sent long, glistening branches stretching out over the river, desperately competing for rare, direct sunlight.

"There's our spot." Elizabelle's dad pointed to the clearing beside the stream. "At your post, Rip." Working together in rhythm, as they had practiced many times, dad and son formed loops and tied rope knots, readying the balloon for a soft, safe landing.

They neared the surface. Elizabelle's heart beat like the big bass drum in the circus band as she caught flashes of the exotic life forms awaiting them. A twiggy nest of red-beaked curlibirds. Slithering green things that might be snakes or lizards, or even giant worms. Whiskered bushhogs rooting in stinky mud. A glistening spider web as large as their basket. Giant strangler trees that sucked the life out of smaller plants.

Elizabelle's mom whispered to her husband, "You sure this is a safe place to land?"

He paused a moment, then answered. "I'm sure of one thing. We'll never get another chance like this. We're in the Spitfire, equipped for any emergency. What could go wrong?"

King Donovan's Mighty Jefferson Spitfire was the most famous hot air balloon ever to tease the clouds. The shimmering image of a red-scaled dragon wrapped around the air bag. When the burner flared to heat the air inside, the floating dragon appeared to be breathing fire. The passenger basket imitated a drakkar—the ancient Viking longship whose dragon masthead symbolized the king's power. And unlike all other balloons, the Spitfire had a three-fingered mechanical claw—which Ripley had nicknamed "Pincher"—that made targeted landings possible.

Elizabelle's mom grabbed the claw gun and carefully aimed it down at the big black boulder beside the river. She drew a deep breath and slowly squeezed the trigger until the claw shot out from its lock. Fingers closed, the Pincher zipped through the fog, hissing like an angry snake. Elizabelle nervously bit her lip and held her breath. If the fingers opened too soon, they could throw the claw off balance, risking a miss. If the fingers opened too late, the claw would crash. Or tangle in the trees, stranding them in a dangerous, isolated, wild place where rescue was impossible.

At the last possible second, Elizabelle's mom hit the zapper. Pincher's fingers flipped open and tightened around the boulder. The scraping sound gave Elizabelle goose bumps.

"Bull's-eye!" Ripley joined his sister and mom in cranking the winch, pulling the balloon toward the boulder.

The basket jerked when it touched the ground. Elizabelle's dad left the starter flame burning but locked the main gas line off. "Let's put up the tent. We'll stay the night. We don't wanna fly this balloon into the afternoon rainstorm." Elizabelle shivered at the thought of their balloon getting fried in mid-air by a sky-ripping bolt of lightning.

They all jumped out of the dragonhead basket. Elizabelle's dad pulled his machete knife from its sheath, hacked off several branches, and then looped tie-down ropes around the branches. Her mother and brother unpacked the tent and positioned it on the ground.

Elizabelle wasn't much help, though. As her brother and parents worked at setting up their little camp, she kept eagle-eyeing the kid and its wild family in the trees. She caught a glimpse of the kid imitating the motion of her dad cutting the branches. When she waved and smiled, the creature raised its arm, copying her movement, too. "Look, it's waving at us!"

Her parents and brother dropped their tent work and turned to watch the wild family.

The runt in the wild family rode on the back of the tall creature. Behind them, a few branches away, other reddish tree-dwellers chattered madly, flailing their arms. The tall one pulled the runt off its back and passed it to the mother; she caressed it and let it nurse from her breast.

The tall creature bobbed from vine to branch, jumped down to the forest floor, and zigzagged toward them in fits and spurts. Several times it stopped and looked back; each time the wild mother kept pointing to the humans.

Elizabelle wanted to see the kid up close. But as it drew closer, she started to wonder. The kid had bits of fur all over its body, and a tail. *A real human would not have a tail. Maybe mom was right. Maybe it is a Yerkoza half-breed, half human, half . . . yikes! A freak for the circus sideshow? Not really the kind of new circus star I had in mind.*

The creature snagged its tail in a crack between two rocks. It stopped, then turned, grabbed the tail, and yanked it free. *It's not a real tail at all! A vine? A rope? A tail stolen from some dead animal?*

Soon the wild creature stood directly in front of them, smiling.

Elizabelle put her hands on her hips and proudly announced, "See. I told you. It's a kid." She took a deep breath and was nearly knocked over by his earthy aroma. "A very dirty boy who needs a bath!"

"Naked as a goony!" Ripley laughed.

Elizabelle shot a disapproving glance at her brother and then turned to Wild Boy. As he meandered toward Elizabelle and Ripley, their parents jumped in front of them. "Whew! You're right about that bath, Belle," their dad said. He loaded his tranquilizer dart gun and held it ready steady. Wild Boy stared at the gun, and raised his eyebrows, blinking.

With a flourish of his dirty hand, Wild Boy reached into his long, matted hair and drew out a squirming, kicking grasshopper. The bug was snot green with dark brown spots, fatter and longer than her dad's thumb. Flicking its legs wildly, the hopper spat yellowish juice from its mouth in sticky pulses. Wild Boy smiled, smacked his lips, then held out his hand, offering the hopper to Elizabelle.

Ripley laughed. "Lunch with your new boyfriend, Dizz!"

Elizabelle recoiled. *Is he trying to trick me into eating a poison bug?*

Wild Boy raised his eyebrows and popped the hopper into his mouth. He chomped on it, then spat out the hard legs while they were still kicking.

Elizabelle sputtered her tongue. "Oh yuck! Bugs are not food."

Wild Boy sputtered his tongue, too. "Oyuck. Bugs . . . foo." He licked his lips.

"He's imitating." Elizabelle's mom nodded. "No threatening movements. Good signs."

"Very few animals will share food with a stranger," her dad said. "He wants to be friends. I'm ready, just in case." He clicked the dart gun, and moved aside. "You saw him first, so go ahead, give him a chance."

Give him a chance how? Though Wild Boy appeared human and friendly, he was also a dirty, stinky, naked, bug eater. With a fake tail, a bush of tangled hair, and fur patches. Elizabelle didn't know whether to shake his hand, pet him, or put him on a leash. "Do I treat him like a kid or a wild animal?"

"Yes, give him a chance," her mom said softly, nodding. "But be careful. If he's been living wild, he may have learned some dangerous behaviors just to survive. Hard to tell what he might do. Wait. I have an idea." She strode to the clothes bag near their tent and dug into it. Wild Boy followed her. While pulling out a khaki rain coat, she accidentally dropped a colorful cape. She offered the rain coat to Wild Boy. He pushed it aside, nabbed the color cape, and ran off.

"Mom, no! Don't let him take it. I need it for the parade." The cape was a gift from Kiko's Guild of Royal Weavers on the Lavender Moon. Of all the craft guilds in Empire Luna, only Kiko's group had mastered the secret of making fabrics that changed colors in shifting light.

Standing in the shaft of sunlight, Wild Boy rubbed the cape in his fingers, sniffed it with his nose, and patted it on his cheek. As he turned the fabric in the narrow beam of sunlight, the colors rippled like a rainbow. He laughed joyfully, then wrapped the cape into a little bundle.

"He's gettin' it dirty!" Elizabelle protested.

"It's okay, Belle," her mom said. "If that's what he wants to wear, show him how to wear a cape."

Elizabelle moved slowly toward Wild Boy. "Can we be friends?"

Wild Boy rhythmically rocked his eyebrows, like a clown bouncing on a teeter board.

"Friends?" She pointed first at him, then to herself. "You and me, friends, okay?"

"Fren zokay." He smiled proudly and pointed first at her, then at himself.

"Oh, you can talk, a bit! Good." She took the cape from him and wrapped it around her own shoulders. "Here. Do it like this."

The Wild Boy ran his fingers around his own lips.

"Say it again," her mom whispered.

Elizabelle obliged, this time speaking precisely. "Do . . . it . . . like . . . this."

Wild Boy twisted his head again. "Rike . . . dis."

Elizabelle clapped her hands in approval, and her family joined in. "Good, good!"

Wild Boy clapped his hands, too, and then repeated, "Good, good."

Elizabelle's mom took the cape and wrapped it around Wild Boy's shoulders. He did not resist when she tightened the vine around his waist, converting it from a poor excuse for a tail into a make-do belt. "Much better."

As Wild Boy turned in the sunlight, the cape flashed from maroon red to rippling purple.

With his nakedness covered, Elizabelle decided it was time for introductions. Opening her palm and pointing in turn to her parents, she said, "My dad, Braden. My mom, Althea." Then she nodded toward Ripley. "My little brother. He's ten." She held up ten fingers. "His name's Ripley, Rip for short."

"Rip. Shore." Wild Boy seemed to enjoy making the sound.

Pointing to herself, "I'm Elizabelle. I'm thirteen." She flashed all her fingers, then held up three more. "I like to be called Belle because bells make beautiful sounds. I want to sing in the choir at Crestival."

Wild Boy just stared at her with a puzzled look on his face.

"She's Dizzy Mizz Lizzy," Ripley interrupted, buzzing the zees. "Dizz for short."

"Dizz," Wild Boy repeated, buzzing the zees even more than Ripley.

"Ignore him," Elizabelle shot back. "We are the Hawken family from Seven Moon Circus. And who are you? What does your ma call you?" She pointed to his wild family.

Wild Boy looked up to his home in the trees. The wild mother stared back. He blinked his eyes and answered. "Maar." Or something close to that. His sound buzzed at the end.

Elizabelle couldn't quite match his sound. "You need a name people can say." She paused. "What do you like? Mark? Marcus? Markham? Hmmm. How about . . . Marz?"

"I like it," Ripley said, nodding and pointing at Wild Boy.

"It could fit him," Althea said. "The sound is the same as Mars, one of the sister planets of Ol'Terra. Far as we can tell, he is a child of this moon."

Ripley clapped his hands together as he chanted, "Yes, Marz! Marz!"

Wild Boy joined in clapping and chanting, "Marz, Marz."

Braden smiled and nodded his head. "Okay. Marz it is. For now, anyway. How old do you think he is?"

"Hmm . . . early adolescence," Althea said. "Probably somewhere between twelve and fourteen. Under all the dirt on his face he has the beginnings of a mustache. He's so thin it's hard to tell. He needs some quality protein."

"And a haircut and a bath," Elizabelle added, chuckling. "And clean clothes that fit."

"Let's see if he likes hats." From the clothes bag Ripley pulled a round, black hat, decorated with the sparkling symbol of Seven Moon Circus. Plunking it on his own head, he marched around, as he often did in parades when their circus traveled to other moons. He flipped the hat to Marz. "Here, you try it."

Wild Boy Marz snatched it, spun it in his hands, and plopped it on his head.

"Lookit that catch! He's a natch," Ripley shouted. "He's a born juggler."

They all laughed and applauded. "Marz, good, good!"

He repeated after them, "Marz good good."

Braden passed a small hand mirror to Elizabelle and whispered, "Test him." From helping her dad train circus animals, Elizabelle knew that most animals cannot recognize themselves in a mirror. Most will either attack the face in the mirror, or run from it.

Elizabelle made a show of admiring herself in the mirror, swiveling to give Marz a few teasing peeks. He approached, walking tall and proud in his cape of many colors and his 7MC hat. She stood beside him and angled the mirror, showing him his tree home across the clearing, the Spitfire balloon tied at the edge of the river, and her parents.

Then she offered the mirror to Marz. "Try it."

First he aimed the mirror at his own face. His eyes widened.

He stuck out his tongue. Lifted up the cape and shook it in the sunlight.

"Yes, Marz, it's you." Elizabelle smiled at her dad, who gave her a thumbs up.

As Marz continued learning and admiring his own face, a sudden, bright ray of sunlight speared the fog and struck the mirror. The flash hit the mirror precisely at the moment that a bolt of lightning flared across the cloudy part of the sky. Marz reacted by flinging the mirror and his 7MC hat onto the gravel. A split second later, thunder cracked the air and rolled through the forest, making the leaves tremble and the ground rumble.

The wild family erupted in howls. The mother and the runt both hooted and madly waved their arms. Pivoting, Marz loosened his vine belt so the cape would hang free. With the cape flying wildly behind him, he sprinted across the clearing and up into the trees, where his wild family greeted him. They formed a rain shelter out of big leaves, and huddled under it. He wrapped the runt in his cape and cuddled him.

A second thunderbolt ushered in a light drizzle. The Hawken family quickly finished setting up the tent, and then took refuge inside it. They gathered around a portable table and snacked on dried jackleberries.

"You seem unusually quiet," Althea said to her husband. "Whatcha thinkin'?"

Braden rose and paced around the tent. "Something strange is in the works. Lots of rumors. The king's advisor has been meeting with the Lunar Council. He wants this Crestival to be about something more than a party about moons aligned in the sky. We could be part of something historic. I wonder if Marz could help us put on our best show ever. We need it."

Elizabelle understood. With everyone watching, a spectacular performance would make 7MC the hottest circus in the empire. But if they disappointed the king, or the audience, word-of-mouth badvertising would mean the end. Their performance at Crestival would be a "shine or die" show.

Braden continued. "Maybe, just maybe, our new star . . . isn't an animal." After a few turns, he stood tall. "Try to imagine Bucky in the center ring." He broke into a booming hullaballoo voice like their Master of Spectacle. "Ladies and Gentlemen, Seven Moon Circus now proudly presents, the boy who grew up living with wild animals in the Verdanta Cloud Forest, the amazing Marz the Monkey Boy!"

Ripley clapped his hands. "I knew it. Marz's our new star. We have a freak monkey!"

"No!" Elizabelle blurted. "He's not a monkey. Don't you dare call him a monkey."

Althea frowned. "Hold on. He's a lost boy, a human who needs to find his real family."

"He thinks his real family is up there." Elizabelle pointed through the rain, to the trees.

"Yeah, and they don't care if he wears clothes or not," Ripley said. "Real parents would just make him go to boring schools and obey stupid rules!"

"As they should," Althea added. "He's a human child living with wild animals. We must find him a home. Give him a chance for a life with his own kind."

"How?" Elizabelle asked. "The lady governor said we can't take any living thing out."

"Right," Althea said. "We have to report to her. Maybe she knows how he got here."

The rain grew louder, pounding on the tent. Braden stroked his long sideburns. "Marz is a human in the Cloud Forest without a king's permission." After a pause, "So . . . he's got—"

"No right to be here." Elizabelle finished her dad's thought. "So we can take him out!"

"Yeah!" Ripley cheered. "Marz gets to join us!"

"Careful there, kids," Braden warned. "He may know nothing beyond this forest. Probably can't even imagine a circus. May not like it. We won't kidnap him."

"He'll choose us," Elizabelle said. "I can tell from the look in his eyes, he—"

A loud bellowing sound interrupted her. Braden rushed to the windflap of the tent and peered out. Over the pouring rain he groaned, "Oh, no! Now we have real trouble."

Chapter 2

BLUEMIST

Elizabelle grabbed the binocs and peered through the tiny view hole of the expedition tent. In the middle of the river lurked four dark green crocodiles, their yellow eyes and nostrils bulging just above the waterline. The biggest, a huge bull croc, muscles pulsing, surged toward them, his tail swishing in powerful beats. More crocodiles followed in his wake. Soon the river churned with dark green scales. Heavy rain pummeled the whole scene.

Braden ripped open the tent door and dashed out. "We gotta get outta this place! Back in the basket, now! Forget the tent. Look alive! I mean it, move, move, move!"

The crocs swam toward them, their yellow slit eyes glaring.

Althea and her kids bolted to the basket and jumped over the railing. Braden loaded his dart gun with eight max-power cartridges.

From the basket Althea yelled, "We're in! Come on!"

Braden raced to the basket, drew his machete and hacked the tie-down ropes.

"Hurry, Dad!" Elizabelle shouted.

"Gotta release the claw!" Braden called back. He rushed to the boulder where Pincher held tight, and pulled the release pin. The claw fingers opened with a loud *snap!* He ran to the balloon, jumped over the railing and slid into the basket.

Althea fired up the main burner. "Hold on!" she yelled. As the balloon began to rise into the rain, the bull croc roared, leaped up out of the water and slashed the side of the basket with its razor teeth. Terror filled Elizabelle's heart as she stared directly into shining yellow eyes.

Braden drew the baton from his tool belt and whacked the bull croc on its neck. The croc grunted and slipped back into the river.

With her family rising in their dragon balloon, Elizabelle looked to Marz. He and his wild family huddled together under the giant leaves of their tree home, staring back at her.

A lightning flash splattered across the sky. The clouds seemed to shiver.

With the balloon's air heater sputtering in the rain, the balloon struggled to lift off. Pincher, metal fingers open but still attached to the rope, dragged behind. Braden and Ripley cranked on the winch to pull the bouncing claw back to the basket. But just as the basket skimmed the tallest tangle of trees, the claw snagged on a gnarled branch. When Braden yanked on the rope, the claw's fingers snapped shut.

"Full blast on main!" Braden shouted. "Trimmers straight up! Rip free!"

Althea opened the main burner wide, and red hot flames leaped into the air bag. The rain poured down in cascading sheets. When the rain hit the hot air bag, it turned to steam.

Pincher gripped tight on the branch. The balloon pulled on the rope, but the wet branch would only bend. The roaring dragon balloon and the moaning branch were caught in a tug of war. "Just cut the rope!" Althea shouted.

"No! We need Pincher for landing!" Braden yelled back. "Turn the burner down."

Even surrounded by all the mad, wet confusion, Elizabelle kept glancing at the wild family. Her eyes widened in disbelief as Marz suddenly stood up, handed the screeching runt back to the wild mother, wrapped the cape around the runt's neck, and crouched to jump.

"What's he . . . ?" She broke into a shout. "No!"

Marz, wearing only vine tail and fur bits, dropped down and dashed toward the river. He ran to the tree limb where Pincher was snagged. Soon he was only an arm's length above the roiling water, with the bull croc circling directly below him, just beneath the surface.

"Marz, No!" Elizabelle motioned with her hand. "Get out! Move away!"

But Marz did not move away. He crept further out, where the limb grew thinner even as the water below grew deeper. He grasped Pincher's rope and pulled on it.

With a deafening roar the bull croc surged up, its toothy snout gaping, water spraying everywhere. Marz jumped barely in time to escape the sharp teeth. Still gripping the rope, he landed on a higher branch and scrambled to get a grip on a wet bough. But the harder he pulled on Pincher's rope, the tighter the claw gripped the branch.

The bull croc bellowed again and lunged for Marz's feet.

"Dad! Help!" Ripley yelled as the basket rocked in the air.

Braden aimed his gun at the big croc and shot. The tranco dart hit another croc instead. That scaly beast shook for a moment, then went limp and floated down the river, twitching.

"Try again, Dad!" Ripley hollered.

"No! We're rockin' too much. Might hit Marz."

"Dad, look!" Elizabelle called out. Marz clasped his hands together, making a swinging motion against the branches. "Toss him your big knife."

"I'm busy keeping this balloon in the air!"

"I'll do it," Ripley shouted. He unsnapped the sheath on his dad's belt, attached the machete to a rope, and dangled it down. Marz could not reach it, so Ripley added more swing.

As the knife swung by, Marz reached out for it. It was so wet and slippery that he bobbled it several times before finally nabbing it.

"Great catch, Marz!" Ripley shouted as he applauded. Elizabelle wondered if Marz could hear anything above the steady rain. Or, even if he could hear, could he understand?

Crouching, Marz cautiously worked his way back to the place where Pincher was stuck. With each step, the branch shook. All the time, the big bull croc loomed below, tracking Marz's every move, with several more crocs prowling nearby.

Marz took a giant swing with the knife and chopped away at the snagged branch. The claw opened and dropped straight down. Toward the open mouth of the big croc.

The giant croc quickly turned its head and batted the claw off to the side. He lurched toward Marz, bellowing angrily, caught Marz's tail in his jaws, and began pulling.

"Dad, save Marz!" Elizabelle shouted. Braden took aim and shot the tranco dart gun. This time the dart landed in the big croc's neck.

The croc thrashed angrily in the water for a few moments, then collapsed and floated down the river, with swirls of blood following him.

Wiping the rain from his face Braden said, "He'll wake up with a headache he'll never forget." Elizabelle understood. Her dad was following his basic rule: we will kill an attacking animal only when there is no other way to stop it from killing or seriously injuring a human or another animal. We will not kill when a stun will stop the attack.

"Marz, you're safe!" Ripley shouted.

Elizabelle could not contain her joy. She called out, "Now come with us!" Ripley joined her in frantically waving their arms in invitation.

Up in their tree home, Marz's wild family still huddled under their giant leaf umbrella. The runt let out a sad, mournful cry and stretched his skinny arms out to his big brother.

Marz had only a few seconds to decide. Elizabelle recalled her fantasy about the cloud-whale leaving its natural home and ending up as nothing. *Will Marz stay with his wild family or jump at his only chance to join his own kind? And just where is his natural home?*

Crouching on the branch, Marz turned first to the snorting crocs circling directly below him, then to the circus family high above in the balloon, and finally to his wild family.

"Climb the rope, Marz!" Ripley thumped on the rope and made climbing motions.

Althea kept adjusting the burner to keep the balloon at the same height while a canyon breeze tugged the balloon downstream. The rope, no longer weighted down by Pincher, dangled behind. Marz stared at the balloon rope, slithering away from him.

Giving in to impulse, Elizabelle grabbed her mirror and flashed it over the railing. "Marz, it's your only chance! You're one of us!" She knew he could not understand her words, but still she had to try to get him to understand, if only from her movements and tone of voice.

Suddenly Marz stood straight up and drew the machete again. He cut the vine from his waist and cast it into the river. Then he pulled the bits of fur from his chest and threw those to the crocs below. Finally he leaped out of the tree, bounded onto the sandy beach, turned to face his wild family, and held his arms open.

Squealing, the runt grabbed the colorful cape, dropped down from its tree home and scampered through the mud and rain toward Marz, with its mother in hot pursuit. The little one reached Marz first, jumped into his open arms, and desperately wrapped his tiny shaking hands around Marz's neck. Moments later, the wild mother arrived and pulled the little one, screeching in protest, away from Marz. She hoisted the runt up on her back, and gripped its hands.

Marz caressed the runt's head, hugged him, fastened the cape around his own neck, then turned and ran to the dangling rope.

Elizabelle's heart wrenched in pain as she watched the little runt squealing and squirming, desperately trying to break free and cling to Marz. But the wild mother held firm, and clutched her baby tightly. Elizabelle appreciated the wild mother's determination. *She may be a wild animal, but she understands. Marz belongs with us. Her baby belongs with her. All creatures belong with their own kind.* Still, she was sad that the little runt was losing his big brother. And she was glad that the rain hid her tears.

Marz wrapped his fingers around the rope and struggled to

climb, but his fingers slipped on the wet rope. He scooped up some grainy sand and rubbed it between his palms and then, gripping the rope tightly, hoisted himself up.

"Let's drift at this height," Braden ordered. "Give him a chance."

Althea again adjusted the burner to hold the balloon at a steady height.

To Elizabelle's amazement, Marz made no effort to reach the basket. She called out to him, and motioned with her hands. "Marz, climb the rope!" Ripley and the parents joined in, and they all chanted together, "Marz, climb the rope!"

But he didn't. Instead, he cackled loudly and pumped his knees, leaning back and pushing forward, urging the rope into a long figure-eight pattern, letting the cape swing wildly down his back, fluttering with each gust of wind.

"What's that goony doin'?" Ripley asked.

"No time for games!" Althea looked over the railing and scowled.

Elizabelle grabbed the bullhorn and shouted through it. "Marz! Up! Climb up!" She and Ripley both made the hand motions of climbing up the rope. But Marz seemed happy just to swing high in air, far beneath the balloon, cape dangling and swaying, changing colors in the wind.

The Spitfire balloon continued floating down the canyon, just above the river, gradually gaining speed. Soon they came to the point where two rivers joined. The combined waters sped down the canyon, rushing ever faster until they spilled over the rock ledge and crashed straight down into a plunge pool. Soon the din of the falling water drowned out the sound of the rain.

Marz, hanging by rope below the balloon, whooshed over the waterfall, dangling like a dizzy spider swinging from a strand of web silk. His strange cackling sound was new to Elizabelle, but his big grin told her it was the sound of a thrill. *This crazy Wild Boy thinks it's fun to hang from a rope in a lightning storm!*

Floating in the mist above the plunge pool, Marz reached out with his left hand and grabbed a small, sparkling thing. Then he pressed his fist to his chest.

"Marz, are you completely nutso?" Ripley shouted. "Get up here, now!" Again he motioned for Marz to climb the rope. A rainbow shone in the mist above Marz.

Ripley and Elizabelle chanted together, "Marz, climb the rope!"

"Let's haul him up before he falls," Braden said. Dad and son cranked the winch.

When Marz finally reached the basket, he grabbed Braden's outstretched hand and jumped in, still clutching the treasure from the mist in his left hand.

"Welcome to the Spitfire, Marz!" Ripley said.

Elizabelle whispered to her mom, "That's one way to get him to have a bath!"

Once Marz was firmly inside the basket, he and the circus family gazed over the railing. "Have a look!" Elizabelle opened her palms to the scene below. "It's a fabulous view from here." The breathtaking vista fell away from them—the misty forest, the rushing rivers, the roaring waterfall, the rainbow, Marz's old home. Even the runt, pointing to the balloon, still struggling to escape from its mother.

"Good boy, Marz!" Althea tried to replace the cape with a raincoat. But Marz clung tightly to the cape, even though it was soaking wet. So she simply straightened it on his shoulders and showed him how to fasten the belt. "That good, Marz?"

"Good Marz." He then faced Elizabelle and held his hands together, forming a box.

Remembering his grasshopper gift, she took a step back. "What now, Marz?"

Smiling and rocking his eyebrows, he moved his thumbs aside as if cracking open double doors leading to a dark chamber, teasing her to take a peek inside.

"A present for me?" Elizabelle leaned in to look, ready to pull back in case a spitting grasshopper—or something worse—should spring out. But it wasn't a grasshopper. This time, Marz held a live Bluemist Dragonfly, one of the rarest insects in all of Empire Luna, and the only bug known to live in plunge pool mists. They often brought high prices from makers of custom jewelry. In the proper light, a pair of their wings would shine and scintillate just like the rainbow. "Oh, it's so beautiful! Thank you! Good Marz!"

"Good Marz."

"Just don't eat it, okay?" Elizabelle covered her mouth with her fingers and shook her head. She hoped that Marz had learned an important lesson. "Bugs are yuck, not food."

"Bugs yuck." He rocked his eyebrows and licked his lips.

"Up, up, and away!" Braden called out. "Full burn! Let's get above this storm."

With the burner in full power blast, the Mighty Jefferson Spitfire rose rapidly. The painted dragon seemed to spring to life, eager to do fiery battle with the storm looming above.

Braden piloted the balloon, so sure with his movements, so

natural at the controls. Up ahead of them a lightning bolt split and lit the sky. They were sailing straight into a gathering gloom of rain clouds and darkness. And thunderbolts that could strike an airborne balloon, and fry it in a blinding flash.

Elizabelle cast her eyes down to Marz. With his cape wrapped around him, he sat on the floor of the basket munching away. The shining wing of a Bluemist Dragonfly dangled from his lips.

Chapter 3 ᒐ ᒐ ᒐ ᒐ ᒐ ᒐ

MAI-KELLINA

Elizabelle dreaded the thought of reporting, once again, to Governor Lady Mai-Kellina for their exit interview. But she knew it was their duty, and that her parents always did their duties.

When they arrived at the governor's office, two stern-faced guards stood by the main entrance; high-power stunners hung from their belts. The guards escorted them into the room. Two rows of view-gems sparkled on the shelf behind the governor's desk. Elizabelle wondered what scenes and secrets might be saved within them, just waiting for a chance to be seen. She scanned the ceiling and all the walls, looking for lenses that might be recording their meeting.

As Mai-Kellina entered the room, the guards snapped to stiff attention. Elizabelle and her family rose from their seats. Marz stayed on the floor, roaming around, massaging the carpet with his bare feet, feeling all the leather furniture with his hands, and sniffing everything.

The lady governor's solid stride radiated confidence and control. Miniature chains connected the rings on each of her fingers to a row of gold bracelets encircling her wrist.

A small dagger, with three gems mounted in the handle, hung from her neck. She took the high-back seat behind her raised desk, and glared down at the Hawken family and Marz.

"Mr. Hawken." Mai-Kellina impatiently tapped her fingernails. "Did I, or did I not order you to harm no living thing, leave nothing behind and take no living thing out of the Forest?"

Braden stood at attention. "That you did, governor."

"Then why did you damage the trees, injure the crocodiles, leave your tent and your mechanical claw behind, and remove this . . . wild *boy*?" She spat out the word "*boy*" like it was an insult.

Elizabelle piped up. "He decided to join us."

"I called out to him," Ripley added. "Climb the rope—"

"Children . . ." The governor's voice sounded cold as the ice caps on the Moon of Clouds. "In this office, adults decide important things. Children remain silent until I ask a question. Didn't you learn that lesson last time you were here?"

Elizabelle felt all the bad memories of their first meeting coming back again.

"I just asked you a question. Answer me."

"Yes, ma'am," Elizabelle mumbled.

"I'd like to tell you the whole story, governor," Braden offered.

Mai-Kellina trained her dark eyes on Braden. "Everybody has a story, Mr. Hawken. But I have many pictures, and very little time." She rubbed the brightest of her ten rings. Addressing one of the guards, she ordered, "Bring me the view-gem."

"Which one?"

"Veegee seventeen forty."

The guard left the room, and returned in a moment, carrying

an emerald-encrusted jewelry case. "As you ordered, governor." He positioned the case on her desk, removed a purplish view-gem, and mounted it on the cradle of the pierce-light. A magenta-colored beam emerged from the lens and rotated like a miniature searchlight. As it circled, the narrow shaft quivered and then expanded into a small light-frame. Inside the frame, a thin cloud, faintly purplish, glowed and pulsed.

"Play." On the governor's command, the little cloud began forming moving images. The Hawkens and Marz all gathered around to watch the show.

The Mighty Jefferson Spitfire could barely be seen through the clouds as a red dragon balloon twisting and thrashing its way through a thunderstorm. Blasts of heater flame argued with occasional flashes of lightning. Marz pointed at a tan speck crawling up a line toward the balloon, cape flowing behind. "Marz."

Elizabelle patted Marz on the back. "Yes, Marz, that's you."

The governor frowned. "Not very clear. I need more spy-eyes. Something that can see through the clouds." Using her pointed fingernails as precision tweezers, she turned the view-gem in the cradle. *She looks like a spider positioning to eat a captured fly,* Elizabelle thought.

Inside the light-frame, the scene faded from forest rainstorm to a hot, dry, desert scene, endless rolling sand dunes. The Spitfire balloon coiled and contorted like a brave dragon battling with a whirling, dry wind. The circus family and Marz clung desperately to the ropes while trying to shield their faces from the spinning dust devils. One of the support ropes frayed and then snapped, sending the basket into a lurching twist. Finally the basket crashed onto the desert and skidded along, spraying blistering sand into their faces.

The basket, plowing through the dunes, dragged the balloon down until it, too, collapsed on a crest. Then the image froze.

"Long way from the wet forest to the dry desert," Althea said. "We thought we'd die of thirst before your guards rescued us. We thank you for sending them."

"I did not send them," the governor said coldly. "They were just doing their jobs, patrolling the border lands." She turned back to the pierce-light. "Off." The image dimmed and swirled the light back into the lens like water sucked down a sinkhole.

"My question still stands, Mr. Hawken. Why did you disobey my orders?"

Elizabelle noticed her dad nervously clenching his fists behind his back. "We had to tie down the balloon so it would not float away. The crocodile episode was self-defense, and we were careful to stun, not kill. Leaving the gear behind was the only way to escape."

"So. You admit that you violated every order I gave you. Why did you kidnap the boy?"

"He was a human in the forest without a king's permission. He had no right to be there. We did not kidnap him. It was his decision. He risked his life to join us."

"Don't play word games with me, Mr. Hawken."

"We were looking for an animal, not a kid," Elizabelle blurted. "We didn't plan this."

The lady governor glared at Elizabelle. "Young lady," she said slowly, carefully pronouncing every word, "when I want your story, I will ask for it. Now you all hear me. Maybe this boy belongs in the forest. He could be part of a very important experiment."

"No human should be the subject of an experiment like that,

forced to live with wild animals, completely cut off from all people," Althea said defiantly.

"Mrs. Hawken, I run this moon, remember? Did you encourage him to join you?"

"Yes, the kids called out. He seemed to understand their hand motions. He saw his big chance and took it."

"Does he have a name?"

"We've been calling him Marz."

The governor snapped her fingers sharply at Marz. "Boy! Go sit in your chair."

Marz blinked at the governor, then shifted his gaze to Elizabelle. She tilted her head toward the chair. Still Marz did not move. He just sat on his cape.

Using her forefinger as a baton, the governor pointed at Marz, and then at the empty chair. "Marz! Move, now!" He rose from the floor and moved toward the chair, but then suddenly sprang forward, grabbed the model of Empire Luna from the governor's desk, and began playing with it. As he moved the seven moons circling New Roma, Elizabelle wondered how the little moons could just float in the air, and stay in their orbits.

"No! That's a map, not a toy. Put it back." With her longest finger, the lady governor pointed first at the model, then at its stand on her desk.

Elizabelle felt relieved when Marz replaced the model.

The governor turned back to the parents. "Did you even try to return him to his home?"

"Impossible," Braden said. "We barely escaped alive. We sailed in clouds, lost, for several days. We nearly starved to death." He relaxed a bit. "By the time he finally climbed in the basket, we were already far from his home, and we couldn't make the balloon float upstream. His only home was in the trees. That's not a home for a boy."

Mai-Kellina scowled. "But a space traveling circus is?"

"We circus people love our children just like other parents," Althea insisted. "We make sure they go to classes, even when we're touring. Most circus kids train to take over their parents' jobs."

Elizabelle glanced at the pictures on the wall behind the governor. In almost every shot, Mai-Kellina looked cold and serious. But there was one shot where she smiled happily as she and Donovan—when he was still the prince—waltzed in the grand ballroom. The seven moons, all aligned for Crestival, glowed in the background. Elizabelle recognized the ruby tiara that marked Mai-Kellina as the lunar princess from the Blood Moon.

"How did he get there?" the governor asked. "Any idea who his parents might be?"

Braden shook his head. "None. Do you know?"

The governor cleared her throat. "The forest is not far from Yerkoza. I wonder—"

The sound of Marz clapping his hands together interrupted the conversation. Marz had captured a fly and was munching it. He rocked his eyebrows at Elizabelle, and stuck out his tongue so that she could see the fly squirming in his saliva. "Bugs yuck."

"Boys are so gross," Elizabelle whispered to her mother. "They're all beasts at heart."

"Seems he grew up surrounded by wild animals," Braden said. "We live and work with animals all the time. If he likes the circus, maybe his tree climbing skills could be used on the high wire or the acrobats' scaffold. And there seems to be a bit of the trickster in him . . . maybe he can be a clown. He might adjust to circus life much more easily than a townie kid would."

"The circus is no home for any child. Especially a wild orphan who can't even talk."

"I can be his tutor," Elizabelle said proudly. "He's a good learner. He has already learned some words. He just needs a chance."

"Did I ask you a question, Miss Hawken?" the governor snapped.

Elizabelle cast her eyes down to the floor. "Sorry. Quiet is not easy for me."

"Children belong in a real school, not some vagabond carny that bounces from one moon to another. Children need tough lessons and strict rules with serious punishments for breaking them. It's all for their own good. It teaches them to be obedient citizens."

"Is that how you raise your own children?" Althea asked.

The governor's voice turned icy. "If I had any children, they would be none of your business. But I am far too busy running this moon to bother having children."

Elizabelle tried to imagine Mai-Kellina as a mom. *Horrible.*

The governor pulled a paper from her desk drawer and signed it. "I'm doing all of you—especially this rude, crude boy—a big favor. He's going to Yerkoza."

Elizabelle jumped to her feet again. "Not fair!" She knew all the rumors about how stubborn animals got "broken" at Yerkoza. "He's used to being free!"

"That is exactly the problem," the governor said.

Braden set a firm hand on Elizabelle's shoulder. She was bursting with anger, yet she knew that Mai-Kellina would win any argument. As long as they were on Luna Verdanta, Mai-Kellina was the governor. The boss. Both her dad and mom said so.

"What about finding his real parents?" Althea asked.

"You leave that to me. The first step is to get him under control." The governor handed one copy of the signed paper to a guard and another to Braden. "You are going home."

"But he wants to go with us!" Ripley protested.

"Young man. No interrupting and no whining!" Mai-Kellina slapped the desk. "You circus people will board the next relay looper back to New Roma. Bug boy will go to Yerkoza for the training he needs. I have more important matters to deal with. That is all."

The governor nodded to a guard, who then moved forward and grasped Marz by the nape of his neck and pushed him. They were near the door when Marz broke free, grabbed his cape and fastened it over his shoulders. The guard tightened his fingers around Marz's neck and led him out the door.

After he was gone from the room, Althea asked, "When can we see him again?"

"That's up to him. He must unlearn his wild ways, and learn to obey rules. If he cooperates, he won't have to stay long. If keeps his beastly ways, we could have a long battle. Once he learns to obey rules, then he can be adopted by a family that will give him a safe home."

"That's us!" Elizabelle's heart leaped for joy. "We want to apply for that!"

"If he's ever ready, he will need a stable home. With a family who stays in one place."

"But Dad—" Elizabelle started. She didn't finish. Her father's look told her to keep quiet.

There was nothing more they could do. After just a few days with Marz in their family, he was being taken away. They had given Marz a choice and a chance to be with his own kind, and the governor had destroyed it in a moment, with just the stroke of a pen.

The Hawken family, glum faces on every one, shuffled out the door, following their guard. Elizabelle whispered to her mother: "I could civilize him better than she can."

With the circus family and the wild boy gone their separate ways, Mai-Kellina placed her inter-lunar communicator, the Quicksilver Messenger, on the pierce-light, then whispered into it, "QM awake! Walpurgis."

The machine answered back, "Homburg."

The governor then spoke the next password: "Conquistador."

The light beam arose from the pierce-light once again and formed a shimmering wall of grayish light. The governor placed both of her thumbs on the testing pads. An official-sounding voice announced, "Feet." She stepped out of her shoes and stood on a footpad on the floor. "Eyes." Continuing the ritual, she turned her head left. The screen collapsed into a single yellowish light beam that scanned the retina inside her right eye. "Blood." She did not wince as the point punctured her thumb and sucked a tiny drop of blood. "Security clear. Proceed."

The lunar governor unfastened the miniature dagger from her necklace. Using her painted, pointed fingernails as tweezers, she twisted the crimson gem in the dagger handle one quarter turn.

She closed her eyes, clutched the dagger to her heart, and chanted. "Proco, are you there?"

The Quicksilver Messenger crackled. A deep male voice, echoing as if speaking from the bottom of a well, drifted out of the QM. "I am here. Did you meet them?"

"I did."

"Is it him?"

She took a deep breath. "Could be. Can't be sure, yet."

"Who else could it be?"

"The forest attracts many desperate people with dangerous secrets."

She placed the QM on her desk and opened the projection screen. The shadowy image of a man in windswept dark glasses appeared. "How'd they get in?"

"King Donovan gave them permission. I could understand a scientific expedition, but a circus family looking for a new trick pony? Lunacy."

"Donovan's a fool. Worse than his father. A whole family of lunatics."

"I already sent the boy to Yerkoza."

"Good. They will test him. Hard. When we're sure we have the right one, then I want to take him out while everyone in the empire is watching. Flash me the veegees of their balloon escape. Did you record today's meeting?"

"Of course. Every word."

"Send that, too. Let me know when the family has broken orbit on their flight back home. Keep veegees of everything they do in the looper station."

"Certainly." Mai-Kellina inhaled deeply. "When will we be together again?"

"Soon. Just keep your eyes on the prize."

Then they chanted together, "All the powers shall be ours."

Chapter 4

QUAGGA

Marz awoke alone. He lay on a tattered mattress on the floor of a small, stark room. A narrow cot, a cracked table, a rickety chair and a small window streaked with dust and dirt; nothing more. The place had no people, no animals and no plants. Not even a bug.

His bare feet contrasted with the khaki jumpsuit that covered most of his body. Rope rings were sewn into the seams of the sleeves and legs, and all down the back. He chafed at it, but could not get it off.

He rose and jiggled the door handle. It would not open. He pounded on it. "Yuck bug!"

Soon the door opened and a woman appeared. Atop her head, a huge mound of black hair twisted into a beehive shape. Her arms and legs were even skinnier than Marz's, and covered with tattoos of colorful lizards.

Bighair Woman entered the room, carrying a steaming bowl. "Good morning, Marz." Her voice had the sticky-sweet, singsong sound of fake friendliness. "Welcome to Yerkoza, your new home sweet home. You'll love it here. My name's Maleeza. I'm your personal tutor." She winked at him. "We're gonna be the very best of friends."

When she offered to shake hands, Marz reached up to explore her hair. She drew back. But when his eyes fixed on her tattoos, she held out her arms to him. "Ah! You like my lizzies do ya? Blue tail here is Lizardee, orange nose is Lizanne. This big guy is Jimmo the Lizard King, Miss Two-Tail is named Lizona, and this cute baby is Lizbeth. They're with me always." Marz ran his fingers over her arms, outlining the lizards.

"Let's get your first day started with a nice bowl of hot groat-mush. Yummy! It's got zest of remona and rich creamy milk the momma hippo gave us just minutes ago." She proudly offered the steaming bowl. "Here, Marz, real people food. No more bugs for you."

He sniffed the gloppy goo. Stuck a finger in the mush, then quickly pulled it back.

"Okay, time for your first lesson. How to use a spoon. Here, it's very simple, you just dip it in like this, and then put it in your mouth. Even monkeys can do it. Ummm, good. Here, try it."

The stuff reminded Marz of forest mud. He dipped the spoon in the mush, then placed the spoon on his lips and dabbled at it with his tongue. His face blanched; his nose crinkled. He took a spoonful into his mouth, and held it there as his eyes circled the room.

"See, I told you it's yummy," the tutor said. "Dee-lishus, no?"

Marz spat out the mush, spewing gobs of gunk all over her beehive hair. "No lishis!"

The tutor wiped the dripping mush off her hair and tossed it toward the dusty window. She flashed him some bad face. "They warned me about you. Said you look like a boy but act like a beast. I said you deserve a chance. Some thanks I get from you!"

"Yuck bugs food." He threw the spoon across the room.

"Okay. If you won't learn the easy way, we'll do it the hard way. We specialize in hardheads and rebels here. You'll go hungry 'til you're ready to eat people food with a spoon." She stomped out, slamming the door. A moment later she stuck her head back in. "You flunk your first lesson on your very first day. Bad sign. Bad boy." The door clicked and she was gone.

Marz sat on the cot and sputtered his tongue at the bowl.

He wandered to the window and stared out the streaky pane. A bland scene lay before him: dry ground with a few bushes between his room and a fenced area, a stone's throw away. But a smile crept across his face when he spied a few crickets on the ground just outside, crawling into a rusty old container. "Yuck. Bugs." He smiled.

Marz pushed on the window, but it did not open. He dumped the mush on the floor in front of the door. With the bowl on his fist like a boxing glove, he smashed the window, spraying shards of glass out into the yard. A stub of glass nicked his finger when he tried to climb through. Using the bowl as a mallet, he trimmed off the bits of glass, then crawled out the broken window. He was determined to get out and find his way back to the forest. After food.

He made his way to the rusty container, captured some crickets, and sat cross-legged and happy in the morning sun. "Mmm yuck. Bugs. Marz good."

While he was enjoying the fresh crickets, a noisy ruckus broke out somewhere behind him. He turned to investigate. Beyond the dorm, toward the plain, a large animal circled inside a round enclosure. Though it had four legs like the tigers he had seen in the forest, it did not crouch close to the ground. Instead, the legs were long and straight. Its head, neck, shoulders, and forelegs had stripes, in dark brown, on tan hide. The underbelly was dirty white; the black mane stood straight up. The animal moved nervously within the pen, charging forward, then pulling back and pushing on the fence with his nose. Marz had never seen such an animal.

Two men shuffled up to the corral. Inching from bush to bush, Marz crept ever closer to the corral. He found a good hiding place behind a leafy bush and crouched behind it to watch.

One of the men, rope in hand, scaled the fence and entered the corral. Rope Man curled his tongue and whistled, splitting the air with a shrill, warbling sound, and then shouted, "SunKing!" The striped animal faced the men and snorted, blowing hot snot out of his nostrils.

From his hiding spot, Marz quietly repeated. "SunKing. SunKing."

Rope Man turned to the other man. "Get yer gun ready."

Marz's eyes widened as the second man pulled a gun from its holster and clicked it. It was the same kind of gun Braden had used to shoot the crocodiles in the river.

Gun Man adjusted his hat. "How'd he get this silly name, SunKing?"

"I heard about that." Rope Man spat on the ground. "He's named after some fat old king who wore long curly wigs and rouge on his cheeks. Real fop."

"Fop?"

"Dandy. Pretty boy. A girlie man who wears more makeup than

QUAGGA

an old beauty queen. His people called him the Sun King. Story goes he had the last quagga zebra in his personal zoo."

"That true?"

"Dunno. It's probly jus' one more crazy Ol'Terra story. Anyway, this here quagga's jus' about the meanest critter ever uncorked. The lab guys are trying to brew up a girlfriend for him. They think it might calm him, but his kinda pretty girl would probly make him wilder than ever."

Gun Man snickered. "He don't look very cooperative today."

"He'll learn." Rope Man approached the quagga. "Well, now, Mr. SunKing, you ready for the halter? That's the key to everthin'." He dangled the halter from his hand. "Come to shuga daddy, now." He threw two sugar cubes to the animal. The tan zebra sniffed the cubes, and then drew them into its mouth with nibbling lips.

"Oh, SunKing, you big beautiful boy, you ain't no halfbreed, no zedonk, no zorse. I'm a-bettin' you're a real quagga," Rope Man said. "Soon's you learn to take halter and bridle, realize who's the boss, every circus will be biddin' for you. You'll bring us a sweet payday. One half to the gov'na lady, and the other half to us." Gun Man snickered. "With a little tip to us, of course."

As Rope Man drew nearer, SunKing's nostrils flared, and his breathing grew fast. Marz, leering from his spy place, started breathing faster, too. He felt somehow bonded to the striped animal by something deeper than both of them being prisoners at Yerkoza.

"Okay, now, Mr. SunKing, just relax why don't ya? I got more candy for you now, right here." Rope Man held out more sugar cubes in one hand, with the halter hanging on his arm.

Head down, the quagga eyed Rope Man, head swaying. A deep,

suspicious sound vibrated in his throat. Marz felt a strange stirring in his own throat.

"You got to come an' git it. Come on, now." Rope Man rubbed the sugar cubes together, and then blew the sugar dust toward SunKing. A wisp of it blew toward Marz.

Marz, still hiding, caught a whiff of sugar dust and salivated. "Yuck," he whispered.

Rope Man posed a sugar cube on the tip of his outstretched tongue. Teasing the quagga, he curled his tongue and drew the sugar into his mouth. He then spat the sugar into his hand, and held it out to the quagga, fingers wiggling. "If you don't eat it, I will."

The quagga inched towards Rope Man's hand, twitching his ears. As he began to nibble, Rope Man moved the halter down his arm and toward the quagga's nose.

At the first touch of rope bristle on the pink skin of his nose, the beast bolted. Marz jerked in sympathy. The beast's ears lay back flat against his neck; the whites of his eyes flared in anger. He backed up and kicked the fence with his powerful rear haunches. His assault cracked the timbers and sent large wood splinters flying. Marz, heart thumping, prepared to run.

"Still can't do it the nice an' easy way, huh?" Rope Man traded halter for lariat. "Okay, we have other ways. We noted for our creativity. One way or 'nother, we break 'em all." He spun the lariat until it whistled in the air, then pitched it toward SunKing. The loop sailed through the air and fell around the quagga's head. SunKing fought back, twisting and turning, trying to free himself. Rope Man flicked the rope and tugged on it, making it slide farther down SunKing's neck. Marz grabbed his own neck and rubbed it.

QUAGGA

SunKing reared up on his hind legs, forelegs paddling in the air, making an angry, hissing sound. He was about to stomp on Rope Man when Gun Man aimed and squeezed the trigger. A winged dart shot out, spiraled through the air, and smacked SunKing in the neck. Its needle point burrowed into his muscle, pumping tranco.

The powerful, numbing medicine surged through the quagga's muscular body, sucked deeper into his bloodstream by each heartbeat. His skin shivered. His eyes flickered, dimmed, and closed. First his front legs, then the rear, crumpled beneath him. He slumped to the ground.

When Marz caught the beast's gaze, their eyes met in a bittersweet moment. Hello and goodbye in one glance. The quagga's head swayed and then fell in the dirt.

Marz wanted to jump out from his hiding place, run to the animal's side, attack the evil men, do something! But he hesitated because he remembered what happened to the crocs when Braden shot them with the same kind of gun.

Once SunKing lay powerless on the ground, Rope Man loosened the lariat. "This gonna be the longest night of your solitary life, lonely boy. I recommend you wake up tomorrow with a new attitude. You git no girlfriend 'til you learn who's boss. 'Til you learn to serve and obey!" He climbed the fence and stomped away, Gun Man following.

With the evil men gone, Marz scaled the fence and approached SunKing. The magnificent striped beast lay stretched out on the ground, eyes closed, flies crawling all over his eyelashes. Marz placed his ear to the quagga's chest. The heart was still beating, ever so slowly. He placed his palm up to the animal's nostril. The exhaled air was still warm.

After pondering a moment, Marz climbed over the fence and looked around. In a flash he turned and ran down a little path that led away from the corral. If he took it, he might be free from Yerkoza forever. Maybe find his way back to the balloon family. Or back to the forest.

He started running. The trail soon took him to a point overlooking a lush valley, teeming with red-leafed trees and a winding river. One more step and Yerkoza would disappear.

And he would never again see Bighair Woman. Or Rope Man. Or Gun Man. Or his new friend, SunKing the brown striped beast.

Marz stopped and looked back at the quagga, lying nearly motionless in the corral. For several moments he just stood there. He turned first to the valley, then to the corral. Then, one cautious step at a time, he traced his tracks back to the corral. He climbed the fence and checked the quagga. No change. Helpless, but still breathing . . . slowly.

All through the heat of the afternoon Marz explored the corral and its surroundings, searching for bugs and plants to eat. Every few minutes he would return to the quagga, and check on him. Every time, same result.

When the stars began twinkling, and the moons glowed in the heavens like colored lanterns floating down a river, Marz crouched down beside the quagga. Soon he lay his head on the quagga's belly and fell asleep.

He dreamed of being back in his old home in the forest, watching the moons in the warm evenings, hearing the rising chorus of life in the wild. Birds twittering and cawing. Frogs croaking, crickets chirping, river gurgling. The flapping din of millions of bats departing their cave as a living black cloud, headed for the evening's bugfeast. Fat gozzle berries, ripe and ready to drop to the ground, exploding on his tongue.

Something woke Marz from his dream. The quagga had moved a bit.

The quagga lifted his head in jerks, but was still too weak to stand. Marz tried stroking him, but the animal pushed him away. Salty, dried sweat rippled across the quagga's neck.

Marz carefully pulled the tranco dart out of SunKing's neck; the animal made a soft chirping sound. The boy knelt before the beast. Could they once again find the connection they had shared, for a moment, before the quagga collapsed? They stared into one another's eyes.

A small muddy pond lay just outside the corral. Marz dashed to it and filled his bowl with water, then returned and offered the mud tea to SunKing. The animal emptied the bowl with one noisy slurp, his neck rippling as the water surged down his dry throat. Marz repeated this favor many times, until SunKing would drink no more. Each time Marz went to the pond, he squished the mud between his toes. It was fun, like playing in the mud along the river, back home in the forest.

When the quagga's thirst was finally satisfied Marz knelt beside him again. He ran his fingers through the animal's thick, black, spiky mane. One by one, he pulled long black hairs from the tail, until he had enough to twist together into a string, which he tied around his own neck. He then pulled strands from the quagga's mane, wove them into a second string and tied it to the first. The new string hung down the back of his neck, imitating the quagga's mane.

Marz bounded back over the corral fence and returned to the muddy pond. Using mud from the pond, he painted dark brown stripes on his jumpsuit, to match the stripes on SunKing.

In the field around the corral grew several types of grass. Marz collected a few handfuls and fed them to SunKing, and followed up with a dessert of extra sugar cubes left behind by Rope Man. He treated himself to a couple of them, too. "Mmm yuck." Soon SunKing regained enough strength to stand up, at first wobbling like a newborn colt.

When the sugar was gone, Marz and SunKing lay down together in a corner of the corral. Marz slowly climbed astride, wrapped his legs around the beast's belly and his arms around the neck. "Fren zokay." Soon they both fell back into a deep sleep, with three moons glowing in the heavens above them.

Shortly after sunrise, Rope Man and Gun Man reappeared at the corral. Rope Man carried the halter and lariat as before, but this time he also had a long black whip with a stinger tip.

"You learn anythin' durin' the night, Mr. SunKing?" Rope Man cracked the whip several times and did his ear-splitting whistle again, startling SunKing and Marz.

Marz tried to hide behind the quagga's large body, but he was revealed when SunKing rose in answer to the whip.

"Aha! The Wild Boy is it? We heard about you. Runaway. Fugitive kid. You need a hard lesson, too. Think you can escape Yerkoza? Stupid, stupid boy." His laugh sounded like gravel shaking in a barrel. "You here forever now! You should be almost hungry enough to eat your own finger. Or some bugs. We hear you a in-sec-tee-vore. A bug eatin' boy."

Marz dashed to the fence and clambered over it, out of the corral. He located a hiding spot behind a bush, and crouched down to watch and wait.

"We'll get you later, Bug Boy. SunKing first," Rope Man called out. "He's worth big money; you just another runaway with a better excuse than most."

Once inside the fence, Rope Man held out the halter and approached SunKing. "No shuga today, bad boy. Either you take the halter, or you get an even worse pain in the neck." He cracked the whip, stinging SunKing's ear. The quagga reacted angrily, rearing up, whinnying in protest. Marz grabbed his own ear in sympathy.

"Oh, so you still Mista Nasty, are ya? Guess you want the big bee sting again." Gun Man stood so the quagga could see him, and aimed his tranco dart gun.

SunKing met the old threat with a new display of anger. His ears flipped straight back and his nostrils flared. Rope Man took one more step toward him, and the beast let fly with a mighty blasting kick to the fence. The brown zebra ran crazy inside the corral, bucking, rearing, snorting. Wild enough to hurt himself on the railing.

"Git 'im under control!" Rope Man screamed. "A dead quagga's worth nothin'."

Gun Man took aim and shot, but this time the dart only flew through SunKing's mane, missing the flesh. Gun Man loaded another tranco dart and cocked the gun again.

When the man squinted and aimed at the quagga, Marz grabbed

his bowl, threw it and hit the man, throwing him off balance. The gun fell to the dry dirt.

"You worthless grunt!" the man screamed. "You nothin' but trouble. Maybe you need the bee sting even more'n this crazy zebar." He leaned down to pick up the gun, but Marz was faster. He charged straight at the man, plowed into him and knocked him over. "Hey! Monkey Boy, you flat outta chances now! I own your neck!"

While the quagga continued circling inside the corral, Gun Man scrambled to his feet. Reloading as he ran toward Marz, he cursed wildly. "You get what you are, a big pain in the butt!" He stopped, dropped down on one knee, and aimed at Marz.

Marz bolted back inside the fence and dashed to SunKing. He leaped up on the zebra's back and grabbed his mane. "Marz good," he whispered.

Gun Man waited outside the fence, his gun fixed on Marz. "Good thing you worth big money, Mista Hothead, otherwise you'd be the vultures' dinner tonight."

SunKing recoiled with even more angry energy than before. Marz held tight, arms locked around SunKing's neck, legs strapped around the belly like belts. The quagga snorted, reared up, kicked the fence many times. On the fourth kick, the top two bars on the main gate came crashing down.

Gun Man fired his dart gun. This time the dart passed under Marz's arms and fell into the dirt. Marz laughed and sputtered his tongue at the angry man.

SunKing, the only living quagga in all of Empire Luna, leaped up and soared over the damaged gate, galloped out into the open plain. Marz the Wild Boy, the barefoot kid with no family and no home, clung tightly around the zebra's neck. Their matching manes flowed wildly in the wind as they headed straight for the path leading down to the canyon.

Marz whooped, "Waahaaa! SunKing, Marz. Fren zokay!"

Chapter 5 ☽ ☽ ☽ ☽ ☽ ☽

DONOVAN

"Donovan, my king, the time draws near." It was the crusty voice of Tancreido, trusted advisor to three generations of Arkenstone kings. "We must speak, in private." He hobbled toward the king, grasping his knotted walking staff and huffing with every shuffling step. His white hair and beard hung in a dingy mess, like an abandoned spider web. As usual, he wore a simple maroon robe and sandals.

King Donovan offered his arm; Tancreido gratefully grabbed it with his shaky hand. Even while limping on his left leg, the king steadied his counselor as they climbed down the damp, mossy stone stairs to the old man's humble home. His underground cottage lay hidden beneath the lush greenery of Aldebaran's Garden, at the rear of Castle Tulamarine. The rain-stained oaken door squeaked on its rusty hinges as the king pushed it open. Tancreido doddered through the archway and down the narrow hallway to his study, with the king following.

Embers of gabania wood glowed in the fireplace. Tancreido inhaled deeply, closed his eyes and smiled. "That aroma reminds me of my youth, back on the Blood Moon. Helps me think clearly in my old age." He chuckled. "Or tricks me into thinking I can still think clearly!"

The shelves of the study brimmed with books, many of them ancient, and a rack of multi-colored view-gems in fancy cases. On one shelf rested a model of Empire Luna, the seven moons encircling the home planet, New Roma. A leather book lay on the desk, locked and sealed. King and counselor took their seats.

"How go the preparations for Crestival?" the king asked.

Tancreido sighed. "There's a problem. How can we count on a broke-down circus to do a good job with the grand finale?"

"Depends on how the Cloud Forest expedition goes."

"What's the news?"

"Nothing since they sent a QM flash saying they were in the Spitfire, descending into the forest. The girl sounded excited."

"Can we reach them?"

"I tried yesterday. Nothing but noise."

"Perhaps conditions are better today. Let's try again." The king took out his QM, and entered all the commands for a connection to Luna Verdanta, and then to the Hawkens.

Scratchy noise. Space hiss. Then, finally, "Braden Hawken here. Who's there?"

The king smiled. "Braden, my old friend, where are you?"

"Majesty!"

"Ah, don't majesty me when it's just you and me. Save that stuff for stuffy times."

The screen cleared. The dirty, sunburned face of Elizabelle appeared. Her dry voice almost cracked as she spoke. "King Donovan, it's Elizabelle. We're on our way to the relay looper station. We're coming home!"

"Tell me, young lady, did you find your new animal star?"

The QM signal began breaking up. "We didn't exactly find a new animal, but we did find . . ."

Before Elizabelle could finish, the signal faded back to space noise. Donovan tried to reconnect, but the QM just kept sputtering.

"At least we know they are all right," Tancreido said. "They should be back here soon. Then we'll learn the rest of the story." He folded his wizened hands together and looked directly into Donovan's eyes. "Let us speak of something far more important than moon parties."

The counselor pulled the sealed book to the center of the desk. When he hovered his palm above the lock, it snapped open. "Your good father often spoke of keeping in touch with the people." He began reading from the book. "The duties of loyalty and service flow both ways. A good king betters the lives of all his people, not just his rich friends and family. Kings who abuse their people end up losing their armies, their crowns, their castles." Tancreido closed the book. "And, back on Ol'Terra, a few even had their heads cut off and kicked down the street and into the sewer."

"Are you saying . . ." a tone of suspicion rose in the king's voice. ". . . that I've failed the people in some way?"

"There is an ancient saying about 'a man's home is his castle.' Our people want to see a real family in the real castle."

"Make your point." The king sounded impatient.

"The empire needs a royal heir who can ascend to the throne

when your last sunset fades. A wife who is but specks of smoke in a light-frame, or a bittersweet memory, cannot give you or the empire a princess or a prince. That's why the people long for a new queen. This Crestival."

Donovan rose and approached the picture on the wall, of his own marriage to Galena. "I have a wife. I cannot have children until I find her again."

The counselor glanced at the wedding portrait. "It was my favorite wedding." Tancreido rubbed his teary eyes. "But, our law says that any missing wife—queen, highborn or commoner—is considered dead after seven years. You're free to find a new queen."

"I don't care what the law says," Donovan boomed. "You may call it freedom, but it's a prison to me. Until I have proof that Galena is truly dead, I won't consider a new queen."

The advisor chose his words carefully. "Please, Donovan, listen to a crusty old bachelor. If you hold out for perfection, your prize will be nothing. Two Crestival cycles is a very long time for a man in his prime to be alone. Especially when he is a king whose parents and grandparents are gone, and who has no living brothers or sisters, and no children."

Donovan shook his head. "You are my counselor in running the empire, not family matters."

The aged advisor shook his head. "For a king, there's no difference between empire and family. It is the burden you were born to bear."

"Do you suggest that I enter a fake marriage just to save the empire?"

The advisor nodded. "Many wise kings have done exactly that.

Sometimes, a royal marriage is mostly about holding power. Binding families as a way to avoid war." He hobbled to the fireplace and placed another gabania log on the fire. "But there may be another way."

The king turned and looked doubtfully at Tancreido. "Okay, tell me."

"We could return to the system used by First King." Donovan's great grandfather, the first King Arkenstone, devised the plan. Each moon sent several princesses, and the king chose one from each moon to join his family as secondary wives. His first wife, Aldebaran, dutifully accepted the plan as the only way to end the wars between the moons. The choosing of the lunar princesses was a grand ceremony, the highlight of Crestival. From that time Crestival had been the ideal time for weddings. Especially royal weddings.

"In the old way, each moon had its own queen in the royal family, and each had her own tower in the castle. But you could do it a new way, your way. At your choice, any of the new queens could hold only an honorary title and throne. In public ceremonies, each would be a queen with her own royal sash and the crown for her home world. But in your chambers, you would be free to choose."

"Choose?"

"The mother of your children."

A suspicious tone filled Donovan's voice. "How long have you been planning this?"

"It's been on my mind for a few years. I've presented the idea to the Council of Lunar Governors. They all agree, and approve."

Donovan folded his arms against his chest. "I don't care who approves. Perhaps the seven queen system was needed once, long ago. That time is gone. You remember my choice?"

"Of course. Your mother and I risked our positions to convince your father and the Council that the royal marriage rule had to be changed, that any prince must be free to choose his own wife, and not be limited to lunar princesses."

"Yes, I owe my crown to you, and my mother. But remember, when my choice was between Galena and the crown, I chose her. Galena is wife to me, and Queen Selena to the people. No matter where she may be. No matter how long it takes me to find her again."

"As you wish, my king." Tancreido nodded his head. "Please think about a fresh start."

"Anything else?"

Tancreido's bones cracked as he rose. "Much more. Spy reports. Proco Haruma."

At the mention of Proco, the king's eyebrows furrowed and his breathing deepened.

"His power grows. Especially on the Blood Moon." Tancreido drew a view-gem from its case and placed it in the pierce-light box. The light beam circled in warm-up and then projected an image of a stocky man in a hooded cloak, with a long, deep red cape billowing in a sand storm. Behind him stood a statue of the first King Arkenstone.

Inside the light box, the caped man thrust a staff into the air and shouted, "Who is the reincarnation of the Crimson King?" An unseen crowd roared, "Proco Haruma!" The caped man drew a scimitar sword and thrust it into the air. "Together, we shall restore the power of the ancients. Every Arkenstone must be destroyed!" With one mighty thrust of the sword, he chopped off the head of the statue of First King, spit on it and kicked sand on it as it rolled away. The rowdy crowd erupted in vulgar cheers. "Donovan will be the last of the Arkenstone pretenders." The image faded on the sounds of a delirious crowd.

Tancreido shut the light box.

"He's a traitor!" Donovan pounded his fist on the desk. "A mad man. Where is he now?"

"Between seven moons and this world, there are millions of places he could hide. One captured spy told of Proco's plans to disturb the moon orbits. Something about sabotaging the Higgs Generators, upsetting the gravity balance." He pointed to the model of the Blood Moon. "No more alignment of the moons, no more Crestival. When the symbol of unity is gone, confusion reigns and he takes over. Crazy, but that's how he thinks. Some believe."

"Broadcast the bounty notice. Send out pictures of him everywhere."

"We're not sure what he looks like today." Tancreido moved the lunar model aside and replaced it with a book from the shelf. He slowly turned the pages. "We believe every one of these is Proco in disguise." A series of faces, similar mostly in the eyes, paraded before them. While most appeared to be men, a few seemed to be plain women with far too much makeup.

The king slammed the book shut. "Enough! The day will come when a pierce-light in his eye will betray him, no matter how many face molders he bribes, no matter how many masks he wears. Do we have his eye scan?"

"We do. And tissue samples from his days as a general in your father's army."

"Who are his followers?"

"His spies join the Empire Army. He recruits among the interlunar traders, promises them easy riches from charging heavy tolls for allowing passage between moons. Some of his followers join circuses, pretending to be tent riggers or cooks or truck drivers, or roustabouts, or even performers. They plant their poison ideas with the local troublemakers, leave coded veegees, and then quickly move on to another moon. Be careful issuing lunar travel licenses."

Donovan turned, ready to leave. "On your new queen idea, I will think it over."

"A royal wedding during Crestival, with a grand finale performance by the circus to honor the new queen. That would be a truly historic event."

The king nodded his head. "Indeed it would. What is the bounty on Proco?"

"Ten bricks of gold."

"Make it twenty-one. Spread the word everywhere. Maybe one of his bootlickers will decide to get rich and turn him in. Same bounty, dead or alive." And with that the king left.

It was past midnight when the door handle clicked, and the door creaked again. Donovan stuck his head in. Tancreido lifted his head from his pillow. "Yes?"

"I don't like your advice." The king stroked his forehead. "But I suspect you may be right. You may begin making plans. If I decide to go along, it will be to find a new queen. Just one, not six or seven. Let the governor of each moon name one princess candidate."

Chapter 6 ☽ ☽ ☽ ☽ ☽ ☽

HURRICANE

Elizabelle and her dad were stuck in the relay looper station, jostling their way through the noisy crowds. The family had been crammed in the high security section at Luna Verdanta's space port for two days. They'd slept in their day clothes, waiting for the flight back to New Roma.

"Excuse me, sir," a raspy voice asked meekly, "are you Mr. Braden Hawken?"

"Might be. Who asks?"

A bushy-bearded man sidled up to Braden. "'Twas me, sir." He wore plain blue overalls, a broad-rimmed floppy hat, and windswept dark glasses. He tipped his hat to Elizabelle.

Braden stepped between his daughter and the Man in Blue, but she peered around her dad's elbow. "Make it quick," he said. "We're in a hurry. Trying to find our boarding gate."

The Man in Blue moved his cleaning machine so that the spy cams mounted in the ceiling saw only his back. "Excuse me, young lady, my eyesight is not so good anymore." His voice was so raspy that Elizabelle could barely understand him. "Could you help me read these numbers?" Hunched over, he pointed a shaky finger at the control panel of his cleaning machine.

Elizabelle inspected the dial. The numbers faded into a smoky vapor and a small screen appeared. She gasped when the screen showed the Jefferson Spitfire hot air balloon crashing into the desert dunes, spewing sand. "Where'd you get that?"

"Yes, where?" her dad demanded. "And who are you?"

"Not so loud." The Man in Blue winked at Elizabelle. The corners of his mouth curled. "Follow me, please," he whispered.

Elizabelle and her dad cautiously trailed the Man in Blue as he shuffled down the hallway. He approached a metal door marked "JANITOR ONLY." He stood so that his left eye was directly in front of the "O" in "JANITOR." A tiny light beam flashed out of the "O" and scanned the man's eye. He winked; the light blinked. The door clicked and opened, just a crack. He pulled the door open wide so it blocked the view of the spy cameras, then motioned for Braden and Elizabelle to move behind the door.

The closet seemed to be an ordinary janitor's supply room, a jumble of buckets, brooms, and dusters. A ladder hung on the wall. The aroma of cleaning fluids filled the air and stung Elizabelle's eyes and nostrils.

The Man in Blue stepped into the closet and crab-walked sideways, stepping over several buckets, until he stood directly in front of the ladder. He curled his finger, inviting them to follow.

"What's this all about?" Elizabelle asked.

From inside the closet, the Man in Blue answered in a low but steady voice. "You and your family are on your way back to the Baraboo circus camp on New Roma. Right?"

"How would you know about such things?" Braden demanded.

"In my real business, sir, I learn many things about people in danger. Perhaps you have heard of my service." He flashed a card that read: "ICC, Intra-lunar Custom Charter."

Braden held the card in the light from the hallway. "We don't need a custom charter."

"We're on flight 505 back home," Elizabelle said. "Loading in a few minutes."

"And I'll bet . . ." the man paused for dramatic effect. ". . . you'll be traveling courtesy of our *beautiful* and *charming* Lady Governor."

Elizabelle rolled her eyes at his suggestion.

"We don't know you," Braden said. "Why've you been snooping into our private stuff?"

"I have friends in low places." The Man in Blue seemed almost to brag. "And a few in high places too. Contacts with some of the lady governor's staff." His voice dropped into a whisper. "I have a bit of news that should interest you greatly. Come, I'll show you."

Braden paused. "Make it fast."

The Man in Blue stared into Elizabelle's eyes. "Someone is missing from your family. A young man in his early teens who should be with you. Am I right?"

"Listen, Mr. ICC," Braden said defiantly. "I won't stand for this spying and prying."

The Man in Blue whispered to them. "I can help you find the missing boy."

Elizabelle called back. "How?"

"Elizabelle!" Her father pulled her away and stooped, talking intensely into her face. "This man's not to be trusted. He's a snoop. We don't know what he's really after."

But the idea of getting Marz back made Elizabelle yank on her father's arm. "Dad, what if he can find Marz?" She hadn't seen the Wild Boy in three days, when Governor Mai-Kellina's guards dragged him away to be "civilized" at Yerkoza. "We can at least listen."

Braden turned and approached the closet again, with Elizabelle still beside him. The Man in Blue tightened the ladder and then climbed up and disappeared into darkness. His voice echoed down to them. "Up here, Mr. Hawken. It's quite safe, I assure you."

"You wait right here," Braden confided to Elizabelle. "If I'm not back in ten minutes, alert your mother, call the security police and come looking for me. I mean it, you stay here."

Elizabelle set her QM alarm to eight minutes. "How can you get lost in a closet?"

"I can't . . . I hope." And with that, Braden stepped away. Elizabelle stood at the bottom of the ladder and watched her dad climb. At the top he encountered a hatch—a round door in the ceiling—outlined by a glowing rim of light. He twisted the latch, lifted the hatch, and crawled in. The hatch door closed behind him.

After only a couple of minutes Elizabelle's mind burned with curiosity. She started imagining terrible things. Why did the hatch door close tight? How did this strange man know about Marz? Was he trying to kidnap her dad? Or Marz?

Then on impulse, she stepped back into the closet and climbed the ladder. She was surprised that the hatch door opened so easily. And so quietly. She opened the hatch just a crack and peered in. The dimly-lit room was littered with a few shabby chairs and a couch.

Her dad stood just an arm's length away from her, his back to her. The Man in Blue noisily slurped something. "I keep the light low so I can see out but no one can see in. One way glass. Go ahead, have a look."

Her dad leaned forward, peering out the window. Elizabelle raised the hatch further, straining so she could see, too. The loading station outside was filled with modular carriages, all exactly the same size and all painted in Verdanta green, crammed full of people bustling to board the loopers with their pets, bags, and boxes. Her dad did not notice her.

Braden confronted the man. "Come clean with me. Who are you?"

"My arrest records say Jonathan Hertzicona. Friends, and a few enemies, call me Johnny Hurricane. Pleased to meet you." Braden met his hand suspiciously.

"You offered to show me the boy."

Just then, Elizabelle's grip slipped, and the hatch made a little squeaky sound.

The two men spun their heads in her direction. She smiled and waved. "Hi, Dad."

"Belle, I need you down below."

"I can signal mom from up here." She held up her QM. "Besides, I want to see the show!" She scrambled out of the hatch and looked around, blinking until her eyes adjusted.

"Welcome, Miss." Hurricane chuckled and lifted his hat to her.

69

"Long time since I had a lovely lady here." Then, in sudden movements, he flipped his hat into her lap, pulled off his fake beard and tossed that too. She and her dad gasped at his sudden change of appearance. Hurricane flicked off his dark glasses and released the top of his overalls, pulling out a jelly-belly pad. He handed those to her as well. "Keep these," he said. "Never know when you might want to disguise yourself as a fat old man." He winked at her. "Or a fat old clown?"

Out of costume, Hurricane stood proudly in a bright red jacket and shiny black pants.

"Very dashing, Mr. Hurricane." Braden checked his QM. "We're out of here in five minutes, so cut to it. Show us the missing boy."

Hurricane flipped out his QM and pointed it at the wall directly behind him. A silent, moving image flickered on the wall. A blurry, distant shot of a black-haired, skinny boy in his early teens, with a shock of black hair projecting down his back. The boy leaped onto the back of a tan-striped horse, which galloped a short distance and then bounded over a fence.

"Where'd you get that?" Elizabelle asked impatiently.

"A few years ago, Governor Mai-Kellina invited me to Yerkoza for some special . . . what shall I call it? . . . *Training*. I went along for a couple of moon cycles before I decided the place had too many rules for me. Before I left, I made a few secr . . . *umm* . . . discreet friendships with some of her staff. When I heard about the boy's escape from Yerkoza, I called in a favor, and one of my insider friends gave me the veegee. Recognize them?"

"Sure," Elizabelle said eagerly. "I saw him first. From very far away."

"Where'd Marz get that horse?" her dad asked. "Is it a palomino?"

Hurricane smiled. "It's not a horse. It's a rare kind of zebra. Ever hear of the quagga?"

"I have!" Elizabelle faced her dad. "I studied about them last year. They went extinct back on Ol'Terra. A team of bio-engineers at Yerkoza tried to bring the quagga back."

"That's right, smart girl. Brace yourself, m'dear." Hurricane pointed to the view-gem of Marz and SunKing. "Dr. Rau's team has finally succeeded. The quagga lives again. That's him in the veegee. A proud, hot headed, cranky stallion. The only one. Anywhere. First quagga to live and breathe and kick in many centuries."

Elizabelle narrowed her eyes. "You sure?"

"Watch closely this time." He replayed the scene.

"It does look like the Ol'Terra paintings of quaggas, Daddy." Even in the dim light, Elizabelle recognized the look on her dad's face. The quagga could be 7MC's new animal star. She could almost hear the circus audience going crazy at the sight of a large, beautiful mammal brought back to life after a many centuries of extinction. No other circus could match it.

"Parading that beast would land us in all kinds of trouble . . ." her dad murmured. Elizabelle knew that all extinction revivals were automatically under the king's protection. Revived animals could not be harmed or allowed to harm any other animals or humans.

"Where are they now?" her dad asked.

"They ran away. Together." Hurricane replayed the view-gem showing Marz and the quagga galloping down the trail. "That path leads directly down the ravine and then into the Red River Valley. I went the same way when I esca . . . *left* Yerkoza. You can bet Mai-Kellina will have her chopper cops searching for them. And you can bet that I can find them first."

"And then?" Braden said.

"That's up to you, sir. I run a custom charter. You're the customer. What do you want?"

"Ahhh!" Braden smiled. "Now I see. You're a smuggler looking for a paying customer!"

"Smuggler? Ha! No, Mr. Hawken, I'm just a simple lunar bus driver who does custom jobs. But you are right on the second point. I do expect to get paid."

"Seven Moon Circus can't pay a king's ransom. Or anything. We're broke."

Hurricane turned off the projector. "You just put on a great show at Crestival, starring the quagga, and everything will work out." He addressed Elizabelle in an ominous tone. "If my Yerkoza reports are correct, this magnificent animal was being beaten, whipped and shot full of tranco. All because he would not take a halter and let a rider mount."

From her animal studies, Elizabelle knew that even back on Ol'Terra zebras were famous for bucking riders off their backs, and for refusing to be trained to do tricks. And the quagga, when it still lived, was the most cantankerous of all zebras.

Braden stroked his sideburns again. "If a revived animal has been seriously mistreated by Mai-Kellina's people, then she's lost her right of custody."

"She'll never agree." Elizabelle shook her head.

Hurricane laughed. "Doesn't matter. What happens to the quagga is the king's call, not hers. Besides, I owe her a little . . . *return favor.*"

HURRICANE

"What about Marz?" Elizabelle asked.

"Soon's he's seven lunar leagues off the surface of Verdanta, she'll have no power over him."

Elizabelle's heart leaped as she realized that there was still a chance that Marz could come home with them. "Daddy, we can save Marz! He saved us from the crocs." She turned to Hurricane. "How much?"

"Elizabelle!" Her dad protested.

"I've got some circus pay saved up," she said, ignoring her father, "I can get the clowns to chip in some tips. Tricka will donate some old jewelry."

"Elizabelle, you're getting carried away again."

She spun on him. "Daddy, we can get Marz back. And a quagga—the perfect new animal star we need." She saw Hurricane smirking at her. "What? Why are you laughing at me?"

Hurricane threw his hands up defensively. "I'm not laughing, little lady. I like a 'take charge' woman." He regarded the feisty girl and her father. "Tell ya what. You get your dad and his boss at the circus to chip in four bricks of gold and you can keep your circus pay. And the old jewelry."

"Four bricks?" Braden sputtered, his eyebrows rising. "My boss can't pay even one. We'd have better luck with the clowns painting tears on their faces and passing a beggar's hat."

"Mr. Hawken, I will deliver the only living quagga and the missing boy to you at the Baraboo circus training camp on New Roma. Or any other place you name, on any moon except Verdanta. After the Crestival, if you want to keep the quagga, then your circus must pay me four bricks of pure gold, without registration numbers. If

73

you can't, many other circuses will bid for him. I'll deliver the quagga to the highest bidder, and you'll owe nothing. You can't lose."

"You can't sell him," Elizabelle insisted. "You're not the owner of the quagga."

"Don't claim to be. My fee is a special delivery charge for a dangerous assignment. I'm just a lunar bus driver, remember? If I deliver the boy and the quagga to you, I have the right to take the quagga away after Crestival, or get paid in full. Simple deal. Want it?"

"Can we go with you on the rescue mission?" Elizabelle asked.

"And take the risk of your whole family being captured by Mai-Kellina and imprisoned as thieves and kidnappers? No, sorry. For a mission this dangerous, I work alone."

Braden made direct eye contact with Hurricane. "You can't take the boy."

"Don't want to. He's just one more hungry orphan. I hear he can't even talk. You can have him."

"How do we know you can really do this?" Elizabelle said.

"You don't," Hurricane admitted bluntly. "But if I fail, you owe me nothing. If we don't rescue them, Mai-Kellina will capture the boy and the quagga and take both of them back to Yerkoza. She'll keep the quagga for herself and call the boy an animal thief and a juvenile delinquent. She'll keep him 'in training' for a long, long time, maybe locked up."

Elizabelle shuddered.

"What about it, Mr. Hawken? Do we have a deal?"

Braden paused a moment. Elizabelle whispered in his ear, "Remember when you told Mom, 'we'll never get another chance like this'? Same thing now."

Her dad winked at her. "Yes, Mr. Hurricane, we have a deal." The two men shook hands.

Elizabelle felt relieved. For a moment. Until she realized another problem. "Mr. Hurricane, even if you can find Marz, how will he know who you are? How can he tell you're trying to help, or that we sent you? Won't he just jump on the quagga and run away again?"

Chapter 7 ♪ ♪ ♪ ♪ ♪ ♪

CAVES

Johnny Hurricane stood at the mouth of his old hideout cave. The Red River Valley lay before him, a panorama of warm pastels. The canyon walls, scarred with crags and pock-marked with the gaping mouths of caves, framed the valley. A billow of bats rushed out from one of the caves, eager for their evening bug feast. Dokon trails zigzagged from the valley floor up the steep canyon walls. Last time he was here, just after escaping from Yerkoza, this cave had served as a refuge.

The old cave was the perfect place to stash his interlunar spaceship, the Buzzard. Its name was partly a twist on Bozwald Engineering, the company that built it for him, a pure custom job. There was a second reason for the name: the pilot's cockpit, mounted at the tip of a long, flexible neck, looked like a buzzard vulture jerking and poking its head in search of prey.

He pulled the seeker goggles down from his crash helmet and adjusted them for a comfortable fit. With a quick tap on the button on his sleeve, the veegee in his pocket hummed into record mode.

Hurricane wore his brand-new chameleon suit, the latest masterpiece by Kiko's Guild of Royal Weavers. He crouched in front of a reddish-colored rock near the mouth of his cave. In seconds the suit changed to match the color and vein pattern of the rock. "Thank you, Kiko. Let's find that quagga. And that boy."

Through the distance zoom, Hurricane surveyed the valley. First he scanned the cliffs on one side of the canyon, then the other, searching for any sign of a teen boy and a tan zebra.

Nothing.

He adjusted the zoom lens to focus on the valley floor below. Evening mist rose from the river in enticing swirls. The river attempted a U-turn every quarter mile or so, forming a mud pit at almost every bend. Knee-high grasses gently swayed across the meadow; cat-tail reeds lined the river. Spotted deer, toolachies, antelopes, and dokons grazed in the meadow. Other animals swam in the river—muskrats, beavers, rice rats, rio snakes, whitebelly snoutfish.

No sign of a boy with black mane down his back, or a tan and brown zebra.

When night came, heavy clouds muted the moonlight from the four moons floating above. The darkness made it much easier to hide.

Vertijet on his back, trimjets on his ankles and wrists, retractable jetwings on his arms, Hurricane was ready to search.

The sounds of Mai-Kellina's night crew of sky searchers rumbled in the distance. Soon their helicopters, loaded with penetrating searchlights and probes, broke over the horizon. Hurricane pushed the "insta black" button on his chameleon suit, and continued scanning.

A movement in the distance caught Hurricane's eye. Something walking quickly on two legs, not four. At first it was just a greenish blob zigzagging down the mountainside. "Ten X." The right lens magnified the image by ten. Definitely human. "Thatta boy, Marz! Come to Hurricane."

When the dodging figure reached the river, Hurricane leapt from his perch, jet wings extended and flaring. He flew close enough to make sure it was Marz, then swooped down and landed right in front of him.

Marz jumped back, turned, and ran.

"Marz, wait!" Hurricane shouted through his helmet. "Hold on! Your friends sent me. Elizabelle. Dizzy Mizz Lizzy, Ripley, remember? Let's be friends, okay?"

Marz slowed, took a few more halting steps, then stopped. He turned back, facing Hurricane, but still kept a safe distance. His jumpsuit was dirty and torn, but the mane, woven from SunKing's mane and tail hairs, still projected down his back.

Hurricane lifted his facemask. "Hello Marz! I'm Johnny Hurricane. Friends, okay?" He walked slowly toward Marz, arms open. "I got somethin' for ya." He adjusted the lenses of his goggles, positioning them just above his face.

The veegee image of Elizabelle, small but bright, appeared on the outer surface of the goggles. "Marz, it's Elizabelle." She held up a mirror. "We miss you. This is Johnny Hurricane. Listen to him!" She pointed to her ears.

Moving like a cautious cat, Marz took a few steps toward Hurricane, staring at the image on the goggles.

"Hi Marz! Ripley here." He doffed his circus hat, let the 7MC symbol glisten in the light, then donned it again. "Hurricane's here to help you. Be friends, okay?"

"We know about your beautiful new animal friend," Elizabelle said happily. She held up a painting of a quagga.

Marz cocked his head and inspected the strange man-bird with pictures on his forehead. Moving directly in front of Hurricane, eyebrows furrowed, Marz stuck his forefinger out to touch the goggles. The screen switched to Hurricane and the Hawken circus family huddled together. They chanted, "Marz, go with Johnny Hurricane."

When the image on the goggles faded, Hurricane pointed to his chest. "Hurricane." Then to Marz, "Marz, friends, okay?"

"Fren zokay?" Marz repeated cautiously.

"Where is your friend, SunKing?" Hurricane tapped on his goggles, and the image of Marz escaping from Yerkoza, riding astride SunKing, flashed for a few seconds.

Marz's face lit up at the sight. Gazing up the canyon wall, he pointed to his own hideout cave. With his fingers in his mouth he made a shrill whistling sound. The quagga stuck his head out and barked his *qua-haa* sound.

At that moment one of Mai-Kellina's sky-searcher copters broke through the clouds; its searchlight beam swept across the darkened meadow, nipping wide swaths with mist-filled light.

Hurricane crouched and held still. "Down, Marz. Don't move." He pushed down with his hands. Marz crouched near him. Hurricane's chameleon suit turned the color of the ground. They froze in position just as the chopper's searchlight flashed overhead. And passed by.

It seemed the danger had passed, but then suddenly the chopper stopped. Its roaring engines screeched as it banked hard, doubled back and re-scanned the area. Soon the chopper hovered directly above them, its searing beacon focused right on them.

A voice blared from the chopper. "Ah, we see ya now! Caught us a thief!"

It was the voice of the Rope Man from Yerkoza. "Hey Monkey Boy! We got dee-licious food, much better'n raw bugs. A warm bed. Nice room of yer own. You can get civ'lized, talk right an' all. Where's your partner in crime, that hothead ze-bar?"

Marz broke and ran for the dokon trail winding up the canyon wall. Hurricane, still holding motionless, shouted to him, "No, Marz! Don't lead them to him!"

The searchlight beam locked right on Hurricane. In the intense light his chameleon cloth began changing colors like a rippling rainbow.

From the chopper's loudspeaker several voices filtered down to the surface. "Whoa! Who's that?" "It's the fugitive Hurricane." "Triple bounty." "Bigger reward if we bring 'em im back alive!"

The tool box on the underside of the chopper popped open. A black ball of netting shot toward Hurricane, unrolling as it flew.

"Run, Marz!" Hurricane pointed upstream, then turned and ran in the opposite direction.

Too late. The net caught Hurricane. The sticky netting rolled in on itself, trapping him like a fly in a spider's web. He fired the vertijet, but it only lifted him off the ground a few feet. The jets choked and died. Hurricane fell back down to the ground, rolling in the dirt, squirming to unravel the net. But with each turn the netting stuck more firmly to itself, trapping him tighter.

Hurricane touched his QM and entered the passwords that allowed him to listen in, undetected, on the cabin conversation of the chopper. "We got Hurricane!" "We gotta get the kid, and the ze-bar! That beast is worth even more than Hurricane."

CAVES 🌙 🌙 🌙 🌙 🌙 🌙

The noisy chopper held steady, whirring in the air above Hurricane. A rope tethered the sticky netting to the cabin of the chopper.

"Where's that bug boy?" Rope Man shouted. "Get him and the beast will follow." The chopper's searchlight swept the canyon wall, and pinpointed Marz. "He's up there!"

Rope Man shimmied down the tether and bounced on the ground. He quickly pounded a stake in the ground and tied the tether to it, so Hurricane could not roll away. "Get the boy now!"

Another voice blared through the loudspeaker. "Too windy to fly that close to the canyon wall. Go to RC." The navigator and the pilot jumped out, leaving the chopper hovering in the air with no one inside. The pilot set up the Remote Control on its stand and guided the chopper, sending the huge flying machine over the river and up the canyon wall.

🌙 🌙 🌙 🌙 🌙 🌙 🌙

Marz's cave was concealed high up on the canyon wall, but a sure-footed beast like SunKing could reach it by following the dokon trails. A large boulder perched on an outcropping, hiding the mouth of the cave. Barely enough light seeped in to dimly illuminate the cave entrance.

Deep in the darkness, Marz shivered in fear. Hours before, the cave had seemed a safe place to hide. But now, with the noisy chopper approaching, he felt trapped.

Marz stroked the quagga's neck and led him to the mouth of the cave. Once they were positioned on the cave side of the boulder,

81

Marz went down on all fours. He backed up to the huge stone and kicked at it with his right leg. Then he rose and stroked the quagga's rear haunch. SunKing simply stood there, slowly swishing his tail.

Marz mounted and stretched his arms around the quagga's neck. Extending his legs 'til his feet pressed against the flank, he rubbed the beast's powerful rear leg muscles.

The chopper hovered just outside their cave, whirring noisily. The chopper's bubble windshields made it look like a huge mechanical dragonfly staring right at them. The probe arm, complete with searchlight, camera and speaker, snaked out from beneath the cabin. It frisked the rocks and trails, snooping for the inlet to the hiding place.

Soon the probe arm twisted around the boulder, found the mouth of the cave and invaded. The din of the chopper engine filled the cave, bouncing and echoing off the walls, hurting their ears. A voice on the speaker cackled: "Gotcha! You can't hide from the supa snoopa!"

The long probe, wiggling like an octopus tentacle, searched their hideout. It wove through the air, shining its penetrating glare into every corner of the cave. Finally, the arm came right up to Marz's face, pointed the camera, and inspected him head to toe. Rope Man's voice blared through the speaker. "Gotcha, Bug Boy. Enough hide and seek. Give up."

Marz spat on the camera lens. And threw dirt on the spittle, making mud.

"Still wanna do it the hard way? Okay, your choice."

A thin gas hissed from a nozzle on the probe arm, filling the cave. A starter flame on the probe arm flared; in an instant the gas ignited and formed a dense purplish smoke. Shining through the smoke, the searchlight beams took on an eerie glow. The acrid smell burned the eyes of both boy and beast. SunKing snorted wildly. Marz sneezed as heavy tears flowed.

Though he tried to hold his ground, Marz could bear the stinging purple vapor no more. He darted to the mouth of the cave, where the air was still mostly clear. The quagga followed.

Neither boy nor beast could see much through their streaming tears, but Marz managed to guide SunKing into position behind the boulder. He remounted and again nudged the quagga.

This time SunKing kicked the giant rock. The boulder rocked a bit, but stayed in place.

Then Marz gave a little toe tickle to the beast's haunch. This time the quagga jack hammered the rock. Shards of rock blasted helter-skelter.

Finally, the huge stone broke free. A crunching sound echoed through the cave.

The big rock rolled down the canyon and collided with the whirring chopper. The giant machine jolted, fighting back. The engine choked and sputtered. The rotor blades struggled to grind the big stone into pebbles. The blades scraped against the stone, and bent. The tail rotor whacked against the canyon wall. The probe arm broke off, writhing like a beheaded snake.

The chopper body twisted out of control. Split in half, ripping metal.

The main body of the chopper tumbled down the canyon wall, crushing everything in its path, heading straight toward Mai-Kellina's men. The pilot dropped the RCU and raced to escape, with the navigator following. They bounded right into the river, and ran

ESCAPE FROM LUNA VERDANTA

into a mud pit. Rope Man ran the other way, out into the meadow, toward Hurricane.

The chopper crashed into pieces on the valley floor, its searchlights flailing wildly, smoke billowing. The last whack of a rotor blade pinned the pilot and navigator in the river mud.

Rope Man grabbed his QM and shouted into it. "Emergency! Chopper down. Help!"

No response. He pocketed his QM, pulled a jetpack out of the smoking cabin of the chopper, strapped it on his back and zoomed up and away.

The chopper pilot and navigator struggled to escape from the mud. But no matter how much they grunted and pulled, they sank ever deeper into the quicksand.

The body of the chopper exploded, sending bright red flames leaping high into the air.

Hurricane lay on the muddy bank where Rope Man had tied and staked him. The knotted strands of netting bit into his cheeks and pressured his legs and arms. He was too close to the burning chopper body, and tried to wiggle away from it. But failed.

A purple haze floated out of the mouth of Marz's cave. Hurricane called up to him. "Marz, are you there? Can you hear me?"

Up at the mouth of his cave, Marz called to Hurricane through the purplish fog. "Marz Hurrcane." Mounted tall on SunKing, he rode out of the mouth of the cave. Together they charged down the dokon trail. The quagga deftly turned all the switchbacks in the trail, and jumped over the pika colony holes. When boy and beast reached the valley floor, they bypassed the pilot and navigator, who were still stuck in the mud, and dashed to Hurricane.

"You made it! Amazing!" Hurricane shouted. "I'm proud of you. Help me out." Marz tried to pick away the netting, but got nowhere.

Hurricane grabbed Marz's hand, and gestured for him to hold the netting. The netting fought back, like a roly-poly bug determined to curl into a ball. Marz stepped on the net, holding it to the ground as Hurricane gradually rolled his way out.

Finally Hurricane emerged from the netting, stood and smiled. "Good boy, Marz!" They ran away from the flaming chopper body.

Hurricane hobbled to the quagga and tried to stroke his neck. But SunKing backed away, snuffling. "Okay, don't get in a snit, I'm just tryin' to be friends, okay?" He turned to Marz. "We gotta get outta this place. How 'bout a ride on a space bus?" Marz looked at him blankly.

Hurricane ran to the chopper pilot's RCU. He quickly reset the crystals and entered the pass codes so it could control the Buzzard, and guided it to them. When the lunabus arrived, he released the expander clips and let the accordion walls of the underbelly drop down from the main body. The loading door to the cargo bay opened.

Hurricane ran to the cargo bay door, and hand signaled for Marz to follow. "Let's go Marz! The governor's bounty hunters will be here soon."

Marz again caressed the quagga's muzzle. The beast complained with his chuffing sound, and stroked the ground with his front hooves. And refused to budge.

In the distance, another flight of Mai-Kellina's choppers broke the horizon.

"Rumble time. Load and launch." Hurricane strode to a utility box in the corner of the cargo bay, rummaged through it for a minute, then turned and opened his palm with a flourish. "Sugar!" He tossed the cube to Marz, who sniffed it, tasted it, and smiled.

Slowly, Marz back stepped up the ramp and into the cargo bay, teasing with sugar all the way. The tan zebra followed him, and once they were inside, he received his reward.

The bounty hunter choppers streaked toward them.

"Hurry, Marz. This ain't no luxury liner." Hurricane ducked back into the cargo bay. Using some old rags, he blindfolded the quagga, then fastened safety belts around the animal's belly and secured them to ceiling hooks. He shut the cargo bay door and then rushed up the ladder to the cockpit hatch. Marz stayed with SunKing, calming and reassuring him.

Hurricane shouted through the hatch opening. "Marz! Get up here *now*!" Marz responded to his name. He crawled through the hatch and popped into the long-neck cockpit. Hurricane snapped Marz into his seatbelt, then flipped a bunch of switches.

Three bounty choppers appeared on the view screens.

The Buzzard vibrated wildly when Hurricane fired up the engines and let out a ballyhoo. "Woo-hoo! Hang on, Marz. We're off to fly the Buzzard, the wonderful Buzzard of Boz!"

Three hulking choppers zoomed toward them. The lead helicopter, in shining Verdanta green, flashed Mai-Kellina's power symbol on the front panel. Inside the cabin, the pilot gripped the controls and raised the face plate on the flight helmet.

It was Mai-Kellina.

Chapter 8 ☽ ☽ ☽ ☽ ☽ ☽

CONVERTICOPTER

Luna Kayleno dipped beneath the horizon, leaving just three moons hanging in the night sky, with their pale beams flickering through the river fog. The pilot and navigator of the crashed chopper wiggled in the quicksand, clinging to the bent rotor. Just downstream from them, the Buzzard rested on damp ground, engines humming.

Inside the Buzzard's long-neck cockpit, Hurricane grabbed Marz's hands and placed them on the co-pilot's control yoke. "Here, grab hold." Marz flashed a puzzled look at Hurricane and pulled his hands back. "Keep 'em there!" He tightened his own hands over Marz's, and then turned the flight yoke. "Flyin' the Buzzard's fun, right?"

"Fun right." Marz tested the handles.

Suddenly Mai-Kellina's voice blared over the QM. "Johnny Hurricane, you are under arrest!" Her huge V-1 chopper approached; its searchlight slashed through the fog, glaring directly into the long-neck. "You are a fugitive, a kidnapper and an animal thief! And now you are aiding an escapee from Yerkoza. You are a criminal four times over."

Hurricane dipped the Buzzard's long-neck in a bowing motion towards the lady governor. "Evenin', princess! You're late for the party. You missed my net trick. But I saved the last dance just for you. Let's turn up the music!"

When Hurricane touched the accelerator levers, all four engines rumbled. The Buzzard shook, rattled and rolled on its wheels, quivering like a shack in a moonquake. The air blast from the engines blew up a tempest of dirt, grass, and leaves.

"Don't tempt me, Hurricane," Mai-Kellina intoned. "You have exactly ten seconds to release the boy and the quagga."

"Or else . . . ?"

"Or I will shoot you down."

"Ha! I love that lie! Tell it again, please, whisper it in my ear, darlin'. Not even you could explain to King Donovan why you killed the only living quagga!"

"Okay, Johnny. Your choice, we'll do it the hard way. As usual."

The Buzzard's QM readout showed that Mai-Kellina had gone into secret communication mode. Hurricane grabbed his own QM and entered the passwords. He suppressed a laugh as the governor coldly issued commands inside her cabin. "Fry his lead engine. Ground him."

The firing cone of V-1's lightning generator rotated and aimed straight for the Buzzard's main engine. "Ah! She wants to play sparks. Okay!"

Hurricane snapped open the emergency panel and pressed three buttons. A shiny metal rod flipped out from just beneath the Buzzard's long-neck and sprang into an upright position.

When Hurricane twisted another button, the spring gun spat a sleek harpoon toward the river. It zipped through the air and dug into the quicksand with a *schloop* sound, barely missing the pilot and navigator, still squirming beneath the chopper blade.

"You think this old bird still has enough juice to lift all three of us?" Hurricane pulled back on the take-off control. The Buzzard jittered as it lifted a few inches off the ground.

Marz gripped his co-pilot yoke, eyes wide, giggling wildly, feeling for the first time the thrill of huge machine power pulsing through his fingers, racing up his arms. "Buzzard, fun!"

Over the QM, they overheard Mai-Kellina's voice from inside the V-1. "Fire!"

The lightning bolt exploded from the V-1's aiming cone and zapped across the gap between the two aircraft. The Buzzard's sentry rod deflected the lightning bolt and sent the energy scorching down the chain and into the harpoon. Flash! The mud-stuck pilot and navigator lit up like holiday sparklers and flared into memory. Tendrils of acrid smoke rose from the scene, coiling in the eerie, moonlit mist.

Other than a scarred lightning rod, the Buzzard was untouched. Hurricane shouted to Mai-Kellina over the QM. "Wow, hon, that was quite a kiss! Didn't know you missed me so."

"Now you've really done it, Johnny," Mai-Kellina snarled. "Double murder resulting from resisting arrest!"

"Murder? Me? Who fired the gun, hon?"

"Who deflected the shot?"

"Just defendin' ourselves. We have that right."

The lightning generator on the V-1 began whirring again. Hurricane rammed the take-off lever. Roaring and blowing a powerful downdraft, the Buzzard lifted straight up. Hurricane tilted the engines from vertical to horizontal, shifting into supersonic flight mode. The Buzzard quickly gained speed and elevation. The plasma jets kicked in; the Buzzard streaked away toward the horizon.

🌙 🌙 🌙 🌙 🌙 🌙

Inside the V-1, Mai-Kellina coldly ordered, "They are not to leave this moon." Her V-1 rose high above the smoky scene of the wrecked chopper, and set course to capture the Buzzard.

Her co-pilot warned, "Govna, in chopper mode we'll never catch 'em."

"Striker mode, then." Mai-Kellina piloted the V-1 high up above the canyon walls of the Red River Valley, and then choked off the rotor motor. The rotors limped, sending V-1 into a stuttering tailspin. It flailed in the air, like a wounded bird, falling toward the valley floor.

"Fold the rotors," Mai-Kellina shouted amid the noise. The chopper rotors came to rest in their locks. She guided the telescoping aircraft wings, jutting out from their box beneath the cabin. "Jets on." The glow jets powered up and propelled the V-1 out of free-fall.

By that time the Buzzard, with its heavy cargo of escapees, was just specks of red and blue exhaust flares in the distance, faintly lit by three fading moons and the approaching sunrise.

"Force them down. Rescue stand by. V-1 to Yerkoza, prepare to receive the fugitives."

🌙 🌙 🌙 🌙 🌙 🌙

The panorama screens on the Buzzard's control panel showed the V-1 streaking toward them.

"She's loaded for bear," Hurricane said. "Ready for some fun games?"

"Fun games!" Marz gripped the control yoke. He jiggled it slightly, and laughed when the Buzzard responded by shaking a bit. It was so easy to control such a giant flying machine with tiny movements of his fingers. It took only seconds for the power to go to his head. He yanked the yoke hard right. The lunabus groaned and banked 'til it was flying on edge, sideways to the horizon, like a saucer rolling down the sidewalk.

"No, Marz! No sideways, no jerking." Hurricane took control of the yoke and muscled the Buzzard back with a gentle turn. "Easy, easy. Smooth. Got it? No jerking."

"No jerky." Marz nodded.

On the QM, Mai-Kellina broke in again. "Johnny, don't make this hard. You can't outrun us now. Your hostages belong at Yerkoza. Turn them over and I'll cut your sentence."

Hurricane switched the QM off, turned a knob labeled "DB5," and then said, "Ink." Strange creaking sounds, like large pieces of metal scraping against one another, rose from the cargo bay. The sounds of SunKing braying and stomping on the floor floated up to the cockpit. Lights blinked green above the DB5 button. The speed of their blinking kept increasing until an alarm sounded. Hurricane spoke into the command microphone. "Ink. Three."

One by one, three Decoy Birds—hollow imitations of the Buzzard—dropped away from the underbelly of the real Buzzard. Clouds of smoke, in dark shimmerings of cobalt, carmine and coral, pumped out from their fogger vents. Tiny specks of reflective metal, churning in the colored clouds, sparkled in the rays of breaking dawn.

Mai-Kellina's V-1 was soon engulfed in the thick, inky smoke from the decoys. Her craft swerved wildly, barely avoiding two of the fake Buzzards. The third one missed widely. Her voice crackled over the QM. "Cute trick, Johnny."

"Trick? It's a gift, just for you. I know you love smoke and mirrors!"

On the panorama screen, the V-1, now flying alone, closed in, ready to overtake the Buzzard. The V-1's grappler arm snaked out, reaching for the Buzzard's cargo bay door. Marz panicked. Yanked the yoke hard left. The Buzzard veered into sideways flight and glanced the V-1 at an odd angle, knocking it out of its flight path.

The hard bank turn pulled Hurricane out of his pilot's seat and slammed him hard against the wall. "Marz! No jerking!" He pulled himself up, rushed back to his pilot's chair, and scanned the kadar tracer screens. The V-1 was no longer chasing them. The V-1 seemed to be streaking straight down, toward the Sea of Karoo.

Hurricane grabbed his QM. "Hey, Princess, land softly now, I want the first dance with you at Crestival, okay?"

No response.

He leaned back in his captain's chair and beamed at Marz. "Thanks, Marz, for jerking the Buzzard just when you did. You saved our skin." He reached under his chair, pulled out the captain's hat. "Here, you deserve it." Marz grabbed the hat and happily plopped it on his head.

Chapter 9 ☽ ☽ ☽ ☽ ☽ ☽

LOOPER

The Hawkens had spent two days and nights sleeping in their day clothes in a cubicle at the relay looper station on Verdanta. "How long 'til we get home?" Ripley asked. "My socks stink."

"We were supposed to leave yesterday," his dad answered.

"Can Hurricane really find Marz and the funny zebra?" Ripley rubbed his eyes.

"Shh! Quiet about that!" Elizabelle whispered.

Rumors said Mai-Kellina's spies lurked everywhere in the looper station, dressed like ordinary tourists.

"We don't know anyone named Hurricane." Althea winked at her son. "Breakfast— "

She was interrupted when the door burst open and a uniformed marshal strode in, followed by another officer in uniform. "If you eat now you'll just throw it up during the launch. You'll get breakfast after you're gliding smoothly in space. Better hurry, your car launches in ten minutes. Your big bags are loaded. This is Sergeant Idonya, your guard."

"We can take care of ourselves," Braden said. "We've flown the looper countless times."

"It's an order from Governor Mai-Kellina. You're to have an armed guard accompany you all the way to New Roma. For your own protection. Idonya is our best."

Even after her platform boots lifted her four inches off the floor, Idonya was shorter than Elizabelle. Her face was as plain as a bucket of sand, but still she stood out from the crowd in her Verdanta green uniform, with its double yellow striping down the seams. Her square-toed black boots, flashing a row of golden buckles up the sides, reached almost to her knees. The symbol of the Governor's Security Service sparkled on her cap.

Braden glanced at his wife. "Let's get these tired kids home."

They grabbed their hand bags and totes, and scurried to the door. Braden tried the handle. It rattled a bit, but would not open.

Sergeant Idonya marched smartly to the door, clomping as though she were smashing bugs with every step, and brushed Braden aside. She waved her palm to the blinking light above the handle. The door hummed and clicked open. The Hawkens followed her.

It was not yet sunrise, but already the looper station was crowded and noisy. Whenever the crowd saw Sergeant Idonya approaching, or heard her boots clicking, they stepped aside.

The boarding deck was crowded with looper cars in multiple colors, each with fourteen body mold seats. All were crammed full of people, busily tightening up their space suits and strapping their boxes to the floor.

Idonya directed them to a looper car with an embossed "GV" sign above the airlock door. Once inside, they all wiggled into their space suits. Ripley and Elizabelle scrambled to the seats with the panoramic viewing windows.

Their parents belted up. "Helmet on tight? All QMs on?" Althea asked.

"I hear you," Elizabelle said. "I can turn left or right, but not much up or down."

"Good. That's what we need. No whiplash. How about you, Captain Loopernaut?"

"Just like a robot," Ripley answered happily.

"Cut the silly chatter," snapped Sergeant Idonya. "And get fastened in."

Althea and Braden plopped down in their seats. Elizabelle heard the cushion pockets whispering as air rushed in, conforming the seats perfectly to her parents' bodies. They fastened helmets to their space suits.

Sergeant Idonya took her own place at the door. She strapped her black boots into the floor molds, then fastened ceiling straps to D rings on her uniform. Moments after she spoke into the QM built into her space helmet, all the other cars moved aside.

Their car switched into position. It clicked rhythmically as it rode the steep belt up to the loader, high atop the tower. At the peak of the ramp, their car shunted into the launcher chute. Elizabelle kept staring out the window as they rose, smiling. She knew what was coming.

"Hang on, kids!" Braden shouted. Their car jerked as it locked into position.

Elizabelle's heart pounded in her chest. Ripley's fingers tightened around the arm supports. Suddenly the chute released the car, dropping it straight down, like a boulder pushed off a cliff.

The kids broke into their looper song:

Here we go shoot de loop,
Here we go loop delight,
Here we go shoot de loop,
From the towering height.

"Ya-haaa!" Ripley yelled.

The car vibrated wildly as it plunged straight down, streaking and smoking.

Near the bottom of the drop the car shot out of the launcher like a fireball from a cannon.

The pressure of streaming into space at gravity escape speed crushed them against the body molding of their seats. Soon the looper's booster engines kicked in, adding just enough power to propel the car into orbit.

As she stared out from her space helmet, Elizabelle wondered if anyone could build a spaceship powerful enough to take a crew of explorers back to Ol'Terra, the legendary original home world of all humans. Why had their ancestors left their natural home? What had become of it? The "approaching meteor" story seemed too simple. Would the New Romans ever restore signals with their long lost cousins, the people of Earth? If they had space ships powerful enough for the space exodus, almost seven thousand years ago, why were those space ships not flying now?

In only moments Elizabelle felt the effects of leaving Verdanta's adjusted gravity. Even strapped in her seat, she suddenly felt much lighter.

The kids glued their faces to the windows and stared in awe as the forests, deserts and oceans of Verdanta fell away from view.

Elizabelle looked toward the Sea of Karoo. She noticed something unusual. "Over there. Going down into the sea."

"One wing smokin'!" Ripley shouted.

Sergeant Idonya adjusted her QM so the Hawkens could not hear her. After a few moments of secret conversation, she popped open a panel on the wall behind her and adjusted some controls. Their car jerked as the trim jets kicked in.

"What's happening?" Braden asked. "Is something wrong?"

"This car is going back down," the guard announced. "The governor wants to talk to you."

Braden protested. "What? She ordered us back home. We waited *two days* for this car."

The guard stayed close to the panel. "It's about kidnaping a boy and a rare animal."

Elizabelle's heart sank. Did Mai-Kellina already know about Hurricane's plan to rescue Marz and the quagga, and to meet up with them back home at Baraboo? She whispered to her dad, "She can't touch us here. We're too high."

"I heard that, young lady," the guard said. "Sorry to disappoint you. The seven league rule means nothin' in this car. You're riding in the GV—the Governor's Vehicle—as her privileged guests. This car is under her command, at all times and places." She pulled a long red lever. "You're going back down. You have some serious explainin' to do."

Chapter 10 ꞉ ꞉ ꞉ ꞉ ꞉ ꞉

REUNION

Johnny Hurricane set the Buzzard controls for the space flight to the home planet. The plan was to land at the main looper station on New Roma, refuel, then jump over to the circus training camp at Baraboo. Once there, they would meet up with the Hawkens and deliver Marz and the quagga. Hurricane's special delivery fee would be earned, and he could collect his gold bars at the close of Crestival.

Marz sat beside Hurricane, proudly wearing his co-pilot's hat. Far below them Luna Verdanta turned, a shining ball floating majestically in the infinite darkness of space, the great Cloud Forest forming a rich green belt around the equator. Several other moons and New Roma decorated the sky; distant stars flickered in the background.

Dozens of relay looper cars orbited Verdanta, clustering in the L7 pocket where the gravity from all the moons was equally balanced. The cars were lining up to form a space train, ready for a flight to New Roma. Each train would coast in space until it could hook into the pendulum, an immense rotating slingshot, which would catapult the entire space train onto its destination— another moon or the home planet, New Roma.

But one car—marked "GV" and shining brightly in its brilliant green and gold—moved away from the others, heading downward toward the surface of the moon.

Hurricane chuckled. "Aha! I get it!"

"Buzzard fun!"

Hurricane piloted the Buzzard into the L7 pocket, parallel with the dark green GV. Once lined up, the two spacecraft moved in unison, like a pair of ice skating dancers. He locked the Buzzard to stay on the GV, perfectly matching its every movement, and tuning the QM to hear everything.

Sergeant Idonya appeared in the window of the GV craft. She leered at Marz and Hurricane, and shouted into her QM. "What you doin' here, Hurricane?"

"Doin' you a favor. Takin' some hitchhikers off your hands."

"Too late. The governor says they're goin' back down."

"I think not. We're above seven lunar leagues. Her orders mean nothin' here."

"Wrong again. They're in her personal spacecraft. She controls it everywhere."

"Well, hoop-ti-diddle-oh and kiss my big fat toe. I'm freein' your hostages, like it or no."

"You threatenin' piracy against the Governor's Vehicle? That's serious crime."

"Only if she can catch me. Let's make it a big party!" Hurricane unsnapped his safety belt and signaled for Marz to follow. They glided from the captain's cockpit down to the cargo hold. SunKing, still blind-

99

folded and secured by ropes, chuffed happily when Marz approached.

Rows of color-coded boxes lined the sides of the cargo bay. One box, in bright orange, was labeled "EVA" for extra-vehicular activity. Hurricane pulled himself to it and withdrew a space helmet, a pony bottle of oxygen, cable hooks, and a high-power metal melter. Finally he sealed up his space suit and strapped on a backpack with miniature jet rockets.

The airlock hissed as Hurricane slipped into it. The lock closed and he stepped out into space, floating like a freebird, shining silver in the bright sunlight. "Show time!"

Hurricane jetted to position on the outer skin of the GV looper limo. He rapped on the window and signaled for all the Hawkens to don their space helmets and move away from the window. He fired up the metal melter and, with its white-hot flame, cut a ring all around the window. The moment he punctured the pressure seal everything that was not strapped down got sucked to the opening.

A simple yank popped the window out. All the loose cabin stuff instantly spewed out into space. The danger light on the GV flashed, and the alarm sounded. "Pressure seal broken! Intruder!" Sergeant Idonya pulled the emergency switch and shouted into the system. "Forcible entry. Out pirate!"

Hurricane helped Elizabelle and Ripley crawl out of the gaping hole, then handed cable hooks to them. Once outside, they snapped their hooks to the tether cable and began pulling themselves, hand over hand, toward the Buzzard.

But the circus kids were only part way across the gap when Idonya jerked the controls of the GV, making it shake violently. "You will not hijack the governor's prison . . . passengers! Not while I'm on

REUNION 🌙 🌙 🌙 🌙 🌙

guard duty!" The cable acted like a catapult, and blasted Elizabelle and Ripley out into space, completely out of control. Arms and legs flailing, they drifted ever farther from one another and from the space craft, floating freely in the infinity of space. They were headed into deep emptiness. No food. No water. Only the oxygen in their helmets. Which would run out in ten minutes. Or less.

Imitating Hurricane, Marz ran to the EVA box, snapped pony bottles to his belt, strapped a jetpack on his back, sped through the airlock, and leaped out into space. Without a safety cable. For a few moments he fumbled around with the backpack controls. This made things worse, and sent him zooming away from the Hawken kids. He experimented with the controls until he got the knack and aimed the jet pack to push him toward Elizabelle. With both hands he squeezed the controls for maximum thrust. Swooping and swerving, he streaked away from the two space craft, toward the circus kids.

Elizabelle panicked. A look of terror covered her face, and she breathed rapidly, burning up her oxygen far too quickly. Finally Marz reached her, grabbed her hand and pulled her toward him. Her face lit up with new hope. He pulled one of the pony bottles from his belt and attached it to the emergency air line on her helmet. Soon she calmed down a bit, took a deep breath, closed her eyes, and said, through the QM, "Oh, Marz, thank you. I thought I was about to become space junk."

🌙 🌙 🌙 🌙 🌙 🌙 🌙

Inside the governor's looper car, Hurricane and Idonya, both in their space suits, wrestled. First, one of them would kick the other, sending both of them flying in a new direction. Then the other would punch, and they would bounce off another way, ricocheting like billiard balls smacked too hard. All the time floating, grunting, and groaning. The guard pulled a pen-shaped weapon from her belt. She reached up and tried to jab it in Hurricane's neck, just below the helmet line. But Hurricane twisted sideways, grabbed her hand, aimed the weapon at her arm, and pulled the pressure pin.

Almost instantly she collapsed into a limp heap, floating like a feather in a breeze.

Hurricane signaled to the circus parents. "Let's get back to the Buzzard before she wakes up."

Marz grabbed Elizabelle by gloved hand. Together they turned to look for Ripley. He was off in the distance, with the morning sun glinting off his space helmet, drifting toward the moon below. "Marz, give me a push back to the Buzzard," Elizabelle said. "Go get Rip." When Marz did not follow her instructions, she tried again, positioning Marz's hands on her waist, pointing to the Buzzard, and then indicating "push me" with her hands. He caught on, grabbed her by the waist, from the back, aimed for the lunabus, and accelerated the jets. "Okay, that's good, just release me now," she said. Again, he didn't get it. So she pushed his hands away, pointed at him and then off in the direction where they last saw Rip floating.

When he turned her loose, Elizabelle sailed in a straight line, floating in space, headed for the Buzzard. But Marz's aim was a little off. As she got closer, it looked like she would miss the airlock doors leading to the cargo bay. She ripped the pony bottle from her helmet and used the last spray of oxygen as a miniature jet to adjust her trajectory. It worked. She nabbed onto the airlock handle and shouted into her QM. "I'm on the Buzzard! Get Rip! Hurry!"

By now Marz had much better mastery of the jet pack. He adjusted the jets to allow him to turn slowly in space. There was so much to see—the GV and the Buzzard, all the other looper cars, Verdanta below, several other moons scattered across the sky, the firmament of stars in the background. And three space walkers making their way down the cable, moving from the GV to the Buzzard.

Finally a speck in the distance flashed. Marz changed position and fired the jets.

But as he approached, there was no movement. Just a small space suit, floating limply. Marz grabbed the body and reversed the jets to stop the motion. He turned the body to face him.

It was Rip. Face blue. Eyes closed. No breath.

Passed out? Dead?

Marz grabbed his last pony bottle, snapped it to Ripley's helmet, and turned the airflow switch. Nothing. What to do?

Grabbing Ripley by the handle at the top of his helmet, Marz turned back toward the Buzzard, and pushed the jet pack to max. Together the streaked all the way back to the Buzzard. Braden and Althea waited at the cargo bay door. They pulled their son through the airlock; Marz followed them into the cargo bay.

"Oxygen now!" Althea shouted. Braden ripped the helmet off his son and strapped him to the floor. Althea slapped an oxygen mask over Rip's nose and mouth, snapped her belt to a floor hook, and began pumping Rip's chest. After a few minutes, Ripley coughed, snorted, spit, and took a shivering breath. Normal color began to return to his face. His eyes opened. He sat up and took a drink of water. "Bad dream."

In all the rush to rescue Ripley, the circus family had ignored the quagga. But once Ripley's emergency passed, their attention turned.

"Mom, look!" Elizabelle called out. "Marz's quagga!"

The Hawkens all gathered around SunKing, who was still strapped in by belts connected to the floor and ceiling. Elizabelle reached up and stroked the beast's neck. "He's the most beautiful zebra ever."

"A very fine specimen indeed," Althea added.

"So, all our thanks to you, Marz," Braden said, "For finding our new animal star. Now we just have to get back to Baraboo."

Hurricane stood at the bottom of the stairwell leading to the cockpit. "You're the customers. It's a custom charter. You call the shots. Where do you want to go?"

"Home!" Ripley shouted. His sister, parents, and Marz all joined in, "Home!"

Hurricane pulled himself up the stairs and into the long-neck cockpit. Marz and Ripley followed closely behind. Once inside, Marz pulled out his Buzzard Captain's hat and plunked it on Ripley's head. "Now we're the hat brothers!"

Moments later, Braden, Althea and Elizabelle also arrived in the pilot's cockpit. Althea whispered to Braden. "Do you really think King Donovan will give permission for the quagga to be a circus performer?"

"Why not?" Braden said. "He's asked for the most spectacular circus show ever. Belle told him that a new animal star was the key to the show."

The engines roared as Hurricane rammed them into space flight speed. The Buzzard zoomed on its way to New Roma and the Baraboo circus training camp.

Below them, a train of five looper cars, hooked together, floated majestically toward the space catapult, turning slowly on the far horizon.

But one car, with a gaping hole where there should have been a window, slowly rolled free in space, far out of alignment with the others.

Hurricane placed his palm on a small ball on the control panel. A little light flashed through a series of colors. Soon a tiny screen appeared: "Enter codes." His fingers flashed over a series of keys. The screen projected a new message: "Sound only."

The QM speakers emitted a squawking sound, some stuttering screeches, and then a hiss. Amid the noise, Mai-Kellina's voice, sounding desperate: "Proco! Proco! They are escaping. I need your help. Come in please!"

The story continues in Seven Moon Circus, Book Two: The Rings of Baraboo

BOOK TWO

THE RINGS OF BARABOO

Chapter 1 ☽ ☽ ☽ ☽ ☽ ☽

CANNONBALL

It was not a good day at the Baraboo circus training camp. The owner of Seven Moon Circus, Toberomi, known as "Big Tee," burst into his show master's crowded dressing room. "Where are the Hawkens? They're supposed to be training the big cats for our Crestival show!" No answer. He snooped around in the mess of bizarre costumes. "Bucky, where are you?"

A glittering curtain parted and Boyd Bucklebiter stuck his head out. "I'm here." He squatted on a rickety stool behind the ironing board that doubled as his desk. "I don't know where the Hawkens are. Maybe they got lost in the fog of the Cloud Forest."

"Great! Our big cat trainer and vet disappear just when we need them." Toberomi threw a bunch of orange wigs off a rickety chair and plunked his feet up on the desk.

Bucklebiter sniffed the sour aroma from the hole in the bottom of his boss's boots. "We all agreed," the show master said, "the Cloud Forest is the best place to look for our new star."

"Yeah, yeah, yeah. I remember." Toberomi nervously rubbed the frayed lapels of his threadbare jacket. "But we must never forget.

THE RINGS OF BARABOO

With or without the Hawkens, new star or not, the show must go on." He took the wand from Bucklebiter's desk and rapped it on the calendar date for the alignment of all seven moons. "Two weeks 'til Crestival."

It had taken Toberomi eleven years—and the help of Braden Hawken—to get an invitation to Crestival, the grand festival of the seven crescent moons, celebrated at Castle Tulamarine. He was not going to let some flunky show master ruin his big chance. "Your job, and the future of 7MC, depends on this show. Prove that you are still the master of spectacle!"

"I know what's at stake, Tee." Bucklebiter pulled off his top hat and polished his bald pate 'til it reflected the light. "I put the word out on the circus channel that we're looking for new acts. But . . ." He raised his eyebrows in warning. "Your reputation is out there. Most of the famous performers are afraid you'll never pay 'em."

"Why does everyone think I should be made of gold?"

"It's not just gold," Bucklebiter countered. "It's respect. Show people deserve more than peanuts and rah-rah-siss-boom-bahs. Real talent costs real money. If you'd paid the Flying Valenzias what they're worth, they wouldn't be on the high wire today for Bare Knuckles and Bayleap."

"Money! Is that all these performers think about? Where are the true artistes, the super athletes of the big show, the masters of the Spanish Roll?"

"You wouldn't even spend a hundred sevrins for a fake horn to make the billy goat look like a unicorn! How many times I gotta tell ya? Kids want to see unicorns."

Toberomi grumbled. "Money doesn't float down from the sky!"

But something seemed to be falling out of the sky. A rumbling sound, high in the air, grew into a piercing roar that shook the ground. Bucky and Big Tee rushed to the door.

Outside, the tent riggers dropped their poles and hammers. They looked up, searching the sky. Clowns stuck their heads out of their windows. Was a meteor about to blast them to smithereens?

The eager voice of Johnny Hurricane blared down from his lunabus spaceship. "Attention Baraboo! Clear the grounds, the Big Bad Buzzard is a-coming in!" In the background, a younger voice chipped in, "Buzzard fun!"

As soon as Hurricane's Buzzard came into view, the elephants bellowed in protest; zebras and donkeys brayed loudly; the bonobos huddled together.

"Oh, no," Toberomi moaned. "Not this, not now." He pulled the Quicksilver Messenger from his belt, pressed some buttons and shouted into the communicator. "Go away Hurricane! Go bother somebody else."

"Hey, Big Tee, I have the Hawkens. All six of 'em!"

Toberomi flipped his QM off and turned to Bucklebiter. "Six? Last time I counted there were only four."

Another voice blared from the lunabus. "Listen Boss, Braden here. We're all here."

At the sound of Braden's voice, all the animal caretakers burst into applause. Soon all the performers and crew broke into a chant, "Let 'em land, let 'em land!"

"Mr. Tee, we have a great big surprise for you!" Elizabelle's perky voice brought face-splitting smiles to the faces of the clowns. "We found two wonderful new friends on Verdanta!"

111

"This better be real," Toberomi muttered. He set his Quicksilver Messenger to intercom. "Attention all circus personnel. Clear out the center arena. Make room for Hurricane and his Buzzard to land. Now!"

The whole circus campground erupted in a flurry of motion. Clowns streamed out of their costume dens, wigs flying, makeup smeared all over their faces. They scrambled into their trick trucks, revved the engines 'til they popped purple exhaust, and sped away from the arena. The riggers rolled the tent canopy into a long, snaking reel, hooked their winch tractors to the tie ropes, and dragged the canvas off the staging area.

As the Buzzard descended, the animals in the pens moved out into the big habitat fields. Animals in corrals grew nervous, snorting and braying. The mahouts tried to calm their elephants, but the giant beasts kept thrashing their trunks against the ground, stomping their feet and trumpeting their displeasure. The young bonobos scampered up into their giant tree house.

Toberomi yelled into his QM again. "Okay Hurricane, you can land and let the Hawkens come home. But that's all. Land and unload, then be gone with ya. I don't want you hanging around. And don't make a mess!"

Inside the Buzzard's long-neck cockpit, Johnny Hurricane and Marz, the wild boy from the Cloud Forest, sat side-by-side at the controls. Marz proudly wore his Buzzard co-captain's hat. The Hawken circus family stood behind them, vests strapped to the ceiling, boots snapped to the floor moldings.

"Let's take 'er down!" Hurricane expertly guided the big Buzzard, jiggling the controls, turning the engines from forward thrust to vertical push, extending the wheels as the space bus slowly neared the ground. Its reverse jets blew enormous clouds of dirt, turning the camp into a dusty cyclone zone.

The Buzzard rattled and rocked as it touched down. "Solid ground, my friends." Hurricane's voice was full of pride. The whole Hawken family applauded.

"Hurray, we're home!" shouted Ripley. "Take me to the shoko master!"

Once the dust settled, all the Buzzard passengers unsnapped their safety belts and followed Hurricane down to the cargo bay. Marz greeted his beast friend, SunKing the brown and tan striped quagga, rubbed his neck and cheeks, and whispered to him.

"Remove his blindfold slowly," Althea cautioned. "He's seen nothing during the whole flight from the green moon. Give him time to adjust to the light."

Elizabelle approached SunKing, and tried to untie his blindfold. The quagga reacted with an angry bark, and his right rear leg twitched, like he was preparing to kick someone.

"Careful, Belle," Althea said. "Let Marz handle SunKing."

Marz whispered something in the quagga's ear, which seemed to calm him, and then led him by the halter to the cargo door.

Elizabelle turned the knobs that opened the door. "Welcome to Baraboo, Marz," she said proudly. "This is our home. This is where we work up our new circus tricks and acts. The big project now is getting ready for the Crestival show.

"Cress-val?"

"You'll learn about that soon. It's when all seven moons are lined up in the sky, all at once." Her eyes lit up. "It's a time for a really big party. And our big chance to put on a giant circus show. We're aiming for our most spectacular show ever." She pointed to the two moons above.

Once again, Marz was entering yet a completely new world, unlike anything he had ever seen before. Leading the quagga, he wandered around, taking in the sights. The performance area was lined with circus wagons, all decorated with colorful scenes of daring performers. Train cars showed off pictures of the moons where 7MC had toured, putting on their famous shows. Dozens of giant signs blared their adverts in hot reds and glaring yellows.

Toberomi and Bucklebiter approached Marz and the quagga. "And who . . . and what . . . do we have here?"

When Marz saw Toberomi's shiny bald head, he strolled up and tried to rub it. "Hat fun!" He pulled the Buzzard captain's hat from his own head and planted it on Toberomi.

"Yes, you're right, young man," Toberomi chuckled. "I should wear a hat out here in the bright sun." He tipped the Buzzard captain's hat.

"Mr. Toberomi," Braden said, "it's my pleasure to introduce Marz and SunKing. We found Marz living with wild animals—a tribe of primates we've never seen before—in the Cloud Forest, and he found SunKing at Yerkoza."

"So . . . is Yerkoza still pumping out freak animals that die soon after they leave the lab?" Big Tee and Bucky walked around the quagga, slowly admiring his muscles and brown stripes.

"All we know is that this one is very much alive. And kicking."

"Know what he is?" Elizabelle asked.

"Either a half-baked okapi..." Bucklebiter stroked his chin. "... or a zebra that tried to be an albino, but got very confused."

"Close. SunKing is a quagga," Elizabelle explained. "His ancestors were members of a zebra family who went extinct many centuries ago, in South Africa, back on Ol'Terra. They are named after the *qua-haa* barking sound they make. The old books say that some people used to call them quakkas." She explained how Captain Norzah's scientific team brought tissue samples of the quagga, and many other animals, both extinct and living, on the long space journey from Earth.

Her mom picked up the story. "Some bio-engineers—probably Yerkoza scientists working for Mai-Kellina—used those samples to bring the species back to life. Far as we can tell, SunKing is the only quagga alive today. On any world."

"See, Mr. Tee," Ripley chimed in, grinning. "We did bring back the new animal star!"

The crowd of clowns and freaks—Pastranya the Bearded Lady, Jorjio the Dogface Boy, Harry Muggler the Porcupine Juggler and their friends—moved closer, skeptical expressions on their faces. In the past the they had met plenty of frauds and clever fakers, and so they were always suspicious. Had Hurricane bamboozled the Hawkens with some cleverly dyed horse or bleached out some lost zebra?

Toberomi put his hand on the beast's chest and counted the heartbeat. "He seems strong. Excellent muscle tone." He walked all the way around the quagga. "He's a beauty, for sure. People will pay big money to see him. Especially if you can train him to do some daring tricks. Will he jump through a ring of fire?"

"Tricks?" Braden's voice took on a warning tone. "SunKing is a wild stallion, a pure rebel at heart. He won't let anyone but Marz ride him, and that's only because Marz freed him from cruel trainers at Yerkoza. Even on Ol'Terra, zebras would only let people admire and groom and feed them. They were just too ornery to be trained. People who tried to train them often got kicked. A few even got killed."

"Maybe he doesn't know that," Bucklebiter suggested. "We can at least try to train him for tricks."

Althea stepped forward. "Don't bet on it, boys. As a revived animal, he's automatically under royal protection. Do you really think King Donovan would allow any revived species to be trained for dangerous tricks? Especially an animal as rare and beautiful and SunKing."

Johnny Hurricane, who had been standing on the side, cleared this throat loudly. "Speaking of the quagga, let's not forget our deal."

Toberomi raised one eyebrow. "Our deal? I know nothing of any deal."

"The small matter of my delivery fee."

Braden began explaining the deal he had made with Hurricane when Toberomi interrupted. "Maybe we can pay your delivery fee if our Crestival show is a hit. But today, I couldn't pay you a single sevrin, much less a brick of gold. So you best be on your way."

"All right Mr. Tee, I'll see you and your crew at Crestival. I will expect to be paid in full then." And with that Hurricane sprinted up the loading ramp of the Buzzard and disappeared into the cargo bay. The door lifted up and sealed tight. Soon, the Buzzard engines roared as the lunabus lifted of and sped off into the horizon.

No sooner had Hurricane's space ship departed the scene than a

CANNONBALL

loud explosion shook the area. Circus dogs howled; SunKing barked in protest. A loud whistling sound rose and then fell in pitch, ending a few seconds later with a *plop!* The circus people all ran to the source of the sounds, behind the elephant corral.

In almost fourteen years living in the circus, Elizabelle had never seen such a sight. Tendrils of bluish smoke drifted from the barrel of a huge cannon. A tall, pencil-thin man in a shiny black suit with red piping on the seams pulled himself up from a mound of sawdust. "Ahhh, wunnaful, wunnaful!" He dusted off his jumpsuit, removed his crash helmet, strode up to Bucklebiter and Toberomi, bowed deeply and announced himself. "Meester Toberomi, Meester Buckobida, I am Capitano Zorino Zucchini, zee Hooman Cannonball, at your zerviss!"

"The who?" Tomberomi sputtered. "My what?"

Bucklebiter beamed, pushed his way past his rotund boss, and thrust out his hand. "Pleased to meet you, Captain Zucchini. I've heard so much about you and your beautiful daughter. Welcome to Baraboo! Yes, yes, we want to see your act. Show us!"

"Oh, but of courze!" Zucchini high-stepped back to the huge cannon and aimed it for a high shooting angle. His fifteen-year-old daughter, Zina, wearing a shimmering white dress with red piping, wrapped a shiny black cape around her father's shoulders, and snapped it to his jumpsuit. Then she placed a new bullet-shaped helmet, black and silver, on her father's head and closed the strap under his chin. He wriggled his whole body into the barrel of the cannon, leaving only his helmeted head sticking out.

After curtseying to Bucklebiter and Toberomi, Zina turned to her elaborate set of show gear, mounted behind the cannon. She

117

selected an igniter from the rack and ripped it across the sole of her shoe. A blue flame shot out; she touched flame to cannon fuse, then picked up the drum sticks and played on her snare drum, steadily increasing the tension and the tempo. When the fuse was spent—

BOOM! The giant gun blew Capitano Zucchini out of the cannon barrel at precisely the same moment Zina struck the gong.

The cannon blasted Zucchini high in the air. Whistles, hidden in his glistening shoes, sounded his rise. With her father soaring high, Zina turned to the deremeno, the lost tone generator. She waved her hands around the antenna; the weird machine transformed her hand movements into eerie sound reverberations that matched her father's flight.

High in the air and still rising, Capitano Z snapped his arms above his head and spread his feet apart. Marz stared as Zucchini's cape opened into fabric wings that stretched from his wrists to his ankles, making him look like a huge bat gliding in the air. At the peak of his flight, the piping on the edges of the wings burst into bright red flames. He flapped and turned the wings to guide his flight, pivoting first toward his daughter, then swooping to the audience.

As he neared the ground, the crowd ducked, then cheered as he straightened up. He pulled his arms and legs in to his chest, hit the ground and rolled in the sawdust, extinguishing the flames. He sprang from the dust, smiling. Mr. Man in Black, cape flowing in the wind, and Miss Maiden in White, shining in the sunlight, approached Toberomi and Bucklebiter. Father bowed while daughter curtseyed.

Marz ran to the Zucchinis. "Fun yes! Fun now! Fren zokay?"

"You like it?" Zina asked Bucky.

"Great flying! Excellent! Superb!" Bucklebiter shouted. "I love it. The townies will too."

"You're hired!" Toberomi said. He grabbed 7MC hats from the clowns standing nearby and tossed them to Zucchinis. "Welcome to Seven Moon Circus!"

The Hawkens joined in the clapping and cheering.

"Excuse me, but when do we get paid?" Capitano Zucchini asked.

"After Crestival, after Crestival, everybody gets paid after Crestival," Big Tee answered.

"Thank you Mr. Toberomi, Mr. Bucklebiter." Zina adjusted her new hat and winked at Marz. "We're excited to perform in Seven Moon Circus." She and her father bowed again, hung his flight equipment on the rack, and then headed to the dining hall.

Once they were out of sight, Marz ran to the rack, unhooked Zucchini's cape and tried to make it fit on his shoulders.

"No! Marz, stop." Elizabelle insisted. "We have a rule here at Seven Moon Circus. You never, never, ever mess with the equipment of any other performer, without their okay. And you can't do the human cannonball trick without being trained. It's very dangerous. You could land in the seats and break most of your bones. And maybe hurt some people in the audience."

Toberomi turned and walked toward his wagon, with the show master at his side.

"We might have a new star, but we definitely have a new problem," Bucklebiter warned. "Where do we put them all?"

"The boy can bunk with the Hawkens. Put the Zucchinis in the old Valenzias wagon."

"And what about this quagga beast? Where does he belong?"

Chapter 2 ♪ ♪ ♪ ♪ ♪

MANDRETTA

After the noisy departure of the Buzzard it was time to settle the new arrivals.

Elizabelle volunteered to help Marz. "Let's find out if SunKing likes the horses. And if they like him." She led Marz and SunKing down the path that led to the horse corral. As they rounded the first turn, they came upon the bonobo house. Inside grew one large tree and several smaller ones, with ropes and vines and swings hanging from the heavy branches. Younger bonobos played on the swings, while the older ones rested on tree branches or on the ground. Tables were laid out with fruits and nuts. "There's the bonobo house. They look a lot like chimpanzees. And they are related. But chimps fight all the time, sometimes even have wars. Bonobos just want to have fun. All the time. Just like you."

When they were just outside the bonobo house, Marz immediately stopped. "Fren zokay!" He tied SunKing's halter to a railing, ran to the side of the house, and stuck his hand inside. Soon several young bonobos jumped down from their tree and held out their fingers to him, making their barking sounds. One picked up a big red ball and threw it to Marz. He caught it and threw it up to a bonobo sitting on a high branch. "Fun, now!"

Inside the enclosure, an adult female bonobo climbed up the big tree to a platform mounted on the first large branch. She stood in front of an upright board with several dozen little symbols arranged in rows, and grabbed a pointer stick.

"Okay, Marz, watch Keeli." Elizabelle pointed up to the mother bonobo on the platform. She stood before an upright board that displayed pictures of two bonobos, a human boy, and a red ball. A sound speaker beneath the board announced: "Bonobos boy play ball."

Marz smiled and repeated. "Bonobos boy play ball!"

Elizabelle sighed. "Play ball with the bonobos? Okay, but no monkey business, got it?"

"Yes! Monkey business."

Elizabelle pressed her thumb on the door lock; it clicked and the door opened. She led Marz inside. Keeli swung down from the platform, grabbed her infant and scampered to Elizabelle; she hugged both of them.

"Hello, Keeli. I'm so happy to see you." Elizabelle held out her arms, and the baby bonobo jumped into her embrace and cuddled. "Oh, Manjaro, you're growing so fast!"

Marz rocked his eyebrows, grabbed a ball and held it out to little Manjaro. The young bonobo jumped into Marz's arms, grabbed the ball and started biting it. Marz hugged him, and stroked his head.

The scene reminded Elizabelle of looking down from the hot air balloon and watching Marz's heartbreaking farewell to his wild baby brother, the runt of his wild family. "Keeli is the queen of this tribe, and Manjaro is her first baby boy, so he's their prince." Elizabelle looked at Marz. "You understand mother?

"Mother?"

"Everyone has a mother. Bonobos, people, every kind of animal." She paused. "Well, maybe not SunKing. We're not sure about him. My mother is Althea. Who's your mother?"

"Altee Marz mother."

"No, sorry, she's mother to me and Ripley, but that's all. She's the animal doctor, but that's not the same as mother. Who was your mother before . . ." She made hand motions like climbing the rope.

Marz pointed at Keeli. "Marr." Again, the sound ended with slightly buzzing zees.

Elizabelle thought for a moment. That's the name he gave for his wild mother.

"Marz ma Keeli."

Elizabelle rolled her eyes. "Don't be silly. Keeli is a bonobo. We are people. Your mother must be a human, like mine." Elizabelle pulled Manjaro away from Marz and held him tightly. She then pointed up to the talk board.

Keeli climbed back up to the talk board. Marz grabbed one of the hanging ropes and swung up to join her. The momma bonobo pressed on symbols with the word wand. The screen showed the picture of two bonobos, the same picture of a boy, and a big heart. "Bonobos boy love," the speaker said. Then Keeli touched more symbols. The screen showed a bonobo running and a flashing red light. "Go no."

The speaker said, "Boy bonobos love go no."

Marz laughed and proudly called out to Elizabelle. "Marz bonobos love no go."

Elizabelle took a deep breath. "After everything we've gone through, just to get here, you want to live with bonobos in a tree? Again? Oh, please!"

"Keeli. Manjaro. Fren zokay."

"We can be friends with the bonobos. I love Keeli and Manjaro. But here in the circus, all the animals live with their own kind. Bonobos live with bonobos, and people live with people. And SunKing is going to live with the horses—we hope—because they are most like him."

Elizabelle scaled the ladder up to the platform, and Marz followed her. From there, high up in the bonobo's big tree, they saw the whole Baraboo camp. In the huge central arena, the tent riggers staked out positions for the huge poles that would support the big top. All the animal enclosures were arrayed around one side of the arena. Next in line were Clown Hall and all the performers' wagons and trailers. Behind Toberomi's wagon the 7MC train waited on its tracks, ready to load what remained of Seven Moon Circus. In their glory days, the 7MC train was forty-nine train cars long; now they were down to just seven.

Elizabelle placed the word wand in Keeli's hand and guided it to three buttons: the boy and ball buttons once each, and then the sunrise button. Then she touched the big green button. The speaker announced: "Boy play tomorrow."

"Marz can come back tomorrow." Elizabelle stroked Keeli's back and neck, then tapped on the sun symbol. "But we need to get SunKing to his new home." She climbed down the ladder and then shouted up to Marz. "Boy play bonobos tomorrow. Let's go."

Just as Elizabelle was about to press her thumb on the security key for the gate, a big glob of overripe mandretta fruit plopped right on her head, splattering all over and making a juicy mess. In the background, all the young bonobos hooted in glee. Marz giggled.

Elizabelle turned and wiped the fruit juice dripping from her face. With a tease in her voice, she said, "Okay . . . who's the bad bonobo today?" She quickly turned around, and stared down the young bonobos, trying hard to hide her smile. "Binti, are you the bad girl?" Binti held up both hands and shook her head furiously. "How about you, Kokomo? You look more guilty than usual today." Kokomo put his hands in front of his face and opened his fingers so he could peek at Elizabelle.

Splat!

Another glob of overripe mandretta fruit collided with Elizabelle's rear end. Then a chunk of watermelon glanced her shoulder and bounced over to Marz.

There was a moment of silence as everyone, including the bonobos, looked around. Marz suddenly shouted, "Fun, now!" and hurled the dripping rind at Kokomo.

Shrieks of delight filled the bonobo house. Bonobos ran to food tables, loaded up with wet, juicy chunks of fruit and vegetables and lobbed them at Marz and Elizabelle. And at one another. Elizabelle ducked, using her arms to shield her head.

With food soaring all around him, Marz grabbed a water bucket, climbed up the big tree and crawled out on a branch. He took careful aim and dumped the bucket of water on the bald, fat old grandpa bonobo, Jelly Belly. The Wild Boy then ran to a food table and joined other bonobos who were loading up for another sloppy round.

Up on the platform, Keeli touched some symbols. "Food fight stop."

The shrieks and hoots from the bonobos soon drew a crowd. A few clowns sauntered in the gate, flinging chunks of berry pies. Some cooks brought buckets of peeled tomatoes in a thick, aromatic soup. Marz jumped down from the tree, dug both hands into the bucket and threw globs of tomato paste at Kokomo and his buddies. They returned fire with chunks of thick, drippy pudding. Kokomo's girlfriend, Banjo, landed a pie right in Elizabelle's face. Soon everyone in the bonobo house was thoroughly slimed, licking juice off their fingers with one breath, and lobbing more stuff with the next, and acting crazy as . . . a bunch of drunk monkeys.

A loud whistle blast split the air. "All right, listen up, every one of you." Toberomi, in black boots up to his knees, stomped into the bonobo house. "What's all this monkey business? Stop this food fight now!"

"Food fight. Fun now!" Marz announced, beaming happily.

Toberomi blew his whistle. "You're wasting expensive food. All you clowns and cooks, get this place cleaned up. Elizabelle, get the quagga to his new home."

A rotten tomato hit Toberomi on the top of his shiny bald head. After he wiped the juice and pulp from his face, he looked up, but there was no bonobo—or wild boy—on the branch above. He grumbled, slipped out of the bonobo house and headed back to his wagon. Halfway to the central arena, he stopped, turned back, and yelled at Elizabelle. "You and Marz report to my office tomorrow. Bring your parents, too."

Chapter 3 ꒱ ꒱ ꒱ ꒱ ꒱ ꒱

FREE

Elizabelle and her parents stood nervously before Toberomi. The scene reminded her of the horrible meeting with Mai-Kellina, when she took Marz away from them. At least this big boss did not have guards posted at the door. Or weird rings on his fingers. Or little daggers on a necklace.

"We're in the fun business," Toberomi said. "And yes, a food fight is fun. But we just can't afford to waste food."

"Sorry, Mr. Tee." Elizabelle blushed. "One of the bonobos threw some mandretta fruit at me, and then suddenly food was flying everywhere."

Elizabelle's dad and mom stood behind her. "It was just innocent fun," Braden said.

"No harm done," Althea added. Ripley sat quietly in a chair at the back of the room.

Toberomi gestured to Marz, who sat wiggling in his chair. "I watched the veegee. Your new friend here started the food fight, right?"

Elizabelle answered. "Not exactly."

"Can he speak for himself?"

"He's learning fast. He learned a few words from Keeli."

"Both of you need a special assignment to help you remember not to waste food."

"Assignment?" A look of puzzlement passed over the faces of Elizabelle's parents.

"The assistant mahouts have all quit. So, until I replace them, I'm putting you and Marz on elephant duty. Both of you will feed and water the elephants."

Elizabelle heard her brother snickering behind her. "That sounds . . . okay." She felt encouraged. "I like elephants. Especially the big albino, Queenie."

"Lephants fun." Marz smiled.

"Not just feeding." The circus owner paused for effect, then reached behind his chair and pulled out two dirty, flat-blade shovels. "The other part of the job is scooping up the poop." He winked at Elizabelle, then handed a shovel to her. "It's a bit like a food fight. Especially if you're right there when the elephant . . . delivers the goods. It's a teamwork job. One lifts the tail, the other . . . catches the prize. Good way to learn teamwork."

Ripley snickered. "A dream date!"

Before Elizabelle could respond, there was a loud rapping on the door.

"Later," the boss called out.

"It's an urgent message." The messenger bursted into the room. "Just arrived from Tulamarine."

"Okay," Toberomi said. "Come on in and read it."

"To Jonathan Hertzicona, commonly known as Johnny

Hurricane, and to Braden and Althea Hawken, both of Seven Moon Circus. Lady Mai-Kellina, Governor of Luna Verdanta, charges you with the crimes of kidnaping a child in her custody, theft of a valuable animal, and destruction of the governor's property—her personal looper car and the V-1 converticopter. You are to appear at the Chancellor's Court at Castle Tulamarine within three days and answer to these charges. You are to bring the kidnaped child and the strangely-colored zebra with you."

Elizabelle whispered to her mother. "I thought we got away from her."

Toberomi stroked his chin. "Who sends this message?"

The messenger unrolled the document and showed it to Toberomi. It was signed and sealed by "Tancreido, Chancellor Judge, under the office of King Donovan."

The Chancellor's courtroom was designed to make the chancellor appear tall and powerful, and to make all the guests feel small. The Chancellor's chair sat on a raised stage, decorated with expensive woods. It was a high-back made from toolachie leather, and displayed the king's crest directly above the chancellor's head. Bailiffs—uniformed, armed guards, specially trained to protect judges—stood sharply at attention on both sides. Tancreido sat high above them in a black robe; the chancellor's pendant dangled from his neck.

Below him, Governor Mai-Kellina paced in front of her table, her hair pulled tight behind her head. Elizabelle, sitting with her family and Marz, noticed that Mai-Kellina wore none of her rings, but the emerald brooch—which symbolized her position as governor of Luna Verdanta—glistened from the center of her choker necklace.

Tancreido spoke in a scratchy voice. "I will hear you now, Governor."

Mai-Kellina rose smartly from her seat and addressed Tancreido directly. "Honorable Chancellor, I demand that the wild orphan child now known as Marz, and the strangely colored zebra now called SunKing, both be returned to my custody, on Verdanta, immediately." Her voice was confident, but lacked the coldness Elizabelle felt during their last meeting. "They were both safe on my moon when they were kidnaped."

Elizabelle whispered to her dad. "She doesn't own them!" Her mother shushed her. "The Hawkens took the Wild Boy from the Cloud Forest, after I *personally ordered* them to remove no living thing. I sent the boy to Yerkoza, to be civilized, to get the specialized training he so desperately needs. The Hawkens hired Hurricane to kidnap both the boy and the beast. They are partners in Hurricane's kidnaping crimes."

Tancreido squinted over the top of his spectacles. "Anything else, governor?"

"Yes. I also demand that the fugitive Hurricane be turned over to me so he may go on trial on Verdanta for crimes committed there. Damage to my V-1 converticopter and my personal looper car. I have view-gems showing him in the act of committing these crimes. Even while I was personally piloting the craft."

"How can I turn Hurricane over to you? He is not here. I am a chancellor judge, not a bounty hunter."

"Then I ask for a Royal Order declaring that Hurricane is an outlaw."

"You have already done that, have you not?"

"Yes. But my Order is good only on Verdanta. I ask that you issue a Chancellor's Order, in the name of the king, declaring Hurricane a fugitive throughout all eight worlds of the empire, and offering a reward of twenty-one gold bricks for his capture. Dead or alive."

"Twenty-one bricks?" Tancreido's voice cracked as his head jerked back in astonishment. "That's as much as the bounty on Proco Haruma! Surely you don't suggest that Hurricane is as dangerous as Proco?"

At the mention of Proco, Mai-Kellina's eyes flickered to the floor, and she skipped a beat in her step. She quickly regained her composure, though, and pointed to the Hawken family. "They could bring Hurricane in simply by calling him on their QM."

"Be seated, Governor. I will now hear the Hawkens' side of the story."

Mai-Kellina took her seat, coiled like a snake ready to strike.

The Hawkens' lawyer rose. "Good day, Chancellor Tancreido. I am Jorona Maasai. I speak for the Hawkens." She was a tall, strikingly beautiful, thin woman, with skin as black as ebony wood. She radiated confidence. When she stressed the most important words in her speech, her voice shifted to a slightly lower tone. "The Wild Boy was not taken from his *parents*, so he was not kidnaped. As a human, he had no right to be in the Cloud Forest without the king's *permission*, which he did not have. So, there can be no wrong in taking him out. But more than that, he *chose* to go with the Hawkens.

Indeed, he *risked his life* to rescue them from a crocodile attack, and escape from the wild world. He chose to join his own kind, to be part of a real *human family.* The Hawkens warmly welcomed him. They did not try to run away with him. They took him to Governor Mai-Kellina and asked her permission for him to join their family. When she refused, they *obeyed* her order, even though they thought it was *cruel.*" She took a sip of water.

"When the orphan boy saw that the quagga was being abused at Yerkoza," Jorona continued, "he bravely *freed* the animal from brutal trainers, entirely on his own. No one helped him. Except the quagga himself. They escaped together. The veegee from the governor's own spy-eye shows that. The Hawkens have never paid any money to Hurricane for transporting anyone off Governor Mai-Kellina's moon. The Hawkens have committed no crimes."

"Thank you, Attorney Jorona." Tancreido shifted in his chair, searching for a position that would reduce the pain in his old bones. "And what do the Hawkens request?"

"That they be given custody of the Wild Boy until his natural parents can be found."

Braden and Althea enthusiastically nodded in agreement.

"And what of the unusual zebra?"

"SunKing," Elizabelle blurted, "has to stay with Marz."

"Truly, he is a unique case," Jorona said. "But Miss Elizabelle is right. Neither boy nor beast has any parents or family we can identify. Perhaps that is why they seem . . . bonded in some mysterious way. I suggest, Master Chancellor, that you observe them together before you decide."

"You are a fount of wisdom today, Jorona." Tancreido rapped

his judge's gavel on its pad. "We shall all observe the zebra and the boy together. This afternoon, on the meadow."

☾ ☾ ☾ ☾ ☾

They gathered on the meadow below Castle Tulamarine. Marz, bridle in hand, led SunKing around the small corral that had been quickly assembled for them. On the hill above, Castle Tulamarine shone in all its splendor, with its seven gleaming towers—each representing one of the moons—arrayed in a half circle around the grand ballroom and meeting hall. The meadow sloped gently down to the shoreline of Tulamarine Bay. Elizabelle felt both happy and nervous to be in the meadow, for it was the place that 7MC was scheduled to give their grand finale performance for Crestival.

Tancreido's party wended their way down the path from the castle to the corral. Wearing his usual maroon robe, the counselor arrived first, in his silent carriage, accompanied by his armed guards. Mai-Kellina followed close behind, in her green carriage. Bringing up the rear, a long eight-seater carried the Hawken crew.

Honoring Tancreido's high rank, everyone respectfully waited for the Royal Chancellor to exit from his vehicle. He moved slowly, grunting with each step, huffing with each turn. Once his feet were on the ground, a bailiff handed him his knotted walking stick. Then both guards held his elbows as he shuffled toward the corral.

Mai-Kellina's two burly assistants, broad hats hiding their faces, stayed in their car while their boss made her way to the meadow. Once again, she wore her finger rings.

The Hawkens and their lawyer Jorona followed Tancreido to

FREE 🌙 🌙 🌙 🌙 🌙 🌙

the corral. Braden signaled for Marz to release the bridle, and he did so, leaving the quagga with just a halter on his head.

As Tancreido inspected the quagga, the beast made a few guttural sounds. "So it is true," he whispered. "Astounding. He is the perfect image—the beautiful beast from the old paintings, alive again." He wheezed. "I have waited my whole long life to see this. An extinct mammal from Ol'Terra, brought back to life here on New Roma."

Mai-Kellina seized the moment. "He was brought to life on my moon."

"We—all eight worlds—are one united empire, under one king, Governor."

"Surely, Master Chancellor, we are. But we must not forget that this unique animal needs special protection. We must keep him away from all dangers until my bio-engineers at Yerkoza can create a mate for him. Only then can the species become a herd again. Yerkoza is the only safe place for the quagga."

Tancreido closed his eyes and turned away from the corral. He took a few steps and then turned to face Sanctuary Ardemia, across the bay. The long open sleeves of his maroon robe hung like rippling curtains as he handed his staff to a bailiff, raised his arms to the sanctuary and bowed his head. A quiet nervousness fell upon the group.

"What's he doing?" Ripley whispered to his sister.

"Watch and find out," she answered coolly. She was not about to admit to her little brother that she had not the faintest clue. But it did not seem like something a real judge would do.

The chancellor began humming, chanting, making strange sounds no one could understand. Carried away in his private, trembling bliss, he rocked back and forth, breathing heavily. He lost his

133

balance and tipped to one side, but one guard grabbed and held him; the other then returned the staff to him. He clung to it, wrapping both hands around it, resting his forehead on it. The sunlight made a rippling rainbow in his flowing, white hair.

Ripley giggled. Elizabelle jabbed him and silently mouthed "quiet."

Soon Tancreido's mumbling faded into an ancient ritual song with a chorus about the "root of the royal stallions." After two choruses, he drifted out of his trance, opened his eyes, and turned to face the group. He then issued a command that stunned everyone.

"Release the quagga."

"What?" Braden asked, incredulously. Althea's hand went to her mouth. Elizabelle and Ripley stared at one another, eyes wide in shock. They were worried because valuable animals were sometimes stolen by competing circuses, keepers of private zoos, or poachers.

Mai-Kellina jumped up. "Excuse me, Chancellor." Panic spread across her face. "We cannot know what he might do, or where he might run, or who might nab him, or what trouble he might get into, if he is allowed—"

"Enough! Quiet!" He glared at Mai-Kellina. Then, in a whisper, "You, of all people, should know better than to challenge me." Then he repeated his order. "Set the quagga free."

When the bailiffs unlocked the gate, Marz ran to SunKing's side, ready to mount.

"No rider!" Tancreido shook his walking stick at Marz. "Let the beast run wild. Free. Alone."

Elizabelle rushed to Marz and led him back to the side of the corral. All the people moved aside, opening a clear path for the quagga. "We have to let him go. Tancreido speaks for King Donovan."

Marz glanced at SunKing and grinned. "SunKing, Marz, fren zokay." The quagga made his deep throat chuffing sound, strolled out the gate, and looked around. At first, he seemed to be in no hurry. He stuck his nose in the air and took several deep breaths. Then he bolted out into the open field, galloping toward the shoreline of the bay.

Mai-Kellina closed her eyes and laid her head on the railing, shaking it from side to side in disbelief.

Approaching the water, SunKing slowed to a canter, and then to a trot, then to a walk. He sniffed the sea breeze for a moment, then trotted into the field.

"Now," Tancreido spoke so hoarsely he could barely be understood, "who can bring him back?" He cast his eyes around the puzzled faces in the small group. "Governor, you claim a right to him, so you try first." He pointed at the bridle in Marz's hand. "Hand it to her."

Elizabelle took the bridle from Marz's hand and delivered it to the lady governor.

Mai-Kellina took the bridle and stepped away from the group. "Follow me," she muttered into her QM. Her two helpers—Rope Man and Gun Man from Yerkoza—trailed her.

Bursting from the corral, Marz streaked straight toward his friend. "No! SunKing, no!"

But before he could reach the quagga, Braden caught up with him and turned him by the shoulder. "It's okay. King Donovan trusts Tancreido, and so must we."

Marz pulled free, but he did not run. Instead, he sized up all the

Hawkens with a dark, suspicious look, a look Elizabelle had never before seen on his face. He glowered at the Yerkoza men. With his lower lip quivering, he sadly shuffled back to the little temporary corral.

Governor Mai-Kellina took bridle in hand, and with the Rope Man and the Gun Man tailing her, cat-footed her way toward the quagga. Her hair hung in a pony tail, imitating the quagga's tail. When she was close enough for the animal to hear her whispers, she grasped her miniature sword necklace. She rubbed the crimson gem, then slipped into her breathiest voice, and hypnotically purred, "Oh beautiful SunKing. You magnificent beast. I'm almost your mother. My people gave you life. You were a speck, in a dish, frozen so long, waiting for your chance. Now look at you. First and only." She locked his gaze with her own.

Mesmerized by her rhythmic chanting, the quagga stood tall as a stallion statue, ears at attention, head swaying slowly. Mai-Kellina crept closer, then pulled out her portable QM and showed SunKing a little movie of a female quagga, galloping eagerly through a field. "Look. A beautiful mare. Not quite as big as you, but full of female power. Like me."

SunKing allowed Mai-Kellina to caress his cheek with her right hand, bridle in the left. Her rhythmic whispering continued. "She hears your lonely heart. She needs your wild." As the tips of her ring-covered fingers first brushed his skin, SunKing froze in place. "My people can make her for you. She will be the mother of your colts. You shall be the root of the new herd of royal stallions. Just as I shall be the mother of the new royal family. We will rise in power together."

Mai-Kellina's words hypnotized SunKing. He swayed in the breeze, eyes fluttering. Gun Man and Rope Man doffed their hats.

From his position back at the corral, Marz stared at the evil men from Yerkoza. He began to shake. Althea put her hand on his shoulder, to steady him. It wasn't enough. Suddenly breaking into a sprint, Marz raced out into the meadow and knocked Gun Man over.

"Hey, grunt!" Gun man shouted. "You, again?" He fumbled to recover his hat.

Gun Man's shout was enough to jar SunKing out of Mai-Kellina's hypnotic trance.

The quagga blinked and batted Mai-Kellina's hand away with his muzzle. He moved a few steps away from her, tail swishing nervously, ears pressed back, hissing through his nostrils.

Mai-Kellina turned to her assistants and signaled for them to follow. They crept closer. Rope Man uncoiled his lariat and spun it until it whistled, *woop-woop*, in the wind. He then flung the spinning loop towards SunKing's neck. He easily dodged it.

"Not fair!" Elizabelle protested to Tancreido.

He answered calmly. "Let it play out."

SunKing angrily blew hot snot from his nostrils, then turned his rump towards Rope Man and kicked mud in his face.

Mai-Kellina turned to Gun Man and ordered, "Nap time."

Gun Man ripped his tranco dart pistol from his belt, and began loading. The governor pulled her tiny sword from its sheath, and dipped the tip into a small vial hanging from her belt.

"No!" Elizabelle screamed.

Chapter 4 ♪ ♪ ♪ ♪ ♪

CUSTODY

Tancreido and King Donovan met in the king's private office in the castle, and replayed the veegee of SunKing running free, and Mai-Kellina's attempts to hypnotize him or shoot him full of tranco. The recording began with . . .

"No!" Elizabelle screamed.

"No! No! No!" Marz exploded into action, charging straight toward his beast friend. This time, Braden did not try to stop him. The quagga, galloping away from Gun Man, slowed to a trot and let Marz leap up on his bare back. Once Marz was riding astride, SunKing returned to a gallop and headed straight for the castle.

"*Too-weet!*" A piercing whistle—Tancreido's alarm button on his Chancellor's pendant— split the air. "I've seen enough." He turned and padded toward his carriage.

With the recording finished, Tancreido spoke first. "Lawyer Jorona is right. The boy and the beast are bonded, in some mysterious way that we will probably never understand. We must keep them together."

"I agree." King Donovan paced. "But where?"

"The circus is hardly a good home for any child. Those circus people lead dangerous lives." Tancreido pushed a few buttons on the veegee control, and images of the circus popped up. Clowns spit liquids that burst into roaring, multi-colored flames. Acrobats pranced on high wires with sharks swimming below. "It's not a fit place for an orphan boy who barely speaks, or the rarest animal in the empire. If not the whole universe."

"Still, it's an exciting life," the king said. "I remember my own boyhood dreams of joining the circus. My friend Braden made his dream become real. Sometimes even I envy him. But . . . perhaps Yerkoza is best. Do you believe her story about how the quagga was created?"

The advisor shook his head. "I don't know what to believe. I'm greatly disappointed in Mai-Kellina. My biggest mistake was recommending her as temporary governor."

"How so?"

"So quickly she forgot almost everything her father and I taught her about serving the people. Her power has gone to her head. She thinks the people exist just to serve her."

The king rose and wandered the room, the walls covered with posters for the upcoming Crestival. Artists on each moon had produced a shimmering picture that imposed the smiling face of their moon princess—their official candidate to become the new queen of the empire—over the circle of her home world. All except Verdanta. The poster for the green moon had no face.

"Her time as appointed governor ends at sunset on Crestival day. Then the people of Verdanta can vote and decide if they want her to continue. Or they can choose a new governor."

Pushing another button on the veegee, Tancreido brought up a scene of Mai-Kellina giving a fiery speech to a stadium crowd.

"Who put the robbers in prison?" she shouted.

The crowd thundered, "Mai-Kellina!"

"Who made the relay loopers run on time?" A confident smile crept across her face.

"Mai-Kellina!" the crowd roared again.

"Who will you elect as your govern— "

Donovan clicked the machine off. "Let's decide today's question. Who gets custody?"

They replayed the veegee of Marz leaping quickly onto the back of the quagga, with the Hawken family cheering in the background.

"The boy belongs with his parents," Donovan said. "Can we find them?"

"We have notified all parents who have reported a missing child who would now be between twelve and sixteen. News stories have made the wild boy famous already, so we have dozens of couples claiming him. We'll do tests to throw out the pretenders."

"How long will that take?" the king asked.

"A few weeks. It's also possible that both of his natural parents are already dead."

"What then?"

"He can go into a foster home now." Tancreido put a new veegee in the projector; it flashed through dozens of faces of missing children. "When we're sure that he has no living parents, then he would be available for a permanent adoption."

"Any other possibilities?"

Tancreido paused for a moment, closed his eyes in deep thought, then continued, slowly. "It is also possible—just barely—that he, like the quagga, does not really have parents. If Mai-Kellina's scientists could revive the quagga, many centuries after the last one died, then maybe they could create a human life, using the same methods. Perhaps with human tissue samples from Ol'Terra."

"That's illegal."

"For every law there are law breakers."

The king rose in anger. "This is outrageous. I will destroy any lab that even tries to create children who have no living parents."

"The Hawkens want him. He wants to go with them. Do you trust them?"

"I would trust them with my own children, if I had any." The king stood and turned toward the door. "Give temporary custody to the Hawkens, both boy and beast. Keep them together. And tell the Hawkens to avoid unusual dangers."

"Yes, majesty. What do I tell Mai-Kellina?"

"The truth. This is a temporary answer. We'll take a fresh look after Crestival. When we know the results of the tests for the natural parents."

Tancreido took out a sheet of his official Chancellor's stationery and touched his chancellor's pendant. As he spoke, his words appeared on the paper. "Tancreido to Mai-Kellina, greetings from Tulamarine . . ." He paused a moment and then posed another question to the King. "And Hurricane?"

"He is Mai-Kellina's problem, not mine. She'll have to bring him in."

Tancreido smiled, then chuckled. "She should enjoy that."

The king grinned. "Not as much as he will!"

On his way out, the king reviewed the Crestival posters again. He paused at the green moon. "Has Mai-Kellina announced her governor's choice for the Verdanta moon princess?"

Tancreido chuckled. "Not yet."

Chapter 5 ♪ ♪ ♪ ♪ ♪ ♪

TRICKA

When you're sure I'm really dead
Place my hat upon my head
When I'm gone, and that is that
Just bury me in my hat!

(Chorus)

When my fun is finally done
And I'm down in the ground
Give me peace, and sweet release
Lay me flat, in my hat!

(Repeat Chorus)

I don't care if my shoes don't fit
I don't care how deep the pit
I don't care where my grave is at
Just bury me with my hat!

(Repeat Chorus)

143

Pull that hat down to my ears
Keep me happy for a million years
So when its time to lay me flat
Just bury me in my hat!"

(From "Lunch With Skunks and Other Stinkin' Songs" of the Eefananny Brothers)

Elizabelle and Ripley met Marz on the steps outside Clown Hall. "Are you ready to meet the clowns?"

Marz beamed. "Yes! I meet clowns."

"Good. But I have to warn you about the clown's rule. Only people wearing a clown hat can enter Clown Hall." At her side, Ripley adjusted his clown hat. It was in the shape of a plucked chicken, and its scrawny legs dangled and bounced over his ears as he walked. Elizabelle offered Marz a hat made of fake fur, with a long tail down the back. Both the hat and the tail were solid black, with white stripes that flowed down the sides. "This is a skunk hat. Like it?"

"Skunk hat fun." He donned the hat and adjusted it for fit.

"You make a beautiful skunk." Ripley showed him how to pull the little string on the side of the hat, to raise the tail, like a real skunk when it is angry or upset.

Elizabelle reached into her bag and extracted a bonnet in the shape of a giant sunflower. She wrapped it all the way around her head, and tied the ribbon under her chin. The huge yellow petals formed a bright circle around her face, making her look like a happy sun.

"Okay, boys, now we're ready." Elizabelle rapped on the door of Clown Hall in a strange, stuttering pattern, like a spy tapping out a secret code.

Her pounding was answered by a deep, echoing voice, like a bear hollering out from a cave. "Who seeks admission to the chamber of transformation?"

"It's Elizabelle, with Ripley and Marz the Wild Boy."

"Oh it is?" the voice growled. "What is the secret password?"

"Shall I whisper it into the peep hole?"

The voice lightened up. "Nah! Don't bother! If you know the knock, and say you know the secret password, and are wearing a silly hat, that's good enough!" The door opened and a black dwarf with a beard almost to the floor stuck his head out. His hat was a tall, see-through cone, with a web of wispy wires inside that flashed whenever he spoke. The sparks lit up as he whispered, "We change the password so often we can't even remember it ourselves! Come on in!"

Elizabelle did the introductions. "Sparky, meet Marz, known as the Wild Boy."

Sparky raised his gloved hand to Marz. But, instead of taking Sparky's hand, Marz knelt down so their eyes met at an equal level and began stroking Sparky's long beard.

"Marz," Elizabelle said, "when you first meet someone, shake their hand and say, 'Pleased to meet you.' Show him, Rip."

Ripley grabbed the clown's hand and shook it heartily. "Pleased to meet you, Mr. Sparky. Now Marz, you do it."

When Marz touched the outstretched hand, electric sparks flashed out of the palm of the dwarf clown's glove, and the miniature lightning bolts inside his hat sputtered and crackled. Marz winced and pulled his hand back.

Sparky laughed aloud. "I'm pleased to spark you, Mr. Skunk

Boy! Or should I say, Mr. Stink boy?" He sniffed the air suspiciously. "I love your skunk hat!"

Marz pulled the glove off Sparky's hand and turned it over, inspecting it carefully.

"Come on in, then, Mr. Wild Boy," Sparky said, "and meet the boys and girls of Clown Hall. And maybe, if you promise not to reveal any of our secrets, we might let you meet Tricka!"

Sparky led the way into the men clown's dressing room. One side of the parlor was a long counter. Four men sat before mirrors, applying their funny face makeup and adjusting their outfits in clashing colors. One tested the fake tear squirter attached to the underside of the brim of his straw hat, to make sure it wouldn't smudge the giant toothy smile painted over his face.

A few seats down the row sat Jerry Cherry, a tall, skinny clown with an Adam's apple that stuck out from his long neck like an old fashioned door-knocker. His checkerboard pants were wide enough for three guys his size. Bungee cord suspenders kept his pants from falling down around his floppy shoes. He busied himself cramming his oversize pants full of helium balloons and firecrackers, and guiding his gerbils as they snuggled into the pockets. His hat was in the shape of a large red cherry, and glued to the top of his bald head.

In the hallway behind them, Sammy Stutterfingers struggled with his one-man-band rig.

The room was a tidal wave of bright colors. Clothing racks creaked with costumes in fluorescent colors, polka dots, and metallic stripes. Various headpieces fought for space on the crowded shelves. Rubber caps that made the wearer appear bald, mechanical contraptions, shaggy green wigs.

Marz reached for a clown wig.

"You want the curly wig?" Sparky stepped up on a small ladder and grabbed the wig. He clutched the wig to his chest. "Want it? Want it? Do ya, do ya, huh? Okay, okay, Mr. Wild Boy, I'll trade ya for the skunk hat."

Marz adjusted his skunk hat and looked askance at the short clown.

"Which is it, corkscrew wig or skunk hat?"

Marz ran his fingers through the wig's mass of tight curls, and then rubbed the tail of the skunk hat under his chin. Finally he answered. "Corkoo hat."

"Deal!" Sparky's hat flashed as he stepped up to the top rung of the ladder, grabbed the skunk hat by the tail and yanked it off Marz's head. Then he jumped down and wiggled into his dressing chair, facing the mirror. He waved for Marz to take the seat beside him.

Sparky grabbed the corkscrew wig and adjusted it to fit snugly on Marz's head. The curlicues jiggled over his ears and forehead. "Ah, fabulous! You were born to wear curls, Wild Boy, sure as I was born to walk tall!" Sparky removed his lightning cone cap and replaced it with the skunk hat.

Elizabelle and Ripley crouched on either side of Sparky and Marz.

"Just look at us!" Sparky waved his hand across the mirror image. "A plucked chicken, a curlywig, a stripey skunk head, and a bright sunflower. We should have our own beauty pageant!"

The other men clowns chuckled as they continued applying their face paint. One asked Marz, "You're a natural to be a clown. Wanna join up?"

Marz's eyes lit up. "Clown fun."

Sparky turned to the other clowns. "What'ya say guys, should we let Marz join us, go to clown school instead of boring old book learning school with Miss Elizabelle?"

"He's gonna keep up with his book learning," Elizabelle insisted. "But he can do clown training too."

Mumbles rolled through the room. "It ain't easy being a clown." "Not the same since Bumpsy and his buddies left." Then one voice spoke above the others. "If the girls like him, too, and Tricka thinks he's okay, why not?"

At the mention of Tricka, Elizabelle and Ripley cast knowing glances at one another.

"Maybe he could march with you clowns in the circus parade," Ripley said.

"Ah yes! The Crestival! Our big chance at last!" Sparky said.

"It's our only chance to see King Donovan marry some . . ." Elizabelle paused, "lunar princess."

"All the clowns have to agree before we let in someone new. Let's ask the girls." Sparky led them into the next room, where lady clowns giggled, gossiped and gussied themselves up.

The back side of the room was a glass wall. Just outside, a lady clown, wrapped in a shiny red leotard, rocked back and forth on her giraffe cycle—a high-seat unicycle—practicing juggling with flaming torches. She wore ear beans and a small microphone.

"What d'ya say ladies?" Sparky shouted. "Should we let Marz join up, learn clownin'?"

The lady clowns all spoke at once. "Only if you guys teach him." "We won't make his costume." "No borrowin' our girly stuff!"

TRICKA ☽ ☽ ☽ ☽ ☽ ☽

The giraffe cyclist called out from her high perch: "He has to start at the bottom. I need someone to catch these torches."

"All right!" Sparky pulled on the tail of the skunk hat. "It's almost decided, Marz. You only need Tricka's vote and you're in."

☽ ☽ ☽ ☽ ☽ ☽ ☽

Tricka's private room was at the far end of Clown Hall. The door was covered with faded paintings of famous old fortune tellers. A large sign on the door announced, in fancy gold lettering, "Tricka's Halfling House—No Normal People Allowed." Above the lettering was the ancient ying-yang symbol, curling swirls of black and white inside a circle.

Sparky said, "Okay, kids, now it's up to you. Good luck. Let me know what Tricka decides." He smiled, winked, and walked away.

Elizabelle whispered to Marz, "Tricka's not really a clown, but they always want Tricka's advice on every important decision. Tricka is . . . " Her eyes circled the ceiling as she searched for the right words. "Tricka is the main star of our freak show. You'll see."

Ripley giggled and glanced at his sister.

Elizabelle walked right up to Tricka's door and knocked. The door slowly opened. She signaled for Marz to enter. "Here's your chance. Introduce yourself."

Marz stepped into the room. After a moment to adjust to the dim light, he gazed at the pictures hanging on the wall. In one, a herd of zebras—not tan and chocolate like SunKing, but in the black and white stripes of normal zebras—galloped towards a watering hole. In the next, a high society lady held a black mask to her face as she stroked the black-masked raccoon snuggled on her lap. The third showed black and white piano keys, in deep shadows. The final frame was a picture of a chess board, with black and white playing pieces facing each other.

The person sitting beneath the pictures sat sideways, showing only the profile of the face.

Neat, blonde hair curled under her chin. Her face, white as ivory paper, was made up with glistening lipstick the color of a ripe mandretta, eyeliner echoing the blue velvet of her dress, and just a hint of rouge dusting her cheekbone. Three delicate bracelets adorned her wrist. She looked like a high fashion model past her prime.

Elizabelle stepped inside and announced, "Tricka, meet Marz the Wild Boy."

Tricka smiled warmly. "Oh, wonderful! If he's young and wild, I want to meet him!"

Marz stepped forward eagerly. But when Tricka turned and rose to shake hands, Marz hesitated. His curls wiggled as he shook his head, and took a second look. Behind him, Elizabelle and Ripley struggled to suppress their giggles.

Tricka then turned to face Marz.

"Well, hello there, pardna!" The words rumbled out of Tricka in a voice low enough to make the curtains quiver. "I'm called Tricka. But you kin call me Patrick if ya'll like. That's ma real name. Sir Patrick KirPatrick, to be precise." Tricka firmly offered his right hand to Marz. Like the right side of the face, his hand was black as the deep mines on the Blood Moon.

The bracelets clanged together as Tricka's left hand reached out and smacked the outstretched right hand. The female half said

TRICKA

to Marz, "Ignore that rude old cowboy! I am the real Tricka. You may call me Patricia, or, if you want to impress me, call me *Lady Patrizia.*"

Tricka appeared to be two completely different people sharing the same body, split right down the middle. Makeup, hair, clothing, every part of the two opposite sides met at a line that ran straight from the center of the forehead, down the ridge of the nose and over the chin.

On the left side, Patrizia was white as porcelain, and female. But on the right side, Sir Patrick presented as a black cowboy with a curling mustache and a bluffer's attitude in his eyes. On the right foot, Patrick wore a cowboy boot, while on the left foot, Patrizia wore a lace-up lady's boot in blue suede leather. On the chest, the leather vest hooked into the bodice of the dress. Just below the belt, the velvet dress seamed with rough rider pants in black leather.

When either half spoke, the mouth and lips worked together. In a lilting female voice, Patrizia said, "I'll bet you never met any *one* quite like *us* before, did you? Not even in that foggy old forest with all those strange animals." She smiled and winked at Marz. "We're more alike than you know."

Marz stared at Tricka, confusion in his eyes.

"We're both halflings," the Patrizia voice said. "This body is a chimera—half man, half woman. You are half wild animal, or maybe half wild child, and half . . . something else. Not sure yet. And I know about your special animal friend, too. A zebra that's brown and tan, not black and white. All three—make that all four of us—are confused about who we really are. And normal people can't really figure out exactly where we belong."

Then, in Sir Patrick's voice: "The circus is the only place for freaks like us. People will pay money just to leer at human oddities. What other job could we get?"

Marz stuck out his right hand, then paused and offered the left. Then he rubbed both hands together for a moment, and finally offered both. "Pleased meet Tricka."

The dual person shook both of Marz's hands, and smiled from both sides of the mouth.

"Welcome to the House of Halfling, darling." Patrizia ran her tongue across her lip. "By the way, I love your wig. Perhaps we can trade wigs some evening?

"Tricka is more than our freak show star," Elizabelle said. "Patrizia is our fortune teller."

Ripley added, "Some people pay money to hear Tricka's stories about their future."

"Yes, and they'll pay more for a message from a loved one who's dead and gone to the afterlife," Patrizia said.

"Even if the messenger is just pretending!" Elizabelle added with a little teasing tone in her voice.

"Pretending? How dare you!" Tricka's two voices seemed combined. "There's nothing fake about me, or us, young lady!"

"Okay, sorry. The clowns want to make Marz a student clown, with your approval."

"Why of course I approve," Patrizia purred. "I always appreciate the company of a handsome young man, especially when he has a bit of a wild streak. So much better than this gritty galoot I share my space with." Sir Patrick gruffly objected, "Enough trash talk! The clowns don't need a beginner. We already got way too much curly hair 'round here. We need someone who can catch a high wire dancer who falls."

"I vote yes, yes, and yes," Patrizia insisted. "Let Marz join the clowns."

Sir Patrick objected. "You ain't the voting half. I am the man of this house. I vote no!" Sir Patrick pounded his fist on the table. "If the kid grew up in the forest, swinging through trees with a buncha monkeys, let him swing from the high wire."

"We don't have high wire acrobats anymore," Ripley piped up. "They quit too."

"Then put him in a monkey suit. Marz the Monkey Boy! That sounds right."

"Stop that right now. He's not a monkey," Elizabelle insisted. "His wild family wasn't real monkeys. Just some kind of primates. We don't know exactly what kind."

"I'm the only cowboy 'round here," Sir Patrick said firmly. "I'm the decider. I vote no. That's all."

Patrizia spoke up. "I'm the better half. I have an equal vote. I say yes."

Elizabelle took a deep breath, and stroked one of the sunflower petals of her bonnet. "Hmm. The one half 'no' vote cancels out the other half 'yes' vote . . . so . . . that leaves only the votes of the clowns. And they all agree."

Just then Sparky stuck his head in the door and announced, "Congratulations, Marz, you are now an official clown in training!" His electric cone hat sputtered sparks as he spoke.

"Wonderful!" Patrizia said. "Now, Wild Boy, don't spend all your time learnin' clown tricks. You come on over here and visit me." Tricka's left eye winked at Marz again. "I might teach you a bit of fortune telling. Maybe even some stuff about yourself that even you don't know. Maybe you can be my barker, make a little money selling tickets." The male half broke into the sales pitch. "Ladies and gents, step right this way to see Lady Patrizia, who knows the dangerous secrets of the hidden past, snoops the shadows of the present, and makes clear the cloudy future."

Marz gently pulled away. "Okidoki, Lady Patreezia. Sir Patrick."

"Let's get started!" Sparky said.

As the circus kids turned to follow the long-bearded dwarf clown, Marz inspected Tricka's makeup table. Cups of face paint were arrayed in the order of rainbow colors, from bright red to mysterious, deep violet. Marz stuck his fingers in every colorful gel as he passed. Directly in front of the makeup chair lay two more cups, with their lids open. Both showed the deep, swirling grooves left by scooping fingers.

One was black, the other white.

Chapter 6 ♪ ♪ ♪ ♪ ♪

AROMA

When evening came, Marz saddled up SunKing for a ride out beyond the campground, to the Baraboo Valley. After they cleared the gate, SunKing burst into an eager gallop, power surging from his muscled legs. They were riding free once again, just like the day they escaped from Yerkoza, with the wind flowing through the boy's hair and the quagga's bristly mane and tail.

The light of three moons guided them as they sped toward their favorite watering pool, a resting place beside the stream that meandered through the Baraboo valley.

When they arrived, Marz dismounted and let SunKing walk free. He barked his happy "*qua-haa!*" sound, and swished his tail. Together they approached the stream to drink.

However, before Marz could reach the water, his nose picked up an unusual smell.

He stopped. He sniffed. Bad smell. He followed the scent. Soon he heard a buzzing sort of squeak, behind some bushes. When he crept around the side of the bush he spied a small animal. The squeak sounded like a little dog who had worn out its voice by yelping all night long.

Marz positioned for a clear view. The small animal writhed on the ground. It looked a bit like the raccoon on the poster on Tricka's wall, but it had black and white stripes, like the skunk hat he had tried out earlier in the day.

But this was not just a hat. It was a real skunk. Trapped. He wondered if Sparky knew there were real skunks out here in the meadows.

The skunk had chewed the skin off her own foot while trying to escape from a steel-jaw trap.

Meanwhile, her three little babies kept nuzzling her nipples, squeaking for their momma's milk.

"Friend." Marz inched toward the skunk, whispering. "Marz, skunk, friend." When he was almost close enough to touch, the skunk's squeaks turned to angry hisses. Her white-striped tail rose straight up, pulsing in warning. She kicked her babies with her rear legs, and they rolled away, squealing. She turned her tail end towards Marz, and bent down on her front legs.

Psst! One quick burst. A knockout cloud of pure stink.

Marz jumped aside, barely escaping the spray. The horrid stink burned his eyes. He stepped away to get a breath of fresh air. This calmed the mother skunk, and she allowed her babies to resume feeding. She whimpered, and returned to chewing on her foot.

He gazed at the skunk family. What to do?

Turning suddenly, he mounted SunKing, and together they galloped back to the circus camp. At Clown Hall, Marz jumped off and raced to the door. He tried to imitate Elizabelle's coded knock, but could only manage knuckle stutter.

"Go away! We're gettin' our beauty sleep. No one wants ugly clowns!"

"Sparky, Marz, fren zokay, skunk."

After a few grunting sounds, Sparky's bare head stuck out through a crack in the door. He rubbed his eyes. "Wild Boy, it's time for sleep. Go home."

"Skunk hat."

"You need the skunk hat now? In the middle of the night?"

"Skunk hat now."

"Okay, if it's that important, you can have it." Soon Sparky's hand—this time without a glove—passed the skunk hat through the door. "Here. Just bring back my corkscrew wig, okay?"

Marz put the skunk hat on his head. He then dashed through Clown Hall to Tricka's door, and pounded on that one, too. The female voice answered. "Who be calling on me at midnight? Some handsome young man?"

"Marz, skunk hat."

"Oh, now darlin', you can come up with something sweeter than that." The door cracked, revealing only the female half of Tricka's face. She peeped out. "I see what you mean. Give me a minute to freshen up."

"Makeup. Okidoki?"

Then suddenly the male voice of Tricka took over. "You want makeup? Fergit it. Outta here, now!" Then the female voice insisted, "He's a clown in training. He needs practice." Her delicate hand opened the door wide. She seemed almost to purr. "Come in, my dear." Then, after she took a whiff, "You could use a shower, hon, and a much friendlier cologne."

Marz entered Tricka's parlor, rushed to the makeup counter, and positioned himself before the mirror. Scooping a glob of black face paint from the cup, he rubbed the dark color all over his face, arms and hands. He then wiped one finger clean, dipped it into the white gel, and made a little streak of white down the ridge of his nose. The skunk hat continued the white streak over the top of his head. He pulled the striped tail off the hat, and stuck it to the back of his belt.

Marz smiled as he inspected himself in the mirror. "Marz skunk!"

"Honey, it's a bit strange, even for me," Patrizia said, "but if that's what you really like, it's okay." Then the male half took over. "Disgustin! Ain't no such thing as a skunk clown!"

Marz scrambled out of Tricka's door, his skunk tail flowing in his wake, ran back to SunKing, and mounted. SunKing sped like the wind to bring skunk boy back to the watering hole. There, he dug up a few grubs and placed them in his pocket.

He approached the mother skunk on all fours, prowling like a cat on the hunt. The mother skunk hissed a little, but seemed too tired to fight, or to spray again. Her trapped foot was covered in blood, and a bit of bone shone in the moonlight. She did not position to spray.

Marz reached into his pocket, drew out a few grubs, and tossed two of them toward her. She sniffed them, looked up at Marz with suspicious eyes, and then slowly nibbled the fattest grub. When he offered the water cup, she eagerly lapped from it, and then finished the other grubs. By that time, two of her triplet kits had dozed off, their bellies bulging with warm, sweet milk. The third kit jerked lazily between napping, sucking, and burping.

After the mother skunk stopped drinking, Marz moved closer. "Fren zokay."

AROMA

Her dark, beady eyes stared up at Marz, imploring.

He tried to pull the trap loose, but it was chained to a long stake in the ground. After several minutes of probing, he finally figured out how to turn the release wing. The jaws of the trap opened.

The mother skunk eagerly pulled her bloody leg free, and limped a short distance away from the trap. Then she crouched and quietly licked her wounded leg.

Marz moved in front of her, and tossed her some more grubs. "Bugs. Yum. Lishis." He popped one into his own mouth.

One of the kits woke up and crawled up on Marz. His laughing woke the other two kits. Soon he had triplet baby skunks clambering all over his face, neck and arms, squeaking in delight, and nuzzling him as they searched for a milky nipple.

Marz fluffed his skunk hat into the shape of a nest, and let the kits curl up inside it. He leaned against a tree trunk and cradled the hat full of baby skunks in his arms, rocking them gently. He stroked their tiny striped heads and he hummed until they fell asleep.

Soon he fell asleep too. In his dream he was once again back in his old home in the forest, rocking his little "brother" the runt.

Chapter 7 ♪ ♪ ♪ ♪ ♪ ♪

FARTHING

Bucklebiter and the Hawkens sat before Toberomi in his disheveled mess of an office. "Only ten days 'til Crestival. Do we have a show? A spectacle? Can we take their breath away? Make them squeal in delight?"

Bucklebiter positioned his veegee projector on Toberomi's desk, and snapped his fingers. The light beam emerged, flashed through its color test, and formed a misty screen. The show opened with Capitano Zucchini shooting out of the cannon.

Toberomi nodded. "Good. A big bang beginning. But it takes only two minutes. We must keep them spellbound for two hours. They want spectacle!"

Bucklebiter snapped his fingers again. Clowns appeared, dancing, juggling, spitting fire.

"Not bad." Toberomi nodded. "But they've seen it all before."

Bucklebiter nodded. "Big spectacle costs big money. That's your job."

Dee sighed deeply and shook his head. "It never ends." He swept the stack of bills into the garbage can. "How about you Braden? Can you deliver animal spectacle?

Elizabelle placed her view-gem in the projector. Marz appeared in the light, proudly riding on the back of the quagga. He was costumed as a prince in the legends of Ancient Hindee. A 7MC emblem, mounted on the front crease of his emerald turban, anchored the tip of a peacock feather. On his feet, golden slippers curled at the toes. He rode astride SunKing, who was handsomely decked out with banner skirts in white and gold, and cantered in rhythm with the music.

"Stories about Marz the Wild Boy and the tan zebra have spread throughout the empire," Althea announced proudly. "Many people are eager to see them."

Elizabelle piped up. "People say they just appeared out of nowhere, so they must be magic."

"Ah, yes. *Magic.*" Toberomi chuckled 'til the rolls of his belly fat jiggled. "People love to be tricked. So, let's give them what they want. Make some magic!"

"Such as?" Braden asked.

"Drop them through a trap door and then Bucky will announce that they have magically vanished into a cloud of smoke." Toberomi stroked his chin. "Or, how about, angel wings for the quagga? People love stories about flying horses. They'll go nuts over a winged zebra."

"Great idea," Braden said. "But the king's order says 'nothing dangerous.' And I don't know where to buy angel wings for a zebra."

"They can ride in the parade with us," Ripley suggested, hopefully.

"They must do something exciting." Toberomi glanced again at his dusty old poster of the dwarf ballerina prancing on the back of the Lobanzo stallion. "What else?"

The veegee image faded to Braden Hawken in a golden cage with two tigers. As he pointed a small baton, the big cats jumped through flaming hoops, roared first at one another, and then at the crowd, and finally ran to him, jumped up on him and hugged him. Toberomi nodded. "Sweet. But it's just two cats and a ring of fire. That's not enough spectacle."

"The kids always love the bonobos," Elizabelle said. The misty light faded to Keeli and Kokomo riding bicycles and throwing candy at the kids in the audience.

"That's it? Monkey candy?"

Braden, Elizabelle, and Bucklebiter nodded slowly.

Toberomi nervously rapped his fingernails on the desk. "It's time we consider some nasty medicine." He removed Elizabelle's view-gem and inserted his QM. A round pink face, dominated by eyebrows as furry as caterpillars, appeared. The man flashed a smile broad enough to show off blood-red rubies, arranged in diamond shapes, embedded in both front teeth.

"Hello, Dee!" The man bellowed like a sideshow barker. "So great to see you again!"

"Hello, Largent," Toberomi responded flatly.

It was Largent Farthing, owner of Q&D—officially known as the Quattroni and Diamond Circus, Traveling Exposition, Mobile Museum and Interlunar Spectacular Show. He was a hated man at Baraboo. During the 7MC's last tour season, Farthing had hired spies to steal the 7MC's tour schedule, and then took his own circus to every town shortly before 7MC arrived. Farthing's pickpockets blended into the crowd and fleeced anyone who was too busy gawking at freaks to watch their own pockets. His ticket hawkers short-changed hurried customers. Phony Q&D fortune tellers cheated the townies with made up stories about their dearly departeds. By the time the 7MC arrived, the townies were out of money and grumbling that the circus was a traveling pack of tricksters, thieves, and bunko liars.

"My show master and animal master Braden Hawken, with his daughter Elizabelle, are here with me," Toberomi said. "Give us your ballyhoo."

"Bucklebiter! Mister Spectacle! And Braden Hawken, a man of legend . . . 'the brave one,' right? My sources say you are hurting for some trained animals."

"Hurting?" Braden said coldly. "Try hunting."

"Maybe I can *help* you. We just finished a big tour of Luna Azura, huge success of course. I have a complete menagerie, a large troop of fully trained animals, ready and eager to put on a *fabulous* show." Farthing's face radiated confidence. "Just watch." He popped one of the rubies out of his tooth; soon its image appeared in Toberomi's view-gem projector. The Q&D circus animals performed in three rings, encircled by a hippodrome track.

A caravan of sixteen elephants, each with a small trampoline strapped to its back, did the "tail up" act—circling the hippodrome with their trunks grasping the tail of the animal in front. Meanwhile, moving in the opposite direction, a bevy of acrobatic beauties in flashing rhinestone costumes—one of them wearing a black blindfold—leaped high in the air, flipping, twisting, and somersaulting on the backs of the elephants.

Elizabelle whispered to her dad. "We could do that, if we had lots more elephants."

THE RINGS OF BARABOO

The second stage featured dogs in a cops and robbers play. Raccoons stole a gleaming treasure from a chest and then scampered away. The dogs, wearing police hats, chased them, barking angrily. The "burglars" climbed up into fake trees, out of reach of the "cops." The raccoons pranced along the branches, dangling their ringed tails, flaunting their stolen treasure and mercilessly teasing the frustrated, howling law dogs.

The bonobos worked the third stage, dressed in glittering vests, fez hats in red with golden tassels, and polka dot diapers. They buzzed around the ring on miniature motorcycles, popping wheelies. The smallest bonobo ripped off his diaper, pinched his nose as he smelled it, mounted it on the end of a long stick, and waved it over the howling crowd.

"We have a few bonobos, but only two bikes," Bucklebiter said to Toberomi.

Farthing reappeared in the QM. "That's just a few highlights. We have racing horses, trick ponies, and a huge pride of big cats." He pulled the ruby from the veegee projector and popped it back in his tooth. "Whaddya think?"

Toberomi gave a begrudging answer. "Very impressive."

"That's not all. We also have a full menagerie of show animals—they can't be trained for tricks. Seven giraffes, five hippos, eight or nine zabirs, dozens of birds—even a two-headed dangoo snake."

"It's a good show, I'm sure," Toberomi said.

"How about it, Tee? Would you like to rent my animals?"

Toberomi squirmed in his seat. "Everything depends on price."

Farthing pulled a silky cloth from his pocket and polished the rubies in his teeth. "As you know, I live for the deal, just as you live for the show. How about if you rent my critters now, but you don't have to pay until after the Crestival. Interested then?"

Toberomi's eyes wandered to the ballerina poster. "How much?"

"A complete package. All the animals, full support staff, trainers, feeders, groomers, caretakers, costumes. Even a coupla orphan kids to scoop the poop."

"Why would you want to do me a favor?"

"You got the king's invitation." Suddenly his voice turned from bluster to syrupy sweet. "And you know me . . . always trying to do a favor for a *circus brother.*"

Elizabelle rolled her eyes in disbelief.

"How much is your ticket?"

"It's not a freebie, of course. But, considering what's at stake for you, it's still a real bargain." Farthing rubbed his fingers together. "Only ten thousand sevrins. Ten bricks of gold."

"*Only* ten thousand?" Toberomi snorted. "Ha! For that much I could buy the entire Bare Knuckles and Bay Leap, animals and all."

"I already tried. They won't sell. But my menagerie is for rent."

"At the Crestival show, we can sell lots of shoko and goobers," Elizabelle suggested.

Bucklebiter moved out of range of the QM camera, pacing nervously. Sweat formed on his forehead and the back of his neck.

"And just in case we don't sell quite that much candy," Toberomi asked as his eyes narrowed, "then what?"

"If you can't pay the rent, then I will become the owner of Seven Moon Circus. That will pay your bill in full. We'll go on tour as the combined Q&D - 7MC show, the greatest show in all of Empire Luna!"

Elizabelle shuddered at the thought of performing under the Q&D banner. And getting second billing at that. And worst of all, working for the professional cheater, Largent Farthing.

Bucklebiter pulled his finger across his neck, like a knife slitting the throat.

"Including all your clowns," Farthing continued, "your lunar travel rights, your trainers, your good name, Tricka and the clowns, your Wild Boy, the quagga—"

"I don't own the quagga," Toberomi snapped. "He's under the king's protection. We're just taking care of him until Crestival. And, I assure you, the Wild Boy will not be owned."

"I don't care about him. Orphans are easy to find on every moon. I want the quagga. After Crestival, I'll accept either the gold or the circus—your choice, of course—as full payment. How about it, Tee? Do we have a deal? Yes or no?"

"Give me a moment." Toberomi then turned off the QM camera and turned to the others. "What do you think?"

Bucklebiter spat out his answer. "Complete lunacy. You are out of your mind to even consider any deal with Farthing. I'd rather go down in flames."

"He has beautiful animals," Braden said. "Already trained. We could get them ready in a week."

"Mr. Toberomi, Sir," Elizabelle began. "The only reason we have Marz and the quagga is because my dad took a big chance and landed the balloon in the Cloud Forest."

Braden picked up the thought. "She's right. We'll never get another chance like this. He's offering us a chance to pull off the most important show we'll ever present."

Bucklebiter remained opposed. "He's selling poison candy."

Toberomi pondered. "Maybe this is our chance to skunk Farthing, too. Pay back some of his dirty tricks. Maybe his trainers will join us."

Bucklebiter shook his head. "Making a deal with Farthing is like dancing with a boa constrictor."

"Perhaps," Toberomi said. "But boas can choke to death when they take too big a bite. We can't disappoint King Donovan, especially if he's going to have wedding guests. This chance of a lifetime is worth a big gamble." He turned the QM back on. "How quickly can you get the animals here?"

"Day after tomorrow. I have a special train," Farthing said proudly. "Only need half of it to haul the critters. But I'll bring the whole train if your people want to ride with us to Crestival."

"All right Farthing. You have a deal. Ten thousand sevrins, payable after Crestival."

Farthing smiled and looked Toberomi straight in the eye. "Or all of Seven Moon Circus."

Chapter 8 ☽ ☽ ☽ ☽ ☽

REVENGE

Marz took Althea, Elizabelle, and Ripley out to the watering hole, to see the skunk family. The kits crawled all over him, squirming for the most comfy spot inside his skunk hat.

"Yes, they're cute and lovable. But they'll never survive." Althea shook her head sadly. "Not in the wild, with the mother limping around with one wounded leg. She will soon bleed to death."

"Can we give them a new home?" Elizabelle suggested. "Somewhere close?"

"Their only hope is a protected home," Althea answered.

That was all Marz and the Hawken kids needed to launch the skunk den project. They located an abandoned rabbit warren, just outside the grounds of the 7MC campground. It was easy to convert the rabbit warren into a skunk's dream home, complete with tunnels, logs and stumps, and fresh black dirt teeming with squirming worms and juicy tubers. Elizabelle and Ripley donated some smelly old socks and towels for snuggle blankets.

Right after the skunk family settled in, Elizabelle said: "The momma needs a name."

REVENGE ☽ ☽ ☽ ☽ ☽ ☽

Marz paused for only a moment. "Ma skunk."

"I read in an old book," Elizabelle said, "the word 'skunk' comes from 'segonko,' in the language of the Algon-keen people of Ol'Terra. How about Segonko?"

"Yes. Good." Marz nodded. "Segonko." He continued feeding fat grubs to the kits.

☽ ☽ ☽ ☽ ☽ ☽

By her third day in the skunk den, Segonko's injured leg still had not healed. "We must do something now," Althea insisted. "Elizabelle, please bring me the curtain cage." She ran to the animal infirmary, and soon returned with a box that had roll-down curtains on the inside walls. She placed it near the skunk den.

Marz dropped one of his shoko-covered crickets at the deep end of the cage. When Segonko sniffed the sweet, she walked right in, waving her tail. As she happily feasted, Althea dressed in her sterile gloves, robe and mask, gently closed the cage door, and then opened her veterinarian's bag. Adjusting the sleeping gas in the mist sprayer, she explained to Marz, "This cloud will only let her sleep. It won't hurt her. Okay?"

"No Segonko hurt, okay."

Althea rolled the curtains down, and pressed on the sprayer. The gas hissed as it fogged the inside of the cage. When the timer beeped, Althea rolled up the curtains, revealing the mother skunk sound asleep, with dark brown shoko smeared all over her snout. Althea reached in and pulled Segonko out into the open. "Oh, this trap cut is a very serious wound."

"Altee Segonko help?" Marz asked.

"I'll do my best. But if it won't heal, I may have to amputate the leg."

"Putate?"

"That means cut it off, cleanly." Althea grabbed her surgery knife, and made a motion like cutting off her own thumb. Elizabelle closed her eyes and quivered.

"No! No Segonko hurt!" Marz protested.

"A three-legged mother skunk is better than three baby skunks with no mother." Althea stroked the mother skunk's head. "In the wild, they would all die. But we can save them."

"Yeah, long as we keep her downwind from everybody else," Ripley said.

Althea carefully cleaned the wound. She applied her strongest anti-infection medicine, pinched the broken skin together, and sprayed it with skin sealer. Finally, she wrapped Segonko's leg in a clean bandage. "That should keep the dirt out, unless she chews it off." She then placed the snoozing Segonko back inside the skunk den. The triplet kits gathered around and licked the shoko off their mother's snout.

Althea and Marz were about to pack up the cage when they were interrupted by an urgent shout from a distance. "Mom! Marz!" It was Ripley, calling from the roof of Clown Hall. "Hurry, the Q&D train is coming, with all our new animals!"

Marz, Elizabelle, and Althea dropped the empty cage and rushed toward the Baraboo train station.

REVENGE

The Q&D circus train was a mile-long metal snake slithering along on shiny rails. Four sleek engines in sparkling silver hummed their way toward Baraboo Station. The lead engine had a ruby-colored diamond shape inside a giant golden "Q," mounted on the nose, just beneath the headlight. A red stripe flared out from each side of the diamond, forming a color ribbon streaking down the sides of the engines and continuing along dozens of circus cars.

Marz, Elizabelle, and Althea joined Braden and Ripley on the platform of the train station, where a curious crowd had already gathered.

The giant Q&D circus train pulled into the Baraboo station. The streamlined engines towered above the crowd, slowly rumbling, shaking the ground. Just behind the engines, three curious giraffes craned their long necks out of the top of their car to inspect the new place, all the while wrestling with their long tongues. Four elephant cars were followed by wagons carrying lazy lions, tired tigers, and eager zabirs. Still more animal cars streamed by in a dizzying procession. Horses, kangaroos, kitanzas, tapirs, and toolachies, and a few exotics even the Hawken parents had never seen before. Following the beasts, a dozen or so passenger cars appeared nearly empty.

The train pulled to a stop just as the tail car, the limotel, aligned with the ramp at the station. It was a limousine-hotel on rails, custom built for the personal comfort of one man: the Q&D king himself, Largent Farthing.

Farthing stepped down from the limotel holding his ruby-encrusted cane, followed by four chatty young women wearing short skirts and popcorn hawker hats. Toberomi greeted Farthing and then turned to address the crowd.

"Seven Mooners," Toberomi announced, "this is Mr. Largent Farthing, owner of the Q&D Circus." A low grumble rippled through the crowd. "He has generously . . . *agreed* to let us borrow his menagerie of performing animals, for our grand performance at Crestival. Welcome him and his people. And their animals. Help them help us prepare for the big show."

The Q&D crew used cranes, mounted on flat cars, to lift the animal wagons off the train cars. From there, rigging crews hitched the wagons to elephants, horses, and camels, and pulled them to their parking places. Some of the Seven Mooners tried to help, but they were pushed away by the Q&D people.

At the sound of lions roaring, Marz and the Hawken kids dashed to the cat cage. Inside, Q&D's master trainer, Dane Steele, strode about, cracking his whips and barking commands to the lions. He was a short, muscular man, dressed in a black shirt open to his navel and tight silver pants with four red stripes down the sides. His hat and belt displayed the red and gold Q&D symbol. His shiny black boots went all the way to his knees.

Marz and the Hawken kids stood outside the cat cage, watching nervously.

Inside, about a dozen lions and tigers perched on pedestals. Steele first approached the largest lion, who sat upright on the highest stand. The trainer rubbed his hands around the handle of his whip, blew on it, and then stared intently into the big lion's eyes, challenging the power position of the big cat.

"Dad never does that to our cats," Elizabelle whispered to Marz.

Finally the old lion yawned, blinked and looked away. Steele smiled and laughed loudly. "Good boy, Rexor. You can be king again if you ever get back to the jungle. But here, I am the king of the big cats." He then pointed to the floor with his whip handle. "Down!" Rexor cast his tired eyes around the cage, then jumped down, and sat on his haunches, facing the trainer.

"Very good." Steele patted the old lion on the head and tossed him a bit of raw, red meat. He grabbed the meat, chewed it for only a moment, and then swallowed it whole.

Pivoting sharply, the trainer unsnaked his long whip, sent it sailing out into the middle of the cage, and jerked it back with a sharp *crack!* "Attention cats!" On Steele's command, most of the lions and tigers turned toward him and assumed their most obedient posture. He held up more pieces of meat, dangling them before the longing eyes and drooling jowls of the cats.

Steele rounded the circle, gazing deeply into the eyes of each cat in turn, giving meat to each one who surrendered to his piercing glare. When he came to the last lion, a young male whose mane was just beginning to thicken, he turned his index finger in a rolling motion. "Turn, Duke. Do it now." The young lion fixed his eyes on the meat in Steele's hand, and lunged at it, fangs glistening.

"Tricks before treats!" Steele screamed. His eyes seemed to catch fire. "No meat for lazy lions!" With a sharp flick of his wrist, Steele cracked the whip directly over the head of the young lion. On the next pedestal, a lioness growled. Steele turned to her. "You keep out of this, Saba. This is between me and your son." She growled deep in her throat. He dangled a piece of meat before her; when she reached to grab it, he pulled it back. She hissed.

Steele commanded Duke, "Off the pedestal! You can't be the prince of this pride until you surrender to me. Who do you think you are, some pampered pussy cat who sleeps on a silk pillow? On the floor like your grandfather!" The young lion flared his eyes and nostrils, and displayed his sparkling fangs, dripping saliva. On the next pedestal, his mother shifted into crouching position.

Ignoring Saba, Steele drew the short whip from his belt and flicked Duke's ear. The young lion recoiled in pain, roared and flared his fangs again. Steele hit him again, beating him on the rump, then on his flank, then on his ears. When Duke reached to grab the whip in his jaws, Steele pointed to the floor with the whip handle, and shouted, "Down, now! Surrender to me, Prince Duke."

The young lion refused to budge. He growled slowly, from deep in his throat, his eyes full of suspicion, following Steele's every move.

Steele reached into his belt and pulled out a boxy gadget. He held it tight in both hands, pointed it at Duke, and hit the Fire button. A flash of electric current erupted from the gadget, shocking the young lion. As the electricity surged through him, his whole body shook uncontrollably. When the current stopped, the lion collapsed, tongue hanging out, tail and ears limp. But still breathing.

Marz exploded in anger, ran to the side of the cat cage, shook the bars and screamed, "No, no, no! Stop!"

Steele strode angrily to Marz and lectured him through the bars. "How dare you rattle my cage? If you spook these cats, I could die in here!"

REVENGE 🌙 🌙 🌙 🌙 🌙 🌙

"We must keep quiet," Elizabelle told Marz. "These are not our lions."

"But Dad says no animals will be hurt while in our circus," Ripley protested.

"No lion hurt!" Marz shook the bars harder.

"You're just a silly junior clown," Steele snapped. "You know nothing about wild animals! I train my cats my way. Wild animals understand only two things: food and pain. A little sting saves a lot of time and leaves no scar. Now get out!"

Elizabelle stood beside Marz, shaking nervously. "Mr. Steele, my Dad uses the reward way of training. We're just not used to your way." She wiped a tear from her eye and grabbed Marz by the shoulder. "Let's go."

As Marz turned to walk away, he glanced back toward Duke. The young lion was just lifting himself up, out of his daze, when their eyes connected. "Duke, Marz. Fren zokay?"

🌙 🌙 🌙 🌙 🌙 🌙 🌙

Later that evening, after almost all of the circus people were snoring the night away, Marz crept to Clown Hall. Since he was now officially a clown in training, the door lock recognized the grip of his fingers and let him in. He entered the storage room and located his goal: the squirter he had seen on his very first visit, when one of the clowns hooked it to the underside of his hat to make fake tears.

When Marz arrived at the skunk den, Segonko and her kits were already asleep. He tossed a bit of bread to the mother. She woke up, nibbled the bread, and cozied up to Marz.

He crouched down to her level and looked in her eyes. She let him pet her head. "Help Marz?" She rubbed up against him, and wrapped her tail around his leg.

Marz stood, opened the gate, and walked out. Segonko covered her kits in old socks and towels, then followed Marz, limping on her bandaged leg. He led her to the Q&D wagon that was decorated with paintings of Dane Steele, big whips in each hand, bravely commanding his snarling lions, tigers, and panthers. With the clown hat in between his legs, he carefully stuck his butt in the air, aimed the squirter at Steele's door. And sprayed. Fake tears.

When Segonko did not imitate, Marz dropped a bit of mandretta fruit on the porch. She then climbed up the steps, sniffed the fruit and took a bite. She looked up at Marz, with her beady eyes glistening.

He squirted the door again, then stood up and pounded on it. An angry voice erupted from inside. "Who dares bother me in the middle of the night?"

Segonko positioned herself with her tail towards the door. Steele burst out of the door, rubbing his bleary eyes. "I said, who dares—"

Pssst!

Segonko sprayed. And soaked Steele in stink juice, head to toe.

"Arrgh! Skunk!" Steele recoiled from the attack with angry noises, like a vicious animal in a snarling death fight. He writhed in the moonlight, ripping off his sopping night clothes. "Somebody's gonna pay!"

Marz reached out, yanked the skunk by her tail, and pulled her into a hiding place in the shadows. With one long stroke he petted

REVENGE ☽ ☽ ☽ ☽ ☽ ☽ ☽

her black and white head, back, and tail. He could barely suppress his laughter at Steele howling in the moonlight. But his smirking stopped dead cold when he heard Steele's last curse.

"Tomorrow my cats feast on fresh, raw skunk meat!"

Chapter 9 ♪ ♪ ♪ ♪ ♪

EEFANANNY

"I will get even!" Dane Steele's threat echoed through Toberomi's messy office. "I will not be humiliated!" The lion trainer, legs spread wide, black boots glistening, glared at the 7MC owner. His skunk smell filled the room. Steele had shaved all the hair on his head—even his eyebrows—but he could not shave away the stink.

"Relax, Dane. It goes away in a couple of days. You'll survive it." Toberomi opened the window of his wagon. "Think of it as a bad batch of perfume."

Steele spit out his words one at a time. "You. Owe. Me." His eyes bored into Toberomi's. "One skunk. The exact one who sprayed me."

"Tell me, Mr. Steele," Toberomi said, "ever hear anyone say 'Careful what you ask for, because you just might get it'?"

"You will deliver the stinker to me. By noon."

Toberomi leaned back in his chair and chuckled. "Or what?"

"Or else you will have no Q&D lions in your Crestival Show."

"Okay with me." Toberomi shrugged. "We have dozens of animal acts now. And a couple of lions of our own. And we have something Q&D has never had. We have SunKing the quagga. No other circus has ever had a quagga, in the whole history of Empire Luna. He's the star the people want to see. He's already famous throughout the whole empire."

Steele clenched his whip. "I'm the lead trainer for Q&D. I can load all the animals back on the train—not just the lions—and we'll all be gone by dawn."

"I made my deal with Largent Farthing," Toberomi said. "Not you. He owns the animals. Not you."

"Your fake Wild Boy is the only one crazy enough to keep a spraying skunk for a pet."

Toberomi stood and addressed Steele firmly. "We have no performing skunks in Seven Moon Circus. There are plenty of wild skunks out in the fields and meadows. If you want to spend your time hunting skunks instead of rehearsing lions, and risk getting . . ." He stifled a snicker . . . "a new squirt of perfume, then be my guest." He pointed to the door. "Good day."

The experiment about a home for SunKing did not work out well. Soon after Elizabelle and Marz placed the quagga in the horse corral, he and the dominant stallion started fighting, biting one another on the neck, rearing up and whinnying while paddling their hooves in the air. So, a separate fence was installed, to keep them apart. The corral was part of a series of fenced areas where most of the 7MC animals lived while in training. They all shared one long water trough, and the fences fanned out to give the animals plenty of room to rest and relax.

"*Qua-haa!*" SunKing called to Marz as he approached for their regular morning time together. His tail swished playfully as he acted out his usual tease, twisted and lowered his neck to avoid the halter. Marz rubbed a cube of malt sugar between his palms and blew a whiff of the sweet dust toward SunKing's nostrils. The quagga nickered and nudged the boy's candy hands with his muzzle, sniffing heavily. Marz opened his palms and let the beast nibble.

After strapping the saddle on SunKing's back, Marz attached the wheeled trailer to the saddle. He was adjusting the saddle belt when Steele appeared, striding toward them, fire in his eyes.

Marz quickly opened the corral gate, mounted, and prepared for a quick getaway.

"*Too-weeet!*" Steele blew on his training whistle. "Hold on, boy! We have a score to settle." After a short jog, Steele stood directly in the path leading to the gate, whip in hand.

Marz pulled back on the reins.

"I know you put that skunk up to it." There was an icy glare in Steele's eyes. "I won't stand for it. I have hungry lions, and you . . . you have a pest for a pet. A pest who sprayed me."

Marz reached into the saddle bag, pulled out his skunk hat, and carefully adjusted it on his head. "Segonko friend. Bonobos frenz okay. Lions frenz. All animals frenz."

"I don't care about the bonobos. The lions are mine. Bring me the skunk."

Instead of answering, Marz simply relaxed the reins and pressed his heels into the quagga's flanks. SunKing pushed Steele aside with his muzzle, trotted through the corral gate, and headed for the gate leading out of the circus campground, to the fields beyond.

EEFANANNY ☽ ☽ ☽ ☽ ☽ ☽

Steele shouted, "You will never get away from me! Hear that boy? Never!"

☽ ☽ ☽ ☽ ☽ ☽ ☽

It was only a short ride to Segonko's den. She lay curled in the old towels, nursing her kits. Marz called out, "Segonko!" She shook off her babies and sauntered to him, wobbling. He rewarded her with fresh carrots and dried mandretta fruit.

Their greeting was rudely interrupted by yelping dogs. Marz turned and saw Steele, jerked along by five lunging bloodhounds straining on their leashes, surging toward him and the skunks.

Marz carried Segonko over the fence, pushed her into Althea's travel box, clicked the door and slipped her a shoko candy. Soon the bloodhounds formed a circle around Marz and the box. Yapping wildly, hackles bristling, saliva dripping from their snouts, they took turns lurching at Marz and Segonko.

Inside the box, Segonko shivered. And hissed. And sprayed.

She hit four of the five hunting dogs. The dogs howled in pain as Segonko's greeting gift burned their sensitive noses. Some retreated; others rubbed their noses in the dirt. With the bloodhounds in retreat, Marz put the kits in the box with their mother, and remounted SunKing.

"Wrong idea, Stink Boy," Steel shouted as he struggled to keep the dogs on their leashes. "There's no escape. My lions are hungry for raw meat. We—you, me, the dogs, the skunks, all of us—we're all going to the lion house. Now."

Steele pulled out the electro shock gun from his belt and waved

181

it at Marz. "Listen to me, stupid boy. Either you follow me now, or you and your funny-colored excuse for a horse, and your stinking skunk family will all get a jolt, head to tail. You know I will do it. You saw me do it to Duke. Just watch me." The control knob clicked as he turned the shock gun to full power, pointed it at a nearby tree and blasted it. Electric sparks shot out and hit the tree; instantly it burst into flame, like a torch.

Marz stared at the burning tree and turned to follow Steele. With the whole skunk family in the little trailer, in tow.

The lion house was connected to the cat cage by tubes and tunnels. Steele used the cage to train all his big cats—lions, tigers, panthers, and leopards. Even one liger, rarest of all big cats, a gift from Yerkoza.

Near the cat cage, Sparky the dwarf clown stood on a stool, waving a short baton in his left hand, trying to lead The Eefananny Brothers in song. His efforts were wasted. "The Brothers" took great delight in singing off key, losing the beat, and laughing it off.

Despite their name, The Eefananny Brothers were in fact four fat lady clowns dressed in farmer costumes, complete with oversize overalls held up by bouncy suspenders. They wore fake beards that drooped almost to the tops of their knee-high swamp boots.

The Eefanannies' basic rule was "no real instruments, and vocal harmony only by accident." Occasionally they would carry a tune for a few bars, but they much preferred assaulting the innocent ears of their audience. They replaced drum sounds by bucket kicking, finger snapping, hand clapping, and boot clomping. If the song called for cymbal crashes, the Eefanannies clanged pots and pans together. They were as much like an "a capella" choir as a bunch of pigs in a pen rooting for a new bucket of slop.

In addition to the four lady clowns, The Eefananny Brothers also included one other person, whose head was entirely hidden inside a combination hat and mask in the shape of a brick of cheese. It was a deep, dark secret whether The Fartiste was a man or a woman. Just one thing was certain: The Fartiste never spoke or sang. Through the mouth, anyway.

When The Eefananny Brothers needed the deep punctuation of a tuba they turned to The Fartiste, who would turn backside to the audience, bend over, and—precisely on the beat—deliver a backdoor *oom-pahh*. Or a slow fizz, if the song needed it. On a spicy lunch day, The Fartiste could even imitate a trombonist sliding slowly down the musical scale.

Sparky held his baton high and pointed at The Fartiste. The other Eefanannies held their noses, ready for The Fartiste's grand finale blast. However, just before the odorous moment of gluttonous glory, their nostrils were ambushed by an even more powerful smell.

Steele and the hounds led the way into the cat cage. But the smell came from Segonko and her kits, bouncing along in the travel trailer behind Marz and SunKing.

As Marz arrived at the cat cage, the Eefanannies were rehearsing a chanting song, "We are the bug eaters, chomp chomp chomp." Marz laughed and tipped his skunk hat to the "singers."

He and Sparky winked at one another. Sparky's electric hat lit up as he called out to Marz. "I need the stinking hat!"

Marz yanked the skunk hat off his head, twirled it by the tail, and lobbed it to Sparky. He led the Eefanannies into some rhythmic sounds that could almost be called a song:

I love grasshoppers *(chomp)*
Better than beatles *(belch)*
But you're so proper *(spit)*
We'll just have weevils *(false teeth chattering)*
It's a bug feast, a bug feast for everyone *(underarm fartsounds)*
It's a bug feast, a bug feast, come join the fun! *(laughing)*

"Enough of those stupid songs!" Steele yelled at the Eefanannies. "My lions don't eat bugs. They eat blood-red, raw meat." He tied the blood hounds to a railing and took command of the whole scene. After opening the gate, he strode into the empty cat cage, and ordered his assistant, "Bring Duke. Now."

Clanking sounds announced the opening of a ramp door. Duke, the young male lion, padded from his berth in the lion house, down the tubes. He crept into the cage, crouching slowly, suspiciously eyeing Steele.

"You were a bad boy yesterday. You defied me," Steele said in his most reassuring voice. "Have you learned your lesson? This is your last chance to show me you are a real lion." Duke paced around the cage, head low, constantly leering at Steele. "If you will kill on my command, I will make you the star. But if you fail me, your hide will become some rich lady's fancy purse."

Steele called out to Marz. "Wild Boy! Put your pet skunk in here."

Marz exchanged glances with the Eefanannies, and licked his lip in a sly smile. Sparky pointed his baton at the cat cage door, then at the Eefanannies. Their secret plan was ready.

Once on the ground, Marz lugged Segonko's travel box to the gate of the lion house. Steele opened the gate and Marz opened the travel box door. He whispered, "Okidoki, Segonko."

The mother skunk's twitching nose appeared at the cage opening, sniffing. Outside the cage, the dogs started howling and pulling at their leashes again. Segonko crept into the cat cage. When her kits tried to follow her, Marz grabbed them, forcing them back into the box.

Steele flicked his index finger at Duke. "There's your lunch." He pointed his whip at the skunk. Duke took a few steps toward the skunk.

The mother skunk confronted the young lion, hissing. She stamped her front feet on the ground, raised her black and white tail high, and pulsed it back and forth. The Eefanannies stomped their feet in rhythm.

After several tries, Marz finally made eye contact with Duke. He bent down and whispered, "Duke Marz, frenz okay."

Out of Steele's sight, Sparky jumped down from his stool, slipped his skunk hat under the bars, and pushed it inside.

Marz pointed at the skunk hat. "Mmm. Duke. Lishis." The young lion loped to the skunk hat, smelled it, pawed it, and lifted it in his jaws. A chunk of red raw meat dropped out. Duke lay down, placed the meat between his front paws, and began devouring it, licking his lips after each slurpy bit, happily flicking the tip of his tail. As he feasted, Segonko moved from the far side of the cage back to Marz.

Steele exploded in a new burst of anger, shouting, "Bring 'em all in! Right now!"

Clank! Snap! The cat house doors popped open. The entire pride of hungry lions poured into the cage.

Once inside, Duke's mother, Saba, fixed her eyes on Segonko. Crouching low, the mother lion inched toward the mother skunk. Steele urged her on. "That's right, Saba. You can be my champion of revenge. You are my huntress."

"Sparky!" Marz's call had barely escaped from his mouth when the Eefananny Brothers gathered just outside the cat cage. They reached into the giant pockets of their overalls, pulled out more chunks of fresh meat, and tossed them through the bars and into the cage. The lions caught the scent and reacted in roaring delight, each staking out their own prize and hunkering down to feast.

Steele's dogs, still tied outside, caught a whiff of the meat. They erupted into howls, yanking at their leashes, lurching towards the Eefanannies and the meat in their pockets.

As the dogs yowled, the Eefanannies broke into their favorite hootin' and hollerin' song about a dead skunk in the middle of the road.

Steele covered his ears with his hands. Total confusion reigned as the lions feasted on raw meat, the Eefanannies butchered the Dead Skunk song, and the dogs yowled in protest.

"Stop distracting my cats!" Steele screamed. "And my dogs! Get out of here!" Steele snapped his whip in the direction of the dogs. They responded with more desperate howling, straining, pulling and chewing on their leashes.

Segonko scampered into her travel box. Marz slammed the

door, placed the box on the trailer, remounted SunKing, and rode off. But . . . he left the gate to the cat cage open.

Two of the dogs finally snapped their leashes and broke free. They bounded to the gate, wiggled through the opening, and pushed Steele aside. Once inside, they challenged two of the lions for their meat. The lions snarled and hunkered.

Steele uncoiled his whip and beat the dogs. "No dogs in the cat cage! Outta here, now!"

The larger dog leaped up, twisted on the whip until he pulled Steele to the dusty ground.

Duke attacked by sinking a fang into Steele's leg, cutting a deep gash in his thigh. As his pant leg turned dark red, he grabbed his leg and twisted in the dust. Soon Duke's mother, Saba, and two other lions, piled on, snarling and swiping at Steele's arms and face. The dogs jumped into the fray, lunging at the lions.

Pop! A shotgun blast. All the animals paused their fighting and looked around.

At the first sight of the smoke, Sparky and the Eefanannies broke and ran.

In the center of the cat cage, yellow smoke and fog belched from something that looked faintly like a peach pie. Within seconds, the cats and dogs inside went limp and then collapsed. Steele's body lay motionless in the mess.

Braden and Althea, both wearing gas masks, crawled through the cage door. "Thanks, Sparky, for warning us," Braden said.

Althea rounded the cage, testing each animal for heartbeat. All were deep asleep, but okay. She checked Steele, who lay on the ground, with his leg bleeding. "He'll survive, but he has many wounds. We must get him to the infirmary right away." She took a mask from her vet bag, and placed it over Steele's mouth. After a few minutes of breathing the pure oxygen, his eyelashes fluttered. Braden pulled the QM from his belt and called the rescue crew.

"Proco, is that you?" Farthing looked around his limotel, searching for prying eyes or ears. He held his QM close to his face.

"I'm here. Why are you calling now?"

"We've suffered a disaster. Steele has been seriously hurt."

"How?"

"He was attacked by his own lions. It was a trick set up by the Wild Boy and that dwarf clown. He'll heal, but not in time for the big Crestival show. The animal plan won't work now. I have no other trainer who can handle the cats. Toberomi insists I turn all the animals over to Hawken. I see no other choice."

"Now everything depends on Mai-Kellina. She must convince Donovan."

Chapter 10 ☽ ☽ ☽ ☽ ☽ ☽

GLIDERBIRDS

The Hawken family of animal experts in the Seven Moon Circus met with Toberomi, owner of the circus, in his tumble down office.

Braden beamed as he reported his progress to Toberomi. "The Quattro and Diamond animals are responding well. The young lion, Duke, has already overcome his fear of the flaming ring."

"All he really wanted was some hugs and food rewards," Elizabelle said.

"One lion jumping through a hoop is not enough." Bucklebiter removed his Master of Spectacle hat. "We need some aerial stuff. Daredevils prancing on a wire with no net below. Without aerialists, we'll have a zoo train and some goofy clowns. The crowd will love Wild Boy Marz and SunKing the quagga, but that won't last for two hours."

Toberomi sighed. "Right. We can't disappoint the king."

"Or his bride?" Elizabelle suggested.

"Or his bride. Bucky, get some high-wire fliers in here!"

"Ha! You think that's easy as putting a diaper on a bonobo?"

Bucklebiter snickered. "I've already talked to four different high wire troupes. Everybody knows that time is running out. They know we're desperate. They're all demanding big money."

Elizabelle knew that if 7MC failed to impress the Crestival crowd, soon they would all be working for Largent Farthing. Or doing boring townie work, which could be worse. "How about . . . if we get a brand new company of trapeze people. Maybe they would perform just for the chance to be seen, to start building a reputation."

Bucklebiter nodded slowly. "Good idea! And just where do you suggest we find a new troupe of high wire artists? Who are trained, practiced, and ready to perform? And have their own show costumes?"

Elizabelle paused. "I . . . haven't figured out that part. Yet." She knew it took years of training and practice to be skilled on the high wires, ropes, bikes and swings. There were stories about experienced trapeze artists slipping and falling. Some broke a leg, others a back or a neck. One had even died, right in view of the audience.

"Keep looking," Toberomi said, rubbing his temples nervously. "The show will go on with whatever we have. Whether Crestival is our last show or our best show, the Seven Moon Circus will go on."

Later that night, with five moons moving slowly toward alignment, Elizabelle crept to Tricka's Halfling House. She rapped gently on the door. "Anybody awake?"

"Who's there?" It was the eager voice of Lady Patrizia, the female half of Tricka. "Is that the Wild Boy?"

Elizabelle laughed and whispered. "No, sorry. It's just Elizabelle. I need your help."

The deep voice of Sir Patrick KirPatrick, the male half, answered. "Ah! The sunflower girl. Come on in, shuga."

When Elizabelle entered, Tricka's room was dark, except for a few flickers from a lamp.

"What's bothering you, darlin'?" Lady Patrizia fluttered her eyelashes.

"It's only ten days 'til Crestival . . . and still we have no high wire artists."

"Ahh, now that's a real problem," Patrizia said. "We need some of those daring young men on their flying trapezes. All those muscles soaring gracefully through the air!"

Then Sir Patrick added: "Nah! We need some shapely young women flying and flipping from one high swing to another." The next line was delivered by a voice that seemed to combine both Sir Patrick and Lady Patrizia: "Maybe your friend and mine Johnny Hurricane can help."

Two days later, Elizabelle tutored Marz in their regular early morning class. "This one is called a parrot." She pointed to an image of a bright bird swooping into the trees. "Ever see one?"

"Yes," Marz said. "Many parrot forest. Beautiful. Red, blue, green, yellow."

"Some can talk. Or repeat words. Maybe they understand us . . . maybe they just mimic. We don't know."

Marz paused, listening. "Hear sound?"

It was only a distant rumble, barely noticeable above all the circus noise. But it grew.

Elizabelle smiled and nodded. They ran out of the classroom and looked to the horizon. A red speck appeared over the canyon rim, moving toward them.

"Buzzard, fun!" Marz yelled. "Hurrcane!"

The Buzzard zoomed over Baraboo, flew past it, and then pulled up and banked hard for a complete reverse. The lunabus approached Baraboo once again, and slowed to a hover over the circus campground. "Attention Baraboo, clear a landing area!"

Soon circus people crowded into the central arena. Toberomi grabbed his QM. "What is it this time, Hurricane? No one's missing. We don't want another big mess!"

Hurricane's voice blared out from the Buzzard. "Hey, Big Tee, you're gonna love this mess."

Marz waved his arms, signaling for Hurricane to land.

Toberomi clicked his QM to local intercom. "Attention all Seven Mooners! Make room for the Buzzard to land."

The Buzzard hung in mid-air, over the central arena, but it did not touch down on the ground. Instead, it jerked back and forth, adjusting a little higher, then shaking side to side. With all engines roaring and pushing strong gusts straight down, the cargo bay door opened. But Hurricane did not leap out. The door opened to a cavern of darkness.

"What is this?" Toberomi demanded. "Are you going to land or just hover there, making all the animals jumpy?"

"Patience, Mr. Tee. Turn on your cameras."

Toberomi pushed a button on his QM, and all over the circus grounds, cameras mounted atop light poles and tent poles turned to the Buzzard scene.

A loading ramp slid out of the cargo bay door. A short, muscular man stepped onto it. His long cape looked like bird feathers. On the top, the feathers flared from almost black in the middle to a bright vermillion red on the edges. The underside sparkled in gold. His knee-length pants matched the cape. Tattooed feather patterns in tan covered his chest; his arms and hands were tattooed with blue feathers. A golden helmet on his head had a reddish nose guard.

It took Elizabelle a moment to figure out that he was imitating the curlibirds in the Cloud Forest where they had first found Marz.

The noise from the Buzzard's engines softened a bit. But the space bus still hung in the air, nearly motionless, gently wavering like a falcon in a thermal updraft.

The bird man reached back and pulled out a bow that was taller than he was. His arm muscles rippled as he pulled the string back until the bow bent into the shape of the fluke on a whale's tail. With the taut bow quivering in his hand, he aimed the silver arrow first at one group of gawkers, and then another.

"Hurricane, I don't like this," Toberomi blared into his QM. "You best get outta here now, and take this bird-brain hunter with you."

"Patience, Mr. Tee." The Buzzard rocked a bit even as it continued hovering in the air.

The bird man aimed the arrow at the king post—the center support for the big top tent—and released the arrow.

Sheeeooom!

Midway through the arrow's flight, a small jet, at the tail end of the shaft, flared. Little ailerons popped out and adjusted the flight path. The shaft scored a direct hit on the king post.

"It's a rocket arrow!" Ripley shouted.

"Big fun!" Marz smiled up to the Buzzard. "Hurrcane!"

Toberomi spoke into his QM. "Okay, you have a fancy bow and arrow. But you can't shoot a thing like that over a circus crowd."

"I'll say it once again. Patience, Mr. Tee."

The arrow shaft then went into robot mode. A small winch opened at the connection point, and began pulling a thin fiber that kept getting thicker in stages, until it formed into a metal cable. The winch locked the cable to the king post. The Buzzard pulled back, tightening the cable.

The bird man rode a unicycle, holding a long balance bar in his hands, and slowly pedaled down the cable.

Hurricane's voice blared out from the belly of the Buzzard. "My good friends in Seven Moon Circus, please meet Mr. JoJo Brightfeather, leader of The Gliderbirds, a brand new troupe of high wire artists and acrobats." Brightfeather bowed and the crowd applauded again.

Elizabelle was thrilled that Hurricane and Tricka had made her crazy idea into a reality.

JoJo Brightfeather carefully pedaled his unicycle toward the king post. One by one, the other Gliderbirds—all costumed like brightly colored birds—danced their way down the cable. They shook their tail feathers to the sounds of the Eefanannies stomping out the beat. When they reached the king post, the first six Gliderbirds climbed down to the warm welcome of the Seven Mooners.

Then the last Gliderbird stepped onto the ramp. "Ladies and gentlemen," Hurricane announced, "please meet the youngest of the Gliderbirds, Miss Claire deLuna Taroona, a high flyer from the Blood Moon." Dressed in her glittering parrot costume, she winked and waved to the crowd.

Once out on the cable, Miss Taroona pulled out a jumping rope and began skipping. Soon she was caught up in music, shaking her tail feathers, bouncing on the high wire.

Then, in the middle of a high jump . . . she slipped. She landed on her thigh on the cable, and tried to regain balance. JoJo blew his emergency whistle.

Miss Taroona struggled to stay on the wire. She kept getting more tangled, but somehow kept bouncing, flipping, grabbing the wire with her hands. Several of the clowns gathered beneath her. "We can be your catcher!" they shouted.

But before the clowns could form a cushion circle, a clown cowboy rode into the area on a galloping horse, yelling "*eeh-yah*!" Elizabelle stared in disbelief. "Tricka? No, wait . . . it's Sir Patrick." And indeed it was all of Tricka, dressed completely like a cowboy from Ol'Terra. Only the face and hair colors were divided into Lady Patrizia and Sir Patrick.

"Don't worry, little bird, Sir Patrick KirPatrick is here to save you!" As Tricka rode the horse directly under the wire, Miss Taroona released her hand grip and fell straight down. She landed right on the horse, directly behind Tricka.

Facing backward.

Marz laughed and clapped. "Big fun!" The crowd broke into a spirited applause.

Bucklebiter laughed. "Isn't there a simpler way to get her down?"

JoJo Brightfeather answered. "Sure, but we're in show biz. We don't do simple. We do spectacular!"

"Best audition I ever saw," Bucklebiter said. "We'd love to have you."

Toberomi looked up and tipped his hat. "Hurricane, you're always welcome here."

"Thanks, Mr. Tee! I'll meet up with you at Tulamarine next week, for the big show!" The cable dropped away from the Buzzard, and the lunabus spun in mid-air and roared away. "And my big pay day at last!"

It was nearly midnight when Elizabelle was awakened by a whistle, followed by the sounds of some animal in distress. She sat up and concentrated. It was the braying sound SunKing made when he was upset or angry.

She dressed quickly, ran to Marz's room, and knocked. No reply. So she moved on to Ripley's room. "Wake up! Someone is hurting SunKing. Or maybe he's stuck on the fence."

Ripley's grumbling was slurred. "Don't mess with my dream! Get Mom and Dad."

"They've gone to Tulamarine. It's just us right now."

When Ripley appeared, he and Elizabelle followed the angry braying sounds . . . which led them right to the place where the Gliderbirds had danced on the wire. The birds were not there.

But someone was up there. All alone. With no net below, and no parachute.

Elizabelle rubbed her eyes to make sure. "Marz, what are you doing?"

Marz carefully stepped along the highwire, one foot after the other, swaying to keep his balance. Capitano Zucchini's bat wings were strapped to his shoulders. In his left hand he held a long rope that led down to SunKing's bridle. The quagga had his front feet spread wide, and was shaking his head back and forth, braying and snorting in protest.

Marz let out a shrill whistle and pulled on the rope. "Move under, SunKing. Like Tricka horse."

"Have you been drinking drunk monkey juice?" Elizabelle shouted up to him.

SunKing lay down and rubbed his snout in the dirt, trying to remove the bit and bridle.

"Marz, get down here," Elizabelle demanded. "You don't know how to do this."

"Yes I do!" Marz shouted from the high wire. "Old home forest, I walk trees."

"That's right," Ripley said to Elizabelle. "He did balance on the tree limbs when the crocs attacked." He shouted up to Marz. "I can lead SunKing when you whistle."

"You boys keep forgetting," Elizabelle said. "Nothing dangerous for SunKing."

Bouncing on the wire, Marz responded with his favorite chant, "Rule One—"

"Yeah, yeah, I know, rule one do fun. But not when it breaks the king's rule."

Marz dropped the rope and, spreading Zucchini's bat wings wide, leaped off the wire.

"Marz!" Elizabelle and Ripley screamed together. They were wasting their breath. Even though the wings barely slowed his fall, when he landed in the dirt he just rolled over and got right up. He dusted himself off and bowed, just like Capitano Zucchini.

Marz ran to SunKing, and tried to stroke his neck as usual. But the quagga would not have it. He stood, stomped his feet, and turned his head away from Marz.

"Maybe tomorrow we can talk to the Gliderbirds about teaching you some tricks. No dangerous cowboy rescues, just swings and trampolines and simple stuff like that."

Marz nodded his head. "Yes. Gliderbirds. Cowboy rescue!"

The Story Continues in Seven Moon Circus, Book Three: The Battle of Crestival

BOOK THREE

THE BATTLE OF CRESTIVAL

Chapter 1 ☽ ☽ ☽ ☽ ☽ ☽

CARILLONS

Everything in the room was white as the snow caps on the Moon of Clouds. Behind the First Mother's desk, the white curtains framed a panoramic view of Castle Tulamarine, across the bay. Alabaster busts of all the Arkenstone queens, including the secondary queens of the first two Arkenstone kings, lined the walls.

Elizabelle and her mother awaited the arrival of the First Mother. "Oh, please tell me it is not true," Elizabelle said. "Has Mai-Kellina really named herself to be the lunar princess candidate from Verdanta?"

"She is the governor of Verdanta," Elizabelle's mom Althea answered. "King Donovan's order said that each governor should choose their moon's princess."

"But . . . how could Donovan choose—"

A stately, gray-haired woman entered the room, moving gracefully. "Good afternoon, sisters. I am Jura-Moraine." She too was dressed all in white, except for a simple necklace decorated with colored moonstones. "Welcome to the sanctuary."

Elizabelle and her mother rose and nodded respectfully. Jura-Moraine was King Donovan's aunt, half-sister to his mother.

"Be seated, please. Thank you for answering my call and rushing here on such short notice. I know you're both busy getting ready for the big circus show during the Crestival celebration. But we have an urgent matter. The king's most trusted counselor, Tancreido, has requested that we prepare the Carillons to sing at Crestival. Just in case."

"Just . . . in case . . . " Elizabelle raised her eyebrows in anticipation. ". . . we have a new queen?" On each of the seven inhabited moons of Empire Luna, rumors ran like rabbits in a rainstorm, whispering that their princess had caught Donovan's fancy, and would soon be the new wife of the king. By long tradition, the Carillons sang only at Crestival, and at a birth, death or marriage in the royal family.

"That's right. Just in case Donovan finally decides that he will take Tancreido's advice and marry a new bride. So the royal family can set a good example for all the families in the empire."

"And that will make her—" Elizabelle paused. "The new queen?"

"Almost. First, Tancreido will perform the wedding ceremony, then the king and his bride will meet with the Oracle in the Chamber of Royal Ancestors. When the Oracle announces that the king's ancestors approve of his new bride, and all the dead queens approve the king's bride to wear the crown of Queen Aldebaran, then I, as the senior female member of the royal family, will place the crown on the new queen."

"Oracle?" Elizabelle asked.

"A ghost talker. Someone who receives messages from the royal ancestors."

Elizabelle knew the stories. Some people claimed they could

send messages to, and receive messages from, dead kings and queens who still watched over New Roma from some mysterious place that was nearby, but yet invisible and unreachable to normal people.

Elizabelle blinked. "What if the royal ancestors say no?"

Jura-Moraine smiled. "We perform the ritual to feel connected to the past, and to honor the ancestors. We're following a script, like actors in a play. It's a ceremony. Ceremonies make memories. When you're as old as I am, you'll need memories."

In normal times the queen also held the powerful position of First Mother in the Ardemia Sisterhood. But until the missing queen, Galena Queen Selena, could be found, or there was a new queen, Jura-Moraine held seat of First Mother.

Althea sat up. "How can we help you, Honorable First Mother?"

Jura-Moraine placed a view-gem in her pierce-light; it showed a choir of girls in their teens and early twenties, singing at the wedding of Donovan and Galena. "We need to train a new group of Carillons."

Elizabelle nearly jumped out of her chair. "I want to sing in the choir!"

"Many girls do. But we have rules. You must be between fourteen and twenty-one years of age. Never married, and not yet a mother. How old are you now?"

"Thirteen."

"Ah." Jura Moraine paused. "Then, I will be happy to let you try out . . . next Crestival."

"But I will be fourteen this Crestival. On the very day that all the moons line up."

"Hmm. Only six days away," First Mother said. "I suppose that's good enough. Our second rule is you must be female."

Elizabelle smiled and blushed.

"That one's easy. But the last rule is the most difficult. Carillons are tuned bells. So, you must have a singing voice that is as clear as bells hung from the clouds, and rung by angels."

"I do! That's why my friends call me Belle. Well . . . it's one of the reasons."

"Lovely. Prove it."

"Right now? I haven't rehearsed anything."

Jura-Moraine leaned back in her chair. "Let me hear your favorite song."

Elizabelle rose and stood in her best singing posture. She closed her eyes, inhaled deeply, and broke into "The Rushing River." When she hit and held the high note in the chorus, Jura-Moraine smiled and said, "That's enough. Get ready. Our submarine leaves for Isla Tambora at sunrise."

Elizabelle hugged her mom.

"Bring some warm clothes," Jura-Moraine said. "It can be cold at Tambora. Does the circus have some big drums, and strong young women who can keep a steady beat?"

Elizabelle grinned. "Oh, do we ever!"

Inside Clown Hall at the Baraboo circus training camp, Marz the Wild Boy was getting his first complete clown makeup job.

"Face first. We always start with pure white. Even me. Cover your whole face." Sparky the dwarf clown stuck his fingers into the jar of white face paint, sitting on his makeup table. "We need a smooth, even base. Then the bright colors on top. That way people on the back row can see you."

Marz held steady as Sparky smeared white clown makeup all over his face. He twitched at first, in reaction to the coldness of the makeup. But he sat quietly while Sparky worked.

"Splendid!" Sparky finally said, leaning back to admire his artistry. "Have a look."

Marz stared into the mirror. His entire face was pure white. "Marz clown!"

"Almost. Now on to the design. This is the fun part." Sparky laid out his vials of clown makeup. They covered the whole table, from tiny tubes of glittering metallics in gold, silver, and bronze, to shakers full of sparkles, to jars in colors ranging from the deepest purple to the brightest yellow. "What do you want to look like? With those eyes and eyebrows, you should be a kabuki doll. Bright red lipstick . . . The crowd will howl!"

"Buki?"

Sparky climbed up on the desk, reached up to his top shelf and pulled down his porcelain-faced kabuki doll. The body was tightly wrapped in an elaborate red kimono dress, embroidered in gold with flowers and cranes. The doll was a family treasure, brought from Nihongo on Ol'Terra, by Sparky's ancestors, so many centuries ago.

"Pretty girl." Marz nodded. "Marz no girl. I boy clown. Bug face!"

"Bug face?" Sparky shook his head in surprise. "Never heard of a bug face clown."

THE BATTLE OF CRESTIVAL

Marz grabbed his veegee book and thumbed through the pages, filled with colorful pictures of insect species native to New Roma and its moons, and hundreds of others that had been transplanted from Ol'Terra. "I like bug." Marz tapped his finger on the picture.

"That's a *lady* bug, Marz. You just said you are a boy clown! How about something gross and scary like a hairy spider?" Sparky turned to a page with a trigori spider—native to the Moon of Clouds—that looked much like a tarantula from the deserts of Ol'Terra. When Sparky tapped his finger on the picture, juice dripped from the spider's fangs. Then, in a gravelly growl, Sparky sang, "Igor, spidor, creeping, feeding, crawling, mauling . . ."

Marz joined in the song, forcing his voice down until it cracked.

Sparky reached for the bright red clown makeup. "Suit yourself. Let's get the right—"

He was interrupted by the thunderous sound of a gong strike.

Zina Zucchini stood in the central arena, tightly grasping a long mallet in both hands, smiling gleefully as the giant gong reverberated. She grabbed a pair of long bamboo sticks and joined two other drummers in pounding out rhythms on a set of taiko drums, with two other percussionists from the Seven Moon Circus marching band.

Marz ran straight to Zina's taiko drum. She handed her bamboo sticks to him and he started banging away. The other drummers laughed aloud, nodded in approval, and thumped out the beat. He smiled until his face paint cracked. A crowd of circus people gathered around the furious drummers, clapping and singing, "No more work today, just bang the drum all day!"

When the drum song ended and the applause died down, Elizabelle and her mother emerged from the crowd and approached Zina. "Your timing is perfect," Elizabelle said. "We need some girl drummers to go with us to Tambora for a couple of days."

Zina crashed the largest cymbal. "That means yes!"

Marz interrupted the two chatting girls. "Bang drum all day!"

"Oh, I'm very sorry, Marz," Elizabelle warned, "but this adventure is not for you. Tambora is only for the Sisterhood. That means just girls. No boys allowed."

"I makeup girl clown. Kabuki. Sparky help."

"Makeup might make you a clown, but it doesn't make you a girl. There's a rule about Tambora. It's a king's rule. The whole island is just for us girls. Sisterhood."

"No, Dizz! Rule one do fun. Bang drum all day!"

Althea spoke up. "Not this time, Marz. You work with Sparky on your clown stuff. Work out your bicycle tricks with the bonobos."

Marz threw down his drum sticks and shuffled back to Clown Hall. At the door, the Lady Patrizia half of Tricka welcomed him in, whispering. "I know some secrets about the Tambora girls."

"Attention young sisters!" The inspector's voice bounced off the white walls of the meeting hall of the only building on Isla Tambora. "We have to make sure there are no spies among us. Line up against the wall, hoods pulled back so I can see your faces clearly."

The candidates obeyed. Elizabelle wondered how a spy could be there, since everyone had been inspected before they boarded the submarine. The inspector made her way down the line, examining every face.

"You!" The inspector pointed at a rough-faced girl only four spaces away from Elizabelle. "Sing for me." The girl broke into "The Poet's Quest for a Lost Paradise," in a voice clear enough to shatter a crystalline glass. "Excellent! Welcome to Tambora."

Near the end of the line the inspector stopped again. "You. Why are you wearing red lipstick? There are no men here to impress."

The candidate's eyebrows rocked, and a sly smile spread across the painted lips.

"Sing for me, Miss Lipstick."

The suspect cut loose with an embarrassing attempt at the same song. Elizabelle cringed, wondering how such a poor singer could even get to the island.

"No! Not in falsetto," the inspector snapped. "Natural voice."

The suspect's eyes shifted around the room. The eyebrows rocked. Then, those deep red lips blurted out, in a growly voice, "Igor, spider, creeping, feeding, crawling, mauling . . ."

"Marz!" Elizabelle gulped.

The inspector ripped the wig off the candidate's head. Marz smiled impishly and blushed.

Gasps of disbelief spread through the assembly hall. A few giggled.

"I knew it!" The inspector flew into a shriek. "An imposter. A boy trying to sneak into the girls' chamber!" She looked around the room. "Who knows this . . . trespasser invading our secret place?"

Elizabelle shuddered and shook her head.

"Who helped this bad boy," the inspector demanded. "This boy who thinks he can trick us with bad makeup and a silly wig?"

Elizabelle's mother and Jura-Moraine rushed to Marz's place. The First Mother sternly grilled Marz. "What are you doing here? Can you sing like a bell hung from a cloud?"

Marz said nothing. But he bowed his head, suppressing a little laugh. "Are you between the ages of fourteen and twenty-one?"

Elizabelle's mother spoke up. "I'm his foster mother. No one knows his exact age."

"No males here, except a king or a crown prince," the First Mother said. "He's neither."

"He's just learning about circus life," Elizabelle said. "He has no idea what this is all about." Elizabelle was not sure she understood what Tambora was all about, either.

"I Marz," he declared, in a tone of defiance. Then, as he rhythmically stomped his feet on the floor, he belted out, "Bang, bang, drum all day!"

Jura-Moraine held up her palm. "Stop right there, young *man*. You will stay in the dormitory pantry until the real girls finish rehearsing the royal wedding songs." She locked her eyes with his. "You are not to enter our song chamber. Understand, impudent boy?"

Marz smiled and took back the wig. "Yes, understand."

Chapter 2 ♩ ♩ ♩ ♩ ♩ ♩ ♩

TAMBORA

All the young singers wore robes of pure white. The girls approached the gateway to the volcano, each wearing a shoulder sash and a head band in the color of her home world. Elizabelle's mother placed a lit candle in each girl's right hand, and directed the other hand to grasp the long golden cord which connected all the young singers. When Elizabelle approached, her mother reassured: "Marz will be okay . . . as long as he stays put."

The young singers entered the tambour, the hollow chamber inside the Tambora volcano. They were met by nearly total darkness. It took several minutes for their eyes to adjust to the low light. A thin shaft of sunlight streamed through the oculus—the eye-like opening at the top of the volcano cone. At the bottom of the chamber, a lagoon was filled with ocean water, which entered through a small, unseen inlet beneath the surface. Beside the lagoon, a small musician's stage hid, out of sight.

Jura-Moraine led the new Carillons up the escalade, a walking shelf with safety rail, carved in a spiral on the inner walls of the hollow volcano. Grasping their cord, the young singers wended their way up the inner walls, eventually forming three rising rows of candle-lit, hood-framed faces.

Meanwhile, from her dark station on the musicians' stage, Zina Zucchini and a few other drummers counted out the cadence on huge taiko drums.

Once all the girls were inside, Jura-Moraine stepped onto the speaker's promontory at the high point of the spiral. The spotlight made her appear as a face without a body, glowing in free space, framed by the dark red of her hood. "Little Sisters of Ardemia, new Carillons, as Acting First Mother of the Sisterhood, I welcome you to Tambora. Here, inside the tambour, our songs echo naturally and the darkness enlightens."

The drum beat stopped. Each singer covered her candle, leaving only the light streaming through the oculus. Inside that light beam, Jura-Moraine's cloak shimmered through the hues of the moons. "Young Sisters," she announced, "you are called to be the light in many dark worlds!" The new singers had privately practiced the song before, but this was their first time to sing it together. "Be the choir! Sing the light!"

"We greet the light in the forest, the light on the sea
We sing the light shining on you, shining on me
We sing the light of our new sun
The light that's lost inside of every one."

"After their long pilgrimage through the deep, dark emptiness of space," Jura-Moraine continued, "Captain Norzah and his colonists—our ancestors—realized they had found the new human world at last, when first they beheld this magnificent sight!"

In the middle of the chamber, piercing beams in red and green collided in an oasis of light. The beams twisted, turned, and then gradually formed an image of New Roma, the new home planet, floating majestically in space, with its seven moons circling.

Another hooded figure stepped forward and stood in the spotlight, beside Jura-Moraine. As the hood came off, Elizabelle was thrilled to see the face of her own mother.

"The ancient Greek goddess Artemis was the natural symbol for Project New Worlds. She represented saving mothers and babies at birth, ensuring bountiful crops, success in the hunt, and timing the rhythms of life to the cycles of the moons. We named our Sisterhood after her. Over time, the sound of her name slowly changed to ar-DAY-mia. The ancient Romans called her Selena, queen of the moon. That is why, when Galena was crowned queen, her official royal name was changed to Queen Selena."

Elizabelle wondered if Galena even knew her queenly name. How could she? Galena was not present when Jura-Moraine was crowned in Galena's name, as a stand-in.

Stepping back into the spotlight, Jura-Moraine continued. "Our honored guest today is Mai-Kellina. She is the first Carillon Sister ever to become a lunar governor. Her life proves how far an ambitious, determined young woman can go. Heed her words."

Mai-Kellina took her place in the spotlight, and let her long black hair fall loose. "Young Sisters, I have one message for you: do not sell yourself short. Do not be content with your beautiful singing. Use all of your powers, gently whenever possible, and boldly when necessary. Remember that our role model Ardemia was more than mother. She was also teacher, midwife, archer, huntress . . ." She drew the miniature dagger from its scabbard on her necklace.

When she thrust it into the spotlight, the image expanded to form a glistening sword. ". . . and sometimes, a warrior!" She stepped out of the light.

Jura Moraine's voice echoed through the chamber. "Now hear our Keeper of Myths."

The oculus closed and the chamber went dark again.

From the musician's stage below, several drums played a simple heartbeat sound.

When the oculus reopened it shone directly on the half-hidden face of the Keeper. As the Keeper announced each moon, images of them appeared, floating in the chamber mist. "Behold our Silver Moon, Halcyon, a symbol of hope for better days. She is always bright in the heavens during the darkest and coldest days of winter on New Roma."

Elizabelle wondered if the echo was confusing her hearing. The Keeper of the Myths sounded very much like . . . Patrizia, the female half of Tricka. How could that be?

"Here is Electra, called the Golden Moon because she outshines all the others. She represents the wild woman." Then, almost in a whisper, "My personal favorite."

The next moon appeared. "Verdanta, the Green Moon, is the symbol of gardens and growing plants, and nature's endless command to grow new life. Which women understand."

Elizabelle strained her eyes, trying to see the whole face of the speaker, to find out if it really was Patrizia.

"Our Gray Lady, the Moon of Clouds," continued the Keeper, "honors the ancient Merope, the mother of a blind child, who also adopted several orphans and abandoned children.

"Kayleno, the Blue Moon, represents the mysterious, hidden parts of womanhood, those private treasures that no man can fully understand.

"Azura, the Lavender Moon, shows us woman as artist, the defender of beauty and art, the muse who inspires the creative man."

Now all the moons appeared in their orbits around New Roma, floating majestically in the mist inside the chamber. "All these ancient goddesses dwell within you," the Keeper declared. "All these powers are your birthright as a woman."

This comment was too much for Elizabelle. How could Tricka even speak of a woman's birthright? Was *she* half-man? Was *he* half-woman? Was Tricka's whole act just a trick of makeup and costume? A circus freak to entertain the townies, but out of place at Tambora?

"And last, the Blood Moon reminds us that even in the best of times, life includes spells of suffering and pain, which we must endure, comforting one another."

With a whooshing sound, the oculus closed and the pierce-lights faded, leaving only darkness.

Elizabelle heard scuffling sounds from the bottom of the chamber. Peering through the mist to Zina and the drummers, she thought she saw five drummers. But there were only four when they entered. She had a bad feeling about that extra drummer.

Althea stepped out onto the promontory, the spotlight framing her face. Her hood was gone, and her long hair hung almost to her waist. "Once every seven years," she recited, "when it is summer on New Roma, Ardemia treats us to this vision. Nothing like it may be seen on any other world. It is the most magnificent view of nature's majesty that human eyes can see."

In the center of the volcanic chamber, floating images of all seven moons aligned, one above the other, forming a cascade of crescents glowing in dappled pastels and shadows.

"Young Sisters! This is why we celebrate Crestival—the Grand Festival of the Seven Crescent Moons. The lunar alignment represents connection, especially the love between a woman and a man, and the beginnings of new human lives. It is the most favorable time for weddings. In just a few days, we shall assemble together at Castle Tulamarine. With the Crestival moons shining down on us, we will sing to celebrate the marriage of King Donovan and his new bride."

But who would be the lucky princess? Elizabelle looked up to the promontory, and saw the outline of Mai-Kellina. Did King Donovan understand what a cruel, heartless woman she was? A woman who fancied herself as a warrior, as a way to gain more power? When the words *Queen Mai-Kellina* flashed through her mind, Elizabelle's whole body shuddered in dread.

The time had arrived for the new Carillons to perfect the wedding song and the coronation anthem. Zina and the drummers kept a steady rhythm, punctuating the chorus. But the drumming seemed to add some extra beats that did not really fit the music.

As the girls sang in rounds, standing on the spiral, their songs created a small whirlwind, coaxing the chamber mist to solidify into a block of ice, floating on the surface of the lagoon.

Pierce-light beams carved the face of Ardemia in the block of ice. Once the sculpture was complete, a pierce-light on the bottom of the lagoon projected a beam straight up, into the statue.

Elizabelle's mother spoke softly, but her words echoed around the chamber. "Young Sisters, only we ever get to see Ardemia like this, glowing in ice, with all the aligned moons as a garland above her head." The oculus opened; a new beam of sunlight lanced the darkness. "Soon the air will warm and this temporary statue of Ardemia will melt. That is a reminder. We shall all shall return to the water one day."

Jura-Moraine retook the promontory. "When you witness Ardemia in the ice, your time as a girl child is done. Each of you is now a young woman, a new member of the Sisters of Ardemia. Congratulations to all of you. Now we must return to Tulamarine." She set off on her path down the spiral. The young singers fell in line behind her.

At first Elizabelle joined in the line of girls. But after one turn around the spiral, curiosity overwhelmed her. She ducked out of line and took a side path down to the musicians' stage.

When she arrived at the floor of the chamber, her worst fear was confirmed. Beside Zina stood Marz, in a long robe with a hood, hiding in the darkness. "Marz! You were ordered to stay in the dorm. How'd you get here?"

Marz nodded at the largest drum, smiled and rocked his eyebrows.

Zina whispered to Elizabelle: "He crawled out of the bottom of the big drum."

"You knew?" Elizabelle asked of Zina. "Why didn't you stop him?"

"He was already in. I couldn't interrupt the ceremony."

A look of alarm spread across Elizabelle's face. She glared at Marz. "You're in big trouble!"

Marz pulled down his hood and smiled at her. "Tricka say okay Marz play drums."

"Tricka doesn't make the rules," Elizabelle snapped. "Tricka doesn't follow the rules very well, either." The other drummers were already gone, and the last of the singers were about to leave the chamber. "We'll wait here until all the real girls are gone." She pulled Marz's hood back up and blew out her candle. Which left no light at all on the musician's stage.

♩ ♩ ♩ ♩ ♩ ♩ ♩

From the darkened drum stage, Elizabelle, Marz and Zina stared up to the speaker's promontory. One figure remained, her hood thrown back, standing in the light streaming through the oculus. Elizabelle wondered why Mai-Kellina would linger, apparently alone, in the chamber.

The lady governor looked around and then lifted her QM to her mouth. Even from their spying point, far below, Elizabelle noticed the faint red glow in Mai-Kellina's ears. Elizabelle put her finger to her lips, and then to Marz's.

"Proco," Mai-Kellina whispered into her QM. "Are you there?"

At the mention of Proco's name, Elizabelle shook in disbelief.

"Yes, our plan is on track." Mai-Kellina's whisper voice carried throughout the chamber.

There was a response, but the spies hiding in the darkness below could not pick it up.

"If he makes the wrong choice, it will be his last."

Another muffled reply through the QM.

"Are you ready with the back-up plan?"

Elizabelle strained to hear the response. Did the voice say "above you" or "love you?"

"I miss you. You will be there, promise me."

Marz tried to whisper, "Pro—" Elizabelle slapped her hand over his mouth, and shushed him with a finger to her mouth. And then Mai-Kellina shifted into her chanting voice: "All the powers shall be ours."

Chapter 3 ♪ ♪ ♪ ♪ ♪ ♪

SMOKE

King Donovan slipped out of his private quarters in Castle Tulamarine and went walking, just after sunset. Above him, all seven moons shone brightly, like the moonstones in the necklace of a lunar princess. Tomorrow, the moons would align perfectly. He could delay his decision about choosing a new bride no longer.

The king strolled through Aldebaran's Garden, and stopped at the memorial to his own mother, Queen Rubicania. He bowed his head to her statue. "Oh, my sweet mother. Whisper to me through the wind. Guide me in my heavy choice." She remained silent, resting forever in her marble casket beneath her statue.

The breeze carried a strong aroma from the stack of gabania wood, piled near the stone steps leading to Tancreido's study. Donovan walked to the woodpile, selected a dry log, and split it with an ax. He chose four hefty chunks of firewood and hauled them to his chamber.

The king stacked the wood on a nest of kindling in the fireplace. When he lit the fire, the splintered wood crackled and the bark hissed as it curled away. A fountain of flames licked their way up the chimney. He gazed into the flame.

After the fire had burned down to embers, he tightened the chimney vent, limiting the escape route for the smoke. By midnight, a sweet smokey haze hung in his chamber. He stared into the glowing embers.

The voice of Tancreido pulled Donovan out of his meditation. "Highness," the old advisor whispered, "the princesses, and the people, await your decision."

"I know," the king said. "Tomorrow is the day. Your gabania smoke has disappointed me," the king said. "Neither my mind nor my heart is any clearer."

"Perhaps a fresh review of the candidates would help?" Tancreido's voice seemed raspier than usual.

Donovan simply nodded.

Tancreido thrust his shaky hand deep into his pocket and fumbled around for a minute. Then he withdrew a jewel box, decorated with moonstones. "Somewhere in here is the future of your family," he wheezed, "and all of Empire Luna." He struggled to open the lid.

"Let me do it for you." Donovan took the box and snapped open the lid, revealing a glistening gem inside. He fixed it in the cradle of the pierce-light on the desk. The light beam probed the room and swirled until the smoke formed a miniature screen. "Play."

The first scene replayed Donovan dining with Karianta, princess from the Silver Moon. Not yet out of her teens, she wore large hoop earrings of shining gold, and kept pushing her long hair over her shoulders. Donovan offered a toast, but her hands shook when she raised the goblet.

"A lovely young woman," Donovan said. "Far too young for me. Too young to be wife to anyone. Or queen of anything. Let her finish growing up." He clicked to the next scene.

Princess Orfala, her dark skin shining in the light of candles, stood tall and straight in her deep purple robe, decorated with elaborate gold lace. "King Donovan," she said, "I bring you the warm greetings of my people, and all the people of the Golden Moon." They waltzed together, sweeping across the ballroom floor, synchronized in graceful movements.

Donovan slowed the recording. "She is the best dancer. Far better than me."

"Is Orfala your choice, then?"

"Being queen is much more than dancing."

"She is the granddaughter of Governor Lataan," Tancreido said. "He still holds his position as Commander General of the Army of the Golden Moon. A union between his family and yours would ensure the loyalty of his army. We have reports that some of his generals have been contacted by Proco's spies. A few are listening."

"Orfala will be a great leader on the Golden Moon," Donovan replied. "I hope she can be as good a friend to me as Lataan was to my father, and to you. Next."

The Blue Moon sent Princess Shyama, of the Hindee people. She and Donovan had spent an afternoon boating. As they paddled along, she smiled as if hiding a sweet secret, and remained silent. When their boat passed by a stand of pines, he asked her, "What is the most important goal of your life?"

After a moment's hesitation, she answered. "To know who I was before, and if I have a choice over who I might be in my next life."

The veegee image faded. "Ah yes, a mystic, a destiny dancer." Tancreido chuckled and smiled. "They can be so intriguing. One of them almost tricked me out of my bachelorhood."

"Her natural home is the House of Mysteries on Kayleno," Donovan said.

But when Donovan asked the next princess, Pippa-Luka of the Moon of Clouds, about her life goal, she answered quickly and clearly. "I hope we can have a large family. At least one boy and one girl of our own, and at least one child adopted from each tribe on every moon. That would make us the perfect royal family, don't you think?"

Even on the smoke screen replay, Donovan's surprise showed in the reddening of his cheeks. "I do indeed long for at least one son and at least one daughter. But not so many."

"Perhaps we should help her set up an orphanage, or a foster center," Tancreido said.

"Yes, excellent idea. Get it started right after Crestival."

The projector brightened again. Princess D'Azura from the Lavender Moon, her blonde hair parted in the middle, met Donovan in the library of the castle. "I love books. View-gems are convenient and colorful. But when I read an old fashioned book, I can almost hear the author reading to me, through a time tunnel. When my fingers caress the leather cover, I hold hands with the book binder." She stepped back and pulled the covering off a portrait of Donovan's mother and father. "I painted it myself. Is it close? I never got to meet them."

"D'Azura is the most authentic one," Donovan said. She has a poet's mastery of words and the inspired hands of a painter. She's one of the people who give meaning to life. Perhaps . . . in time."

"She has such strong presence." Tancreido's tone seemed encouraging. "Whenever she enters a room, all eyes naturally turn to her. The people need that in a queen. It's a natural quality, not a learned one. It means she was born to lead and inspire."

The Blood Moon sent Amarna of the Farville tribe, a brown-eyed, athletic woman. An afternoon of horseback riding took her and Donovan to the waterfalls of Nakkona. It was the place where Donovan had last seen Galena, on the day after their wedding, two Crestivals ago.

"It was not fair for me to take her there. Too many memories arguing with the moment," Donovan said. "Let me see your niece again."

Mai-Kellina, regal in her ceremonial dress, wrapped her arm firmly around Donovan's shoulder as they turned in dance. "What can you tell me about the Wild Boy," he asked her.

"There are stories about a boy who was created in a lab at Yerkoza."

Donovan shot her a look of shock.

"It happened long before you appointed me governor," she said. "When that crime was discovered, the lead experimenter escaped, taking the baby. The baby's records were destroyed." She looked Donovan in the eye. "The Cloud Forest would be a good hiding place. It's not far from Yerkoza."

"What's his name?"

Smiling slyly, Mai-Kellina answered, "I never said the experimenter was a man."

Donovan smiled. "Pardon me for presuming."

"She called herself Tanji Moa," Mai-Kellina explained. "Fifty years old, unmarried, childless. I traced the name. Fake. The 'Moa' part means 'stepmother' in some long-lost language."

When the dance ended, they sat at a fancy dining table overlooking Bay Tulamarine.

"Tell me of this strange zebra called the quagga," Donovan said.

"He is not pure quagga, as they once existed on Ol'Terra. The ancient tissue samples were incomplete. After many failures, the Yerkoza life designers filled in the gaps with about fifteen links from two Arabian stallions. That's why he is more muscular, and taller, than any real quagga ever was. Even with the true colors of a quagga, he is a hybrid, a mix of two kinds, the first and only member of a completely new species. But he is mostly quagga."

Donovan pondered her words. "Did his life begin in a tube?"

"In a dish, but only for a couple of days. The vital egg was implanted in a female zebra. She carried and gave birth to him in the normal way, and nursed him as a colt. So she is a mother to him, even though he is not truly her son."

"Can your people make him a mate?"

"They've tried. So far, no success. The ancient samples limit us to stallions, and after many dozens of tries, he's our only success. But we're still trying. We need him back at Yerkoza. He's a scientific experiment, a great achievement in bio-engineering, not a circus act." She paused, and sipped some juice, eyeing him over the rim of the goblet. "How about you, Donovan. Do you need a mate?"

"So says Tancreido."

"Let me speak plainly. I can't hope to replace Galena in your heart, so I won't even try. Still, I've long dreamed of being your wife, even if it's in the old way." She rubbed the pendant hanging from her neck. "Yes, even if I am not your first choice."

Donovan pondered her words before answering. "Thank you for your honesty."

"The throne of Aldebaran should not sit empty. That's dangerous, especially with all the rebellion rumors. The empire is too large for one person, king or queen, to rule. You need a strong queen, a co-ruler. I would be honored to serve the people as your equal partner in running the empire."

The king slowly nodded his head. "You give me much to think about."

Donovan faded the image of his time with Mai-Kellina. The gabania smoke screen dissolved and once again filled the room with a lilting haze.

"The circus performance begins in mid-afternoon." Tancreido said. "Your wedding is scheduled for early evening, at the time of full alignment of the moons. The dressers need to know which princess will wear the wedding gown. And the coronation robe."

Donovan glanced at the formal portraits showing the royal weddings Tancreido had performed in the past. "Whom do you recommend?"

Stroking his long beard, the advisor said, "I am a dried-out old bachelor. Almost ninety years of endless failure with women. Ask me about war, or power plays between moons. Even the need for a royal family to be complete." He grabbed his staff and shuffled toward the door. "But, when it comes to choosing a queen, I can say only one thing. In public, she will be queen to all, but in private, she will be wife and companion to you alone. That choice must be yours alone." He closed the door behind him.

Donovan returned the view-gem of the princess introductions to its case.

Alone in his chamber, Donovan walked to the far side the Carvers' bed. After pulling back the heavy crimson curtain, he stepped into his bedroom. The Carvers' Guild had delivered the new bed only a few days earlier, as a gift for the new queen. They had taken the first

Carver's Bed to the Museum of Artistry in Wood. The new mattress was ready to be installed as soon as a new queen was crowned.

Like the old bed frame, the new one featured gauze curtains hung from the canopy rails, held high by eight columns, each hand-carved from the trunk of a tree. But on the new bed, the view-gem projector system was powered by eight pierce-lights, one atop each of the columns.

Donovan snapped the blue view-gem from his king's ring and placed it in the projector. With a gentle whishing sound, each of the eight columns pulled the gabania smoke out of the air and into the frame of the new bed. Encased by the gauze curtains, soon the smoke cloud began rotating; the space inside the curtains formed a smoky stage.

"Play." The veegee machine projected the images from the blue gem into the gently whirling smoke. He watched in rapt attention, entranced by the life-sized, three-dimensional images of his younger self, Prince Donovan, when he wed Galena, in the grand ballroom of the castle, two Crestival cycles ago.

Within the recorded scene, Prince Donovan's mother, Queen Rubicania, smiled and kissed Galena on her cheek, and whispered in her ear. The recording had been enhanced so he could hear his mother's words to his bride. "Please be a good wife to my son. Bring us happy, healthy children with eager eyes."

Galena bowed and whispered. "It shall be my supreme privilege and honor."

King Donovan stepped inside the gauze curtains, and positioned his flesh body inside the projected image of Prince Donovan. He tried to reshape the recorded wedding; but his present motions could not change the recorded past, or form a new future. The living man of muscle could not dance with a ghost girl.

Within the recording, Prince Donovan took Galena by the hand and led her from the grand ballroom, up the spiraling staircase to the musicians' balcony. There, a grand piano waited; in front of it, a black shroud covered some large object. "And now," he said "my beautiful wife, I have a gift for you." With a flourish, he yanked on a golden tassel that dangled from the ceiling. The shroud rose, slowly revealing a magnificent harp. The crowd, gathered on the ballroom floor below, gasped. With the black pillar of the harp almost invisible, the harp formed a numeral seven.

Galena's cheeks blushed as she beheld her gift. "It is the most beautiful instrument I have ever seen. How can I thank you?"

"Play it." Prince Donovan handed her two keys, one to open the sound box, and another to tune the strings. The radiant future queen, illuminated by the reflected light of seven moons, unlocked and tuned the harp, then wrapped her arms around it. Donovan sat at the grand piano, and together they played the ancient melody "Clair de Lune," Light of the Moon.

While the recording played on, the king noticed his QM flashing on the table across the room. He approached the QM and picked it up. His was about to click the "off" button when an incoming message appeared.

It was the face of Mai-Kellina.

"Donovan I must speak to you immediately," she said in a serious tone.

"I am listening." He turned off the sound part of the wedding recording.

"I've just returned from a visit to my family's home on the Blood Moon. The whole moon is alive with stories about Galena."

Donovan took a deep breath. "And . . . ?"

"I'm so sorry I must bring you sad news. Especially now, on the eve of Crestival. But you deserve to know the truth. Mountaineers discovered Galena's body in a grove of trees."

The king closed his eyes and stared at Galena's harp. He took a few deep breaths, and then returned to the QM. Barely holding his composure, he asked, "Is it true?"

"I was there when they brought the body to the infirmary," Mai-Kellina said. "I recognized her face." She paused. "I'm so sorry."

Donovan shuddered and closed his eyes. "I must go now. Good bye." He contacted Tancreido by QM, told him the news, and asked to be left alone for the night.

The king had a fitful night, pacing the hallways of his private quarters, rewatching the recordings, and trying to play Galena's harp. Sometime after midnight he drifted into sleep.

Shortly after sunrise, a gentle rapping on his door woke Donovan. "Majesty, Crestival is day after tomorrow. This is decision day." Tancreido's voice sounded nervous. "Have you decided?"

Donovan rubbed his eyes, sat up in bed, and called out. "Yes. The answer came to me in a dream."

Chapter 4 ☽ ☽ ☽ ☽ ☽ ☽

PARADE

The entire cast and crew of Seven Moon Circus, along with all the animals and performance gear, traveled all night on the Quattro and Diamond circus train to get to Tulamarine in time for Crestival. The train parked on the Sanctuary side of the bay a couple of hours before sunrise.

Elizabelle awoke and looked out the window of her cramped berth in her family's car. The horizon glowed in the cloudless sky. She could feel the promise of a glorious sunrise. It was a perfect beginning for birthday fourteen, for marking her passage from girl child to young woman.

She watched the seven moons glowing, creeping toward their appointed positions in the sky. Once they reached perfect alignment, they would form a set of stepping stones to the stars. One poet had called it a runaway constellation—heavenly bodies that formed a picture in the sky and then drifted apart after just one inspiring evening. But before the moons broke from formation and wandered away, Seven Moon Circus would perform in honor of King Donovan and his bride. With her father now in charge of the Q&D animals, and the Gliderbirds on the high wire, 7MC was ready—just in the nick of time—to put on a spectacular show.

Even with all these omens of a joyful and historic day, Elizabelle's mood was draped in disappointment. She could not free her mind from the double dose of shocking news she had heard the night before.

Galena, Queen Selena, was dead.

Donovan had chosen Mai-Kellina as his new bride.

Elizabelle tried to understand why Donovan would choose Mai-Kellina, but nothing made sense. On her last day as governor of the green moon, Mai-Kellina would become the wife of the king, Queen of Empire Luna, and First Mother in the Ardemia Sisterhood, all in one afternoon.

Pulling her pillow over her head, Elizabelle shouted, "No!" How could such a promising day suddenly turn out all wrong? The coldest, cruelest woman she had ever met was set to become the most powerful woman in the empire.

While at Tulamarine, all the 7MC people were official guests of the king, so their train car was loaded with the finest, freshest fruits and eggs gathered from the farms on eight worlds. Their breakfast table offered the prickly chertimo from the Moon of Clouds, the kaimeto and the karissa from the Blue Moon, the glackee—sometimes called the "monkey brains" fruit—from the Golden Moon, and Elizabelle's favorite, a bright bowl of curlibird eggs from Verdanta.

Still, these delights were not enough to brighten Elizabelle's mood. Like all the circus performers, she had to eat quickly and get in position for the big balloon launch at sunrise. "I don't understand," Elizabelle said to her dad. "Why did King Donovan choose Mai-Kellina?"

"The empire needs an heir," he explained. "If Donovan dies without a child, the empire will have no king or queen. Just different tribes and armies trying to control the looper lanes between the moons. Maybe even new wars. Only fools want that."

"But any princess could give him a child," Elizabelle protested. "Why would he choose the coldest one? The only one who is mean to kids?"

Her dad took a deep breath and sighed. "I am surprised, too. But sometimes, for a king, duty and power are the most important things. His first duty is to keep peace between the moons and New Roma. That takes power. Of all the princesses, only Mai-Kellina has proven that she is a powerful leader. He may want her advice."

"She doesn't give advice!" Elizabelle shot back. "She gives orders! She threw away Donovan's letter, and gave her own stupid orders. She wouldn't let Marz come with us!"

Her father took a deep breath and looked directly in her eyes. "Donovan is our king. We have a duty to support him in his choice, whatever it is, and to put on our best show."

"Don't we have a duty to help him see his mistake?" Elizabelle said. "She has something going on with that evil guy Proco."

Her parents exchanged quick, doubtful glances.

"Listen Belle, the tambour is a natural echo chamber," her mother said. "Sounds bounce around in there. It's easy to get confused. Perhaps your imagination ran away with you?"

"Yeah, again!" Ripley said.

"I know what I heard." Elizabelle poked at her breakfast, tasted some hot shoko milk, and then spit it back.

"Even if you don't like her, that doesn't make her evil," her dad added. "Yes, Mai-Kellina can be demanding at times, but she is a smart lady, too."

"But when they marry, that'll make her the queen, right?" Elizabelle dreaded the answer.

"Yes, that's right," her mother said. "After the wedding, there's a brief ceremony for Donovan's ancestors to approve her as the new queen. Then the official ceremony of placing the crown of Aldebaran on her head. In that moment she becomes queen."

"Oh, gag! Another boring ceremony!" Ripley stuck out his tongue and tilted his head back, as if he were being hanged from a noose. "More fancy clothes that are too tight!"

"It's no joke!" Elizabelle shouted. "How can anyone celebrate anything? We should be honoring Galena Selena, the real queen. It looks like we're making a party out of her death." She grabbed her jacket and ran out.

For her birthday, King Donovan gave Elizabelle permission to join the balloon marshal, on the Ardemia peninsula. Hurrying to the control tower, dodging the early crowds, she glanced over the misty bay. Soft moonbeams reflected off the water, casting a shimmering trail from Castle Tulamarine to the Ardemia Shrine. "A path of gold, where none go but angels and ghosts," an old song said.

High above Tulamarine Bay, illuminated by the moonglow, hovered a huge airship. Its black and white markings made it look like an orca—a killer whale—floating high above. Cameras mounted on the underbelly of the airship were set to broadcast the circus show, the wedding celebration, and the coronation ceremony throughout the empire. But the airborne whale was not free. A tether line, anchored in the broad meadow below the castle, prevented it from flying away.

In Elizabelle's imagination, the airship's engine pods and propellers looked like flippers. *Not another whale in the sky!* Long, narrow metal arms stuck out on both sides, front and rear. From these arms hung a matrix—a long, woven netting of thin fibers—reaching nearly to the surface of the bay waters below. It formed the largest three-dimensional pierce-light projection system the empire had ever seen.

Across the bay, King Donovan stood on the castle balcony, watching the gathering crowd. To his side stood Boyd Bucklebiter, gleaming in his 7MC Master of Spectacle uniform. On the other side, Tancreido hunched over his walking stick. The king stared into the distance, but did not smile.

"Good citizens of Empire Luna!" Bucklebiter's voice boomed over the sound system, reverberating throughout the castle grounds, bouncing to the meadow below, skipping across the bay, and echoing up and down the full length of the peninsula. "King Donovan and Seven Moon Circus welcome you to Castle Tulamarine. Crestival begins with the first ray of sunlight! Counselor Tancreido!"

The cameras beneath the airship focused on Tancreido, and projected his image into the hanging matrix. He hobbled to the railing of the balcony. Walking stick in one hand, and scepter in the other,

THE BATTLE OF CRESTIVAL

he struggled to perform the ritual of first light. With a quivering arm, he pointed his scepter first to the reddish sunglow on the horizon, and then directly at the gleaming spire of the Ardemia Shrine.

With the down stroke of his scepter, the sun's first ray struck the mirrors atop the central spire of the shrine. Shards of sunlight scattered across the bay. The huge crowd roared in approval. Pounding out the rhythm with his stick, Tancreido recited the rhyme of the ancient mariners in his raspy, almost whispering voice.

"Seven sisters, all ashine, turn and spin
Seven moons, all aligned, let Crestival begin!"

Rod Lightning's Thunder Drummers picked up Tancreido's rhythm. On both sides of the bay, crowds stomped their feet to the same beat, and joined him in chanting, "Let Crestival begin!" The royal trumpeters blared out the rising tones of the Crestival fanfare.

Elizabelle watched the ballunas—free-floater balloons—lift off from the Ardemia Shrine. Rising straight up, they formed an airmada in vibrant colors, glowing from the heater flames inside. Seeing them, she fondly recalled their beloved Jefferson Spitfire, the dragon balloon now shredded and buried in the blistering sands of the desert on Luna Verdanta.

The ballunas took more shapes and hues than all the creatures in the royal zoo. A gray elephant with an ocean blue blanket. A parrot in all the colors of the rainbow. A snarling T-rex. One highlight was a model of Captain Norzah's exodus ark—a space ship with seven solar sails. But the crowd favorite, as usual, was the balloon that looked like the original Luna, the only moon of the first human world, Ol'Terra.

With the ballunas launched, the circus balloons would be next. Elizabelle dashed to the circus balloon area. The tent riggers scurried about, testing taut lines and parachute valves, securing baskets, and lighting pilot lights for the heat blasters.

Soon Elizabelle came upon Marz, polishing SunKing's saddle and slipping him shoko candies. "Marz, are you ready to fly again?"

"Almos' ready." Marz adjusted his zebra-stripe clown suit. "Happy birthday, Elizabelle. Rule one, do fun!"

"Thank you, Marz. No bug candy please." She smiled at him. "Is SunKing ready?"

"Almos'." He tightened the saddle belts around the bulging belly of his beast friend, and adjusted SunKing's blinder flaps so the animal could only see straight ahead. In this way he should not get distracted or upset by all the strange sights and sounds.

Elizabelle's dad checked the gas valve of the Spitfire II. Built to the order of King Donovan, it was bigger, stronger, and longer than the first Spitfire. The new balloon could lift three times as much weight as the original, and was both shaped and painted like a long dragon. A flame thrower, mounted in the dragon's throat, let the pilot frighten the crowd below.

"Marz," Braden shouted, "bring us the new star of Seven Moon Circus!"

With skunk kits squirming in his pockets, Marz grabbed SunKing's reins and led him to the basket. But when the burner ignited, the quagga stomped his feet, snorted and backed away.

Braden whispered to Marz, "Watch."

Closing the flaps on the blinders, Braden took the reins and led the quagga around in circles until the poor beast was so dizzy he could not walk straight. Then he led the wobbling animal right into the basket, and tied the reins to rope hooks on the side. Marz took his place beside SunKing, stroking his neck and whispering to him.

"Quagga on board!" Braden announced. Marz opened SunKing's blinders part way and gave him some grass to munch on.

Althea patted both her kids on their shoulders. "Now or never. Let's fly, kids!"

Elizabelle and Ripley jumped into the basket and fastened their safety belts. Braden flashed his "ready" signal to the balloon marshal.

"Let the dragon chase the moons!" the marshal blared. "Let the quagga fly high in the sky!"

All the Hawkens joined together in singing, "Sail away, sail away, across the bay."

Althea turned the burner to full blast. The New Spitfire rose above the bay, all the way up to the height of the orca airship. From that dizzying height, the Crestival celebrations were laid out in a panorama, far below. All seven towers and the main ballroom of Castle Tulamarine were decorated in the moon colors of Crestival. Flowers gathered from throughout the realm, just for the royal wedding, draped the castle balcony.

On the meadow below the castle, tent riggers worked with elephants to set up the poles and support ropes for the big top. The airship tether was tied to the king pole of the circus tent. Other crews worked frantically to set up the frameworks for the Gliderbirds—swings, trapezes, high wire lines, trick curtains for the Spanish Roll. Clowns sped around in their trick trucks, delivering parts.

PARADE ☽ ☽ ☽ ☽ ☽ ☽

The morning breeze blew the New Spitfire toward the orca airship. When it was close enough, Braden shot the grab line. It flew out like a long-tongue frog zapping a bug on a branch. The tip wrapped around the airship's tether, jerking the Spitfire II.

With the sudden jolt on the basket, SunKing raised his head up, craned his neck, and started making his squeaky bark. Marz rushed to his side. The beast calmed a bit, and then lowered his head over the edge of the basket. He tried to back out of the basket, but ran into the side. His ears flared back and his throat filled with a deep chugging noise.

"We can't have him out of control at this height!" Althea yelled. Marz closed the blinders again. Gradually the quagga calmed enough that they could resume the flight.

Braden flashed a signal to the orca airship. Almost immediately, a tug motor crawled down the airship's tether and nabbed the New Spitfire's grab line. Braden allowed the line tug to pull the Spitfire toward the meadow. "Stand by for landing at Castle Tulamarine!"

Marz donned his skunk hat, checked to see that the kits were happily snuggled within it, and mounted SunKing.

When the New Spitfire hit solid ground, Bucklebiter bowed to the crowd and launched into his ballyhoo. "Ladies, gentlemen, moon kids of all ages, say hello to the new stars of Seven Moon Circus!" Balloon crews rushed out from the prep tents, grabbed the ropes and anchored the New Spitfire to the ground. "First, you've heard all about him, now meet him in person. The boy who spent his young years in the Cloud Forest, the one and only Marz the Wild Boy. He rides astride the only quagga alive today, SunKing!"

Braden opened the basket gate. Marz, sitting proud and tall in the saddle, charged out into the crowd. He unsnapped the tail from his skunk hat, and waved it around his head, as the skunk kits poked their heads out of the snuggle pockets in the hat. The crowd erupted in shouts, cheers, whistling, and wild applause. People near the path crowded one another, jockeying for a closer view. Many reached out their hands, hoping to touch the quagga, or the famous Wild Boy. Crowd control police pushed the surging throngs aside, to clear the path beside the train track.

The other circus balloons followed the new Spitfire in quick order. Sparky and the clowns rode in a giant red balloon. JoJo Brightfeather and Miss Taroona, costumed in their blindingly colorful bird suits, rode unicycles around a small circular track that hung beneath their balloon. When their balloon neared the ground, they dropped straight down, bounced on their unicycles, pedaled up a little ramp, and did a flipover.

Critter wranglers delivered the parade animals, fresh from the Q&D circus train. Elizabelle positioned herself in front of the albino elephant Queenie, who quickly wrapped her trunk around the girl and lifted her up to the padded howdah carriage. Elizabelle held a drumstick that she pressed into the thick elephant skin, to direct Queenie.

Handlers delivered the black stallion, known as the Pride of Baraboo, for Ripley. The horse was so tall that Jerry Cherry the clown had to lift Ripley up to the saddle. Braden, sparkling in his lion tamer's show uniform, wrestled playfully with Duke the young lion, inside a cage car. Althea drove an open air car full of bonobos on swings and trampolines.

Leading the parade, Marz, SunKing and the Hawken kids rode

PARADE 🌙 🌙 🌙 🌙 🌙 🌙

their mounts along the path, toward the castle, gleaming gloriously in the morning sunlight. Behind them, the other circus kids rode on their favorite mounts. The marching band played the anthems of each of the moons and "One Empire"—the unity song.

The circus kids slowed as they neared the castle. "Okay, Marz," Elizabelle called, "this is where we stop and bow to the king, like we practiced. Remember?"

Marz pulled SunKing to a halt. He dismounted, guided the skunk kits into the big pockets of his costume.

"You shouldn't look like a criminal or a skunk, or even a zebra, when you meet the king." Elizabelle climbed down from her elephant, carrying the Kiko cape and her drumstick. She placed the drumstick in her belt and offered the cape to Marz.

He doffed his skunk hat, slipped into the outstretched cape, and marched toward the huge, curving stairway that led down from the castle balcony. Elizabelle and Ripley stood on either side of him, at attention.

King Donovan walked stiffly down the staircase, with Mai-Kellina on his arm, dazzling in her bridal gown and necklace of moonstones. As they drew near, Elizabelle struggled to stay in control of her emotions. She had to keep silently repeating her mother's line about their duty to support the king in his decision.

When the king reached the bottom stair, Marz went down on one knee and bowed deeply. "King Donovan. I Marz, humble servant from Cloud Forest Green Moon." His Kiko cape shimmered in the sunlight, shifting from dark blue to a rippling purple. The scene was projected onto the matrix hanging from the airship. The entire crowd went silent as they beheld the moment.

"Hello, Marz, Forest Boy. I've heard your story from Braden,"

239

the king said. "Everyone has heard it by now. Stand up, young man." Marz did so. "You and your beautiful animal friend are always welcome here at Tulamarine. No matter what color your zebra or your clothes may be."

The baby skunks stuck their sniffing noses out of Marz's pockets and peeked up at the king. "Kits my friends." Marz rubbed the heads of the kits, smiled and rocked his eyebrows. A look of astonishment crossed over the king's face. His eyes widened, and he turned his head to get a deep breath.

"I believe all three of you have already met Mai-Kellina," the king said.

"We have, your highness," Elizabelle answered. She struggled to keep her cool, closing her eyes and clenching the drumstick in her hand. She tried to bow, but managed only to nod.

"Miss Elizabelle," Mai-Kellina purred in her sweetest voice. "I remember you well. It's lovely to see you again, dear child." She stared into Elizabelle's eyes. "It's a new day for you and me. The wild boy and the pet zebra are doing well?"

Elizabelle fought the urge to say, "I'm not a child anymore." Instead she said, "We have adjusted. Your highness."

"Thank you, but I am not officially royal just yet. Until sunset, only a governor. I look forward to hearing you sing with the Carillons."

Elizabelle nervously twisted the drumstick until it snapped. Still, she recited the words her mother had taught her to say: "It shall be my honor, my Lady."

The king and his bride-to-be turned and walked back up the stairway.

PARADE ☾ ☾ ☾ ☾ ☾ ☾

"On with the parade!" Bucklebiter shouted. He blew his whistle and pointed his baton, directing the kids to remount and continue the parade.

As the parade neared the circus tent, the matrix camera focused on Bucklebiter. "Ticket holders, please join us inside the big top at 1:30 for the royal command performance of Seven Moon Circus! All the rest of you can still see the show, larger than life, up there!" He turned and pointed to the huge matrix hanging beneath the airship.

Chapter 5 ♪ ♪ ♪ ♪ ♪ ♪

CIRCUS

M arz and the Hawken kids waited with the 7MC clowns at the performer's entrance on the west side of the big top tent, peering out through the curtains. It was mid afternoon, and the dark walls of the tent shut out most of the sunlight. Still, they needed darkness so the show could include tricks with colored lights, spotlights, pierce-lights and fireworks.

"It's your first real show," Elizabelle said to Marz. "You're lucky. Very few circus artists ever get to perform for the king, and you get that chance on your first show. Are you nervous? Happy?"

Marz adjusted his clown hat. "Yes happy."

"Are you excited?" Ripley asked.

"Big show. Many people." His eyes lit up and he licked his smiling lips.

"Don't get carried away being a show-off," Elizabelle warned. "Here, you might need these." She handed him a set of ear beans and ear protectors. "Sometimes it gets noisy in here. Where's your QM?"

Marz carefully placed the sound beans in his ears and flashed his miniature QM.

CIRCUS

"Are you going to perform with the clowns or the Gliderbirds?"

"Yes." Marz nodded. "Birds, clowns, fun."

"When the lights go down, that means show time." Just as Elizabelle said it, the lights inside dimmed to a faint glow.

Elizabelle was surprised to hear the urgent voice of Jura-Moraine, behind them. "Marz, I have an important job for you," she said. "After your big drop, please present this cape to Mai-Kellina." Elizabelle shone her flashlight on the cape. She recognized it from Tambora as the cape that the queen wore to show that she was also First Mother in the Ardemia Sisterhood. It was woven in the official royal pattern, so only members of the royal family could wear it. Elizabelle's stomach turned at thought of the royal cape around the shoulders of Mai-Kellina.

Marz grabbed the cape and rubbed it in his hand. "I like many colors."

Elizabelle wanted to ask why Marz should present the cape, and why Mai-Kellina should receive the cape even before being crowned queen. But before she could ask, Jura-Moraine disappeared into the darkness.

Mounted high above the crowd, on the high wire rigging, live action cameras sent pictures of the glorious event out to the airship matrix, and from there to all the people on all the moons.

All twenty-one of Rod Lightning's drummers stood at attention, completely surrounding the inner walls of the big top. With a short blast from Rod's whistle, they began a low, slow drum roll.

243

THE BATTLE OF CRESTIVAL

The sounds of the drums awakened the two main spotlights, one red, the other white—at opposite ends of the huge oval-shaped tent. The light beams swept through the crowd, swooping in giant figure-eight patterns.

Finally the lights found Bucklebiter in the center ring. The spots locked on him and reflected off the spangles on his show tuxedo. He strutted around like a fat penguin wearing a tall, stovepipe hat. When he touched the rim of the hat, the top opened like the lid on a teapot. A flock of colorful birds burst out of the hat and flew up into the metal frames for the high wire acts. The kids in the audience hooted and clapped.

Elizabelle tried to steady her pounding heart. 7MC had done so many shows on so many moons, and entertained thousands of people. But all those shows were well-rehearsed. Now they were giving their first royal command performance, and being watched by people throughout the empire. She was worried, because with all the acts added at the last minute, and no full dress rehearsal of the entire show, so many little things could go wrong. "Okay, Mr. Master of Spectacle," she whispered, "this is our last chance. Can you get us through the show?"

"Ladies and gentlemen," Bucklebiter boomed, "looper lunatics and moonshiners, space cadets and townies! Grandmas and grandpas who are still fun-lovin' kids at heart, it's show time!" The Thunder Drummers bashed their cymbals and the 7MC circus band blared out their fanfare.

As the crowd shouted hurrahs and whistled their excitement, Bucklebiter turned to the royal guests, sitting high in their observation booth. The white spotlight focused on the wedding couple. "First, let us all thank our host and sponsor of today's show, King

Donovan." Bucklebiter saluted them with his gloved hand, and bowed deeply. The king, dressed in his military commander's uniform, saluted Bucklebiter, and then the audience.

"And let us now honor his bride, Lady Mai-Kellina." Glistening in her formal gown, she smiled for the cameras and the crowds, showing off her perfect teeth and her glistening red lipstick. She wore the shining tiara of the Princess of Verdanta, and a choker necklace embedded with moonstones. The crowd applauded her too, but not so warmly.

"Watch, Marz!" Elizabelle pointed to the huge cannons, located at opposite ends of the big top.

The drummers kept building up the tension. When it seemed the drums would explode, Rod Lightning grabbed the heavy mallet and struck the giant gong. The cannons blasted the Zucchinis—Capitano Zorino and his daughter Zina—out of the barrels of their cannons. They shot through the smoke and soared high above the crowd, human bullets dressed in black, with red piping on their seams. The spotlights switched to deep purple, and the fluorescent "bones" painted on the Zucchini costumes glowed in the near-darkness. They looked like human skeletons flying and dancing high above the crowd. Meeting in mid-air, directly over the royal seats, they tossed roses to the king and his bride. Then they twisted in flight and opened the bat wings of their costumes. Red flames burst from the seams as they gracefully floated down.

All the lights came on. The Zucchinis bowed to the crowd, and received much clapping and whistling.

Bucklebiter blew his shrill whistle, pointed in turn to each of the four entrances for performers, and shouted, "Shivarrrr-eeee!"

On that signal, clowns poured out from all four performers' gates. Elizabelle knew all the 7MC clowns streaming through her curtain, but the clowns rushing out of the other entrances were strangers to her. She guessed that they were just late joiners. Probably Q&D clowns who didn't want to miss the chance to be part of an historic show. The clown troops spread out, entertaining various sections of the audience with juggling, fire spitting and stilt walking.

"And now, ladies and gentlemen," Bucklebiter blustered, "please welcome the dancing, singing, and musical talents of Seven Moon Circus!"

Sparky the dwarf clown marched out proudly, dressed in his band leader uniform, blowing his whistle and twirling his conductor's staff—which was longer than he was tall. He stood on a high stool in front of the crowd from the Golden Moon, wiggled his butt, put on airs like he was the *la-di-dah* conductor of a symphony orchestra, and held his baton up to the crowd.

The Eefananny Brothers jumped out of their trick truck, stuck their thumbs in their suspenders and stood at attention, ready for Sparky's cue. To their side, Sammy Stutterfingers adjusted the straps for the big bass drum of his one-man band rig. Meanwhile, Peg Leg Meg and Terry Tripple held each other, ready for a waltz.

Sparky flicked his baton, and then gave the downstroke for the music and dancing to begin. With the Eefanannies stomping and Sammy pounding on his drum, they all broke into a "song."

Puttin' on the dog
Party in the bog
Party in the bog til the break of day

CIRCUS ☾ ☾ ☾ ☾ ☾ ☾

Nothin' can be sweeter
Than a mouth fulla mo-skeeters
Party in the bog

Wallowin' in the mud
Floatin' in the crud
Party in the flood til the break of day
Swimmin' with the croakin' frogs
Havin' fun garglin' pollywogs
Party in the bog

Sparky stomped his feet in time with the song, and urged the crowd to join in. Soon all the kids, and many of the adults, started stomping in time with the "music."

Terry and Meg couldn't dance to this because they were trying to do a three beat waltz to a four beat song. They just stumbled over Terry's fake center leg and tumbled into a happy heap.

Kokomo the bonobo clown rushed out, dressed in a glittering vest, fez hat in red with golden tassels, and a polka dot diaper. He buzzed around on a miniature motorcycle, poppin' wheelies, and making the motor do smoky exhaust pops. As he approached the crowd from the Moon of Clouds, he jack-knifed sideways and skidded to a stop.

He made a big show of sniffing the air, then holding his nose. Then he went through a little act, pointing first to one kid in the audience, then to another. He held up a little sign saying "Did you make that stink?" One of the kids pointed back at him.

Recoiling in surprise, Kokomo ripped off his diaper and pinched his nose as he smelled it. He stuck it to the end of a long stick, and waved it over the crowd. All the kids howled. Soon Jerry Cherry arrived, grabbed the diaper, threw it into a trash can, and set it on fire. A huge column of flames roared out of the can, popping and sputtering.

Marz was the last of the 7MC clowns to enter the arena, riding a bicycle with egg-shaped wheels. His friend Manjaro, the young prince in the bonobo troop, clung to Marz's back, hooting, bouncing and waving to the crowd. Each time the oblong wheels bumped them to a high point, little Manjaro threw shoko candies to the audience.

"That's right, kids," Bucklebiter blared, "you've heard the stories about Marz's very special shoko candies, now try 'em for yourself. Verrry juicy!"

Watching from behind her curtain, Elizabelle shuddered and shook her head.

"Attention, ladies and gentlemen, please direct your attention to the main gate, and greet the 7MC animals." A caravan of sixteen elephants, each with a small trampoline strapped to its back, entered the arena. They went into formation and did the "tail up" act, circling the hippodrome. Meanwhile, moving in the opposite direction, a bevy of acrobatic beauties in flashing rhinestone costumes leaped high in the air, flipping, twisting, and somersaulting on the backs of the elephants.

Bucklebiter turned slowly, to face all the different sections of the audience. "We need some brave volunteers, kids who have traveled from far away moons, who are ready to ride the elephants." Eager, young hands shot up everywhere. Elizabelle, Ripley, and the circus kids rushed into the audience, chose a few lucky volunteers, and handed each of them a 7MC hat.

CIRCUS

The mahouts replaced the trampolines with howdah seats. Then circus kids led the townie kids with 7MC hats to the elephants and helped them climb up the steps to the mounting platforms and then onto the backs of the elephants, six kids to each elephant.

The clowns, magicians, and sword swallowers from the other circuses continued to fan out through the arena. Their tricks kept the audience laughing, amazed, and shocked. Elizabelle noticed a lady who had once worked with 7MC, Sabila the Snake Woman, with live snakes wrapped all around her. Elizabelle decided to stay far away.

Jerry Cherry drove the big tractor as it pulled animal cars into the arena, to join the elephants and the bonobos. Many of the critters were descendants of animals brought from Ol'Terra—lions, tigers, real zebras with black and white stripes, a pair of sleepy hippos, camels, even giraffes. But natives of New Roma and its moons were in the menagerie, too. They included dog-like kylazines from the Silver Moon, farzani gazelles from Lectrona, and the pippistrella bat—often called a flying fox. The most popular was the anolay, a large lizard with little stub wings; most people called it a baby dragon.

Braden and Althea Hawken, and their helpers, pulled the big cat car up to the show enclosure in ring three. Braden led the lions into the enclosure, and with his baton directed each to its own pedestal. He led them through their jumping, roaring and rolling routines. Saba did her "friendly wrestling" trick with him. But when it came time for her son Duke to jump through the ring of fire, he refused, and snarled in defiance.

A clown Elizabelle had never seen before limped up to the side of the cat enclosure. He shouted to Braden: "That one's a rebel. He'll never obey. He'll attack you. He understands only one thing—the sting of the whip."

Braden kept his eye on Duke, but called out. "Who goes there?"

Elizabelle and Ripley came running, trying to identify the mystery clown. By the time they arrived at his side of the enclosure, he had already disappeared.

Chapter 6

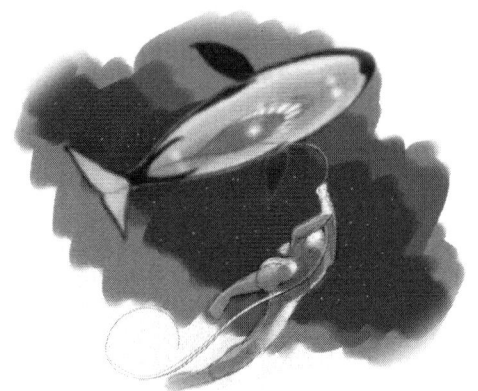

SPECTACLE

"Ladies and gentlemen," Bucklebiter bellowed, "Seven Moon Circus now proudly presents, in their first performance ever, the most exciting new team of high wire artists in all of Empire Luna. Meet the Gliderbirds, led by that daring young man on the flying trapeze, JoJo Brightfeather." He pointed high up into the rigging, where the aerialists, all dressed in their many-colored bird costumes, stretched and strutted.

Brightfeather, on his unicycle and with balance bar in hand, pedaled out onto the wire, backwards. Immediately behind him, a lady bird did the same thing, except she moved forward. As they faced one another, pedaling back and forth on the wire, a rope dropped down from above, and delivered a long, solid bar. They connected the bar to straps over their shoulders.

A third aerialist shinnied down a rope, with a chair hanging from his feet. He balanced the chair on the bar between JoJo and the lady bird, and then carefully settled into it, arms outstretched, constantly adjusting his hands and arms to keep his balance.

"Oh, there's still more!" Bucklebiter announced proudly.

251

"Please greet Miss Loretta Taroona." The spotlight swung up high to Loretta, dressed in shiny red and blue feathers. She grabbed onto the rope and waved to the crowd. Hand over hand, she played out the rope until she descended far enough to place her bare feet on the shoulders of the man on the chair. After a few moments to adjust to the risky situation, she released the rope. The Gliderbirds were now three levels high on the wire—JoJo and the lady bird on their unicycles, the bird man wobbling on the chair, and finally Loretta on his shoulders—all swaying high above the crowd.

In her entire circus life, Elizabelle had never before seen such a dangerous high-wire balancing act. Just the tiniest moment of lost balance would send the Gliderbirds crashing down onto the floor of the tent.

"There you have it Seven Mooners," Bucklebiter continued with his hoo-rah, "the most amazing high wire trick in circus history, the flying pyramid of death! Let the Gliderbirds know you like their stuff." The crowd hollered and whistled and the royal couple rose in applause.

JoJo and the other birds pedaled back to their platforms. Miss Taroona and the chair bird jumped down, bounced on the sawdust-covered floor, and then dashed up the ladder.

The band struck up the Loop de Loop tune. Sparky led the kids in the audience as they sang along with the Eefanannies.

> Here we go loop de loop
> Here we go loop delight
> Here we go loop de loop
> From the towering height.

JoJo leaped from the platform and sailed out on the trapeze. He and the other Gliderbirds did double and triple flips in the air, catching one another in perfectly-timed aerial somersaults, dazzling the audience.

Right on plan, Marz blew his whistle. The real birds, who had escaped from Bucklebiter's stovepipe hat, flew down from the darkness above and into the light. They each landed on the shoulders of the Gliderbird whose costumes matched their own feathers. Then Bucklebiter reopened the top of his hat, and the real birds flew back into it.

"Marz," Elizabelle said, "Ready to put on your big show?" He laughed and smiled.

"Ladies and gentlemen," Bucklebiter blared, "you've heard the stories about the Wild Boy Marz and how he came to join Seven Moon Circus. Now we proudly present to you, a recreation of his brave escape from the crocodile attack! We take you now to the Cloud Forest on Verdanta!"

On the floor of the big top, the 7MC staging crew had created a miniature version of the Cloud Forest, complete with tree branches, a river, a pool of water. Sound effects played over the intercom—bird calls and frog caws, and the gurgling sounds of the river. The Spitfire was represented by the orca airship floating high above. The top of the big top tent opened, so the entire audience could look up and see the orca airship and the matrix hanging beneath it.

Marz donned a wig that matched the hair he had when the Hawkens first discovered him in the forest. To the crowd looking through the mist, Marz appeared completely naked, even though he was wearing a flesh-colored loin cloth. Bits of fur were stuck to his skin, and a ridiculously long vine "tail" dangled from his waist. When the spotlight found him, the crowd roared in approval. He swaggered over to Jura-Moraine's royal cape. The one he was supposed to deliver to the new queen.

Elizabelle grabbed her QM, set it for Marz's earbeans, and warned him. "No, Marz! That cape is for the new queen. You can't wear it." He turned to face Elizabelle, bowed to her, and proceeded to place the rainbow cape on his shoulders. When the spotlight hit him, he pranced and danced around, showing off the shifting colors, to the great amusement of the kids.

Marz climbed up the rigging and stepped out onto the high platform. He held his arms out for balance, and then began stepping slowly down the wire decorated as a tree branch.

Barely visible through the artificial fog, three crocodiles swam in the pool beneath Marz.

When he got to a spot directly above, one of the crocs roared and snapped at him. The crowd let out a mixture of cheers and gasps.

Marz laughed at the croc, and sputtered his tongue. Then he lay down on his back on the wire and pretended to snooze, twitching his dangling tail like a napping cat. Another croc splashed water out of the pool, and Marz woke up.

Elizabelle and Ripley, stationed by the side entrance, held SunKing at the ready.

When Elizabelle saw Marz's antics, teasing the crocs, she spoke into her QM again. "Marz! Don't be a show-off. This is too dangerous!"

Her advice did no good at all.

Marz walked backwards on the wire branch. He lay on his side, then dropped down and grabbed the high wire in his hands. He twirled around the wire, his cape flying. The crocs kept circling and roaring, and the audience kept making their oohs and aahs with each daring flip.

The crocodiles were actually machines. Elizabelle looked over to the control box, expecting to see one of 7MC's own clowns, who had practiced this act. But she didn't. Instead, some unknown clown madly spun the controls, following Marz's every move, adjusting the movements to keep the mechano-crocs on the attack. Was an imposter in control? Even if the crocs were machines, they could still attack and do real damage.

One of the crocs snagged Marz's tail, yanked on it, and bellowed loudly.

Elizabelle set her QM for crew only. "What's going on here? We didn't rehearse this!"

The biggest croc yanked on Marz's tail. The audience gasped at the sight of Marz teetering on the wire branch, about to fall into the pool below. Many in the audience screamed in fear.

Resetting her QM for Marz's earbeans, Elizabelle sounded alarm. "Something's not right! Get out of this mess. Just rip off that silly tail." For once, Marz followed her advice. He pulled off the tail and then replayed the famous moment of his big decision to leave the forest, throwing fur bits into the pool. The kids in the audience yelled in delight.

"We gotta get back on plan," Elizabelle said to Ripley. She clicked her QM to intercom, so everyone in the big top could hear her. "Marz, this is your only chance!" Then she and Ripley alternated on the QM, filling the big top with their famous words from discovery day. "Marz, come with us!" "You are not a monkey, Marz! You are one of us!" "This is your only chance!" Then they broke into a sort of chant, "Climb the rope, Marz!"

The audience picked up the hint and joined in the chanting. "Climb the rope, Marz! Climb the rope, Marz!"

With the audience stomping their feet and chanting, Marz dropped down from the wire branch and dashed to the airship tether. He adjusted the royal cape on his shoulders, and began climbing up the line.

As he shinnied up the line, the royal cape of many colors waved magnificently, blowing in the wind and sun, shifting and quavering from deep reds to purples, violets and lavenders. The audience kept cheering him on, chanting. Once he arrived at the airship, he bowed and waved to the audience below. They went crazy with applause and cheers.

"There you have it, ladies and gentlemen, kids of all ages" Bucklebiter boomed, "with your own eyes you have seen how the Wild Boy escaped from Verdanta!" In the royal observation booth, the king smiled broadly, Mai-Kellina shook her head and then rested her forehead in her hand.

With Marz high above, Elizabelle and Ripley readied SunKing for the cowboy rescue act. She was tightening his saddle straps when she noticed a clown sneaking toward them, dodging around other circus acts. Soon she recognized him. It was the same clown who had shouted at her dad and told him to whip the young lion, Duke. No real 7MC clown, or any lover of lions, would say such a thing. She was about to call the circus police when the strange clown disappeared into a group of clowns all dressed up as animals.

SPECTACLE ☽ ☽ ☽ ☽ ☽ ☽

Elizabelle and Ripley finished adjusting SunKing's saddle straps and glittering head gear. But before they could lead SunKing out into the arena for his big cowboy rescue scene, the stranger clown jumped out of the shadows. "Get 'em now!" he called out. Swiftly, he and four others grabbed Elizabelle and Ripley. Taped their mouths shut. Pulled them through the curtain. Dragged them into the waiting area just outside the tent. The kids kicked and squirmed, trying to break free, but they were overpowered. The fake clowns tied the Hawken kids' feet and roped their hands behind their backs, and then left them squirming on the floor.

The intruders placed a hood over SunKing's head and led him out of the tent, past Elizabelle and Ripley, and toward the circus train.

☽ ☽ ☽ ☽ ☽ ☽ ☽

Sparky was running to the side show wagons when he came upon Elizabelle and Ripley, wiggling in the dirt. "What happened?" The kids tried to talk, but were muzzled by the tape. Sparky quickly removed the tape and untied them. "Are you okay?"

"Yeah, we're okay," Ripley blurted, "but SunKing is gone."

"He's been stolen by some . . ." Elizabelle paused. "I recognized the voice. It was that Dan Steele guy, the cruel trainer from Q&D. In a clown costume. I'll bet he stole it."

"Filthy, stinking rat!" Sparky spat out the insult. "How dare he use a clown costume to hide his crime?" He used Elizabelle's QM to summon the Hawken parents. When they arrived, Elizabelle explained that SunKing was gone, and so the cowboy rescue act could not be done.

"Get the royal police to help us find SunKing," her dad said. "The show must go on!"

Elizabelle ran to the curtain opening and looked up to the airship. Marz was climbing around on the undercarriage, the frame that connected the projection screen matrix to the airship. She called him by QM. "Marz, we can't do the cowboy rescue. Someone has kidnaped SunKing!"

Marz grabbed his miniature QM. "Find my friend!"

Althea answered through her QM. "Marz, you stay there for now. Maybe, if we can find SunKing, you can still do your big trick."

The answer came quickly. "Yes! Cowboy rescue!"

Chapter 7 ☽ ☽ ☽ ☽ ☽ ☽

CROWN

While the 7MC show continued inside the big top, the Hawkens met with the Tulamarine police. They had barely begun working on an emergency plan when Elizabelle received an urgent message to meet with Tricka. "You go on ahead, Belle," her dad said. "We can handle this."

Inside Tricka's wagon, Lady Patrizia invited Elizabelle to take a seat. "The show is almost over. The wedding is next." Patrizia seemed more serious than ever before. "Now, Elizabelle, you listen to me. When you are in Mai-Kellina's dressing room, watch very carefully how she changes into the special jewelry for the wedding ceremony. She normally wears a bracelet with encrusted moonstones. Between each pair of stones there is a small gem. Most are blue or green, but one is crimson red. Wait for the right time, and then pop that crimson gem out of the bracelet, and replace it with this one." Patrizia pressed a small crimson gem into Elizabelle's palm. "Then, get Mai-Kellina's crimson gem to me, before the wedding ceremony is complete."

"I don't understand," Elizabelle confessed.

"Do you want Mai-Kellina to be queen of the empire?"

"No! I would do anything to prevent it." She felt a bit guilty for saying the truth. "But I have no power. I just have orders and duties. Including a duty to support King Donovan in his foolish decision to marry Mai-Kellina. I hate it! I hate her!"

"Cheer up, new Sister. I will give you power." Patrizia winked at Elizabelle. "Here, take this. It will help you remove the gem from her bracelet." She handed a small, tweezer-like instrument to Elizabelle. "Just get the crimson gem to me. I'll be waiting for you."

Sir Patrick, the male half of Tricka, grumbled. "More frilly silly. Junk, jewelry. Weddings. Romantic secrets. Girly goo."

Elizabelle ignored Patrick and spoke to Patrizia. "But how do I get close enough?"

"Play along, hon. Trust your friend Tricka."

Elizabelle recalled Tricka's performance as the Myth Keeper at Tambora, a place that was off limits to men and boys. How could she trust someone who lectured about a woman's birthright, yet was not really a woman? Or, at least, not completely a woman. Or was all this half-and-half stuff just circus makeup, a costume trick? "This sounds dangerous."

Patrizia paused before answering. Then, in a whispering, trance-like voice she said: "Sometimes, the dangerous chance is the only chance."

"Speak for yourself, girly," the Sir Patrick half protested. "We shouldn't even be here. If you get caught, I'm dead too!"

The queen's private quarters in the castle had lain unused for almost fourteen years. Which made it perfect for a quick conversion into a dressing room for the new bride. All the pictures of Donovan and Galena were removed. Gone too were Galena's wedding gown, the tack she had used when riding horses, her books and view-gems on healing plants, and all her wedding gifts.

Only furniture remained: tables, desks, chairs, and chests. But the room buzzed with chatting women. Five of them had been candidates for the bride of the king only one day earlier. Now, instead of brides, they would all be brides' maids. Servants to Mai-Kellina.

Jura-Moraine directed the preparations. "All princesses are to wear the formal gowns of their home moon." She held out a tray covered with glittering jewelry—rings, necklaces, bracelets, anklets, earrings—all coordinated with the official wedding color, azure blue. The princesses and their attendants gathered around the tray.

"It's my duty to perform the coronation of the queen, with the king standing by," Jura-Moraine said to Elizabelle. "Mai-Kellina has requested that you present the crown of Aldebaran to me."

Elizabelle felt deeply suspicious. "Why me?"

"I asked her that myself. She knows that your dad and Donovan have been friends since they were boys. Now that she is joining his family, she wants a fresh start with you. Presenting the ancient crown of Aldebaran for the coronation of a new queen is a great honor."

Like most citizens of Empire Luna, Elizabelle had seen pictures and view-gems of the crown of Aldebaran, First Queen. But she had never seen it in person. When one of Jura-Moraine's assistants delivered the crown, resting on a royal velvet cushion, the shining brilliance of it took her breath away. Above the headband were mounted seven rings of solid gold, in the shape of the orbital paths of the moons. Each ring had encrusted upon it a flawless jewel in the moon color. Together they formed the most valuable collection of precious stones in the empire.

Above the moon rings, a small statue of the ancient "huntress of the moon," Ardemia, held her bow and arrow, reminding all that the Queen of the Empire was also First Mother in the Sisterhood. Even a living, ruling queen wore the crown only on the most solemn occasions, and then only with three armed soldiers from each moon standing guard. Just in case some fool should try to steal the jeweled crown.

"Attention ladies, here comes the bride," Jura-Moraine called out. The princesses and their assistants turned to face the entrance, and bent at the knee when Mai-Kellina entered, glowing with confidence.

Mai-Kellina walked directly up to Elizabelle. "Thank you for agreeing to present the crown." She looked Elizabelle directly in the eye. "It means so much to our future."

Elizabelle took a deep breath, then recited the empty words her mother had taught her to say, "It will be my privilege to honor and serve my king . . . and you." She said the words but her heart was sinking. Empty.

Several assistants helped Mai-Kellina into her wedding gown, puffing and fluffing the train, arranging her hair and makeup.

Elizabelle realized her golden time of opportunity was slipping away. She steeled up her courage and asked, in the most polite voice she could summon, "May I help you with your jewelry, M'lady?" She wondered if anyone noticed the quaver in her voice.

Mai-Kellina's assistant presented the jewelry tray. "Gems of the first order from every moon, for a royal bride." Many of them had been worn by First Queen Aldebaran herself, at the foundation of the empire.

The bride held out her arms to Elizabelle, who carefully removed each of her rings and bracelets, and placed them on the tray. "Which pieces do you wish to wear?" Elizabelle asked.

The bride touched several pieces, including matching earrings from the Blood Moon, finger rings from the Golden Moon and Verdanta, and a necklace from the Blue Moon. Elizabelle picked up each piece in its turn, and placed it on the future queen's fingers, and around her neck. Then she reached for Mai-Kellina's ears.

"I will put in the earrings myself, thank you," Mai-Kellina said, suddenly sounding cold again. "Only my husband, my doctor, and my own fingers touch my ears."

When all the jewelry pieces were in place, the future queen's assistant held up a mirror. Mai-Kellina turned her head, admiring herself from several angles.

"Absolutely royal, a living portrait," Jura-Moraine proclaimed. "I shall be so glad to be free of the duties of First Mother."

"Shall I take the jewelry tray to the safe box?" Elizabelle hinted.

Mai-Kellina answered sharply. "That is the duty of the queen's guard."

Elizabelle panicked. "Pardon me if I'm out of turn, your highness, umm governor, ahh queen, but . . . may I try on one of the bracelets? I've never worn real jewelry, just cheap fake stuff in circus parades."

"Of course. Today is the beginning of a new era for us, too, is it not?" The bride pursed her lips for the photographer.

Elizabelle turned slightly, positioning her body between Mai-

Kellina and the jewel tray. With her heart thumping wildly, she spied the bracelet with the crimson gem, picked it up, and pulled Tricka's extraction tool from her pocket. There was a slight popping sound as the bracelet released the crimson gem. She quickly slipped Mai-Kellina's crimson gem into her right pocket.

"What's that?" Mai-Kellina's voice was suddenly full of suspicion. "Let me see it. That bracelet is very important to me."

Elizabelle's face turned red. She handed the bracelet to Mai-Kellina.

"What have you done? Where is my crimson gem?"

"I . . . I don't know. It must have fallen out." Elizabelle dropped down on her hands and knees and poked around under the furniture. "I'll find it. It has to be here."

Mai-Kellina shrieked, "It better be here! That gem has been a family heirloom for five generations! If you lose it, I will send you to Yerk—"

The maid of honor grabbed Mai-Kellina's arm and whispered in her ear. Soon the bride regained control, but her heavy breathing continued.

While pretending to be searching on the floor, Elizabelle located Tricka's substitute gem in her left pocket. Her heart thumped so hard she feared it would burst out of her chest. If her deceit was discovered, she would be in serious trouble. Stealing an heirloom jewel from a queen! The last thing she wanted on her birthday.

On second thought, no. The last thing she wanted was for Mai-Kellina to become queen. Finally she stood, held out the fake gem, and offered it to Mai-Kellina. "Here it is, good as new."

"Let me have it." Mai-Kellina grabbed the fake gem and snapped it into the bracelet, which she then put back on her arm. She grabbed Elizabelle's wrist and gripped it tightly, boring her steely eyes into Elizabelle. In her coldest voice: "Never, ever do that again."

An icy silence took over the room. No one dared move.

Elizabelle bent her knees again, in the most humble curtsy she could muster. "Yes, M'lady."

Jura-Moraine held up a small tuning fork and struck it. "The Blood Moon is within ten minutes of perfect alignment. We gather on the balcony for the wedding ceremony in two minutes. All in the bride's party assemble behind her. Except you, Miss Elizabelle. You take your place with the Carillons."

Elizabelle rushed to join the other Carillons as they assembled on the balcony. Her golden chance had passed. She could not get Mai-Kellina's crimson gem to Patrizia.

She had failed.

Following royal tradition, the wedding ceremony was set for the balcony just outside the grand ballroom of Castle Tulamarine. The presentation to the dead kings and queens would then take place in private, in the Ancestor's Chamber deep inside the castle. Finally, the coronation would take place in the grand ballroom. The throne of Aldebaran was already set up, polished and waiting in the ballroom, surrounded by an eager crowd of admirers. And armed guards hiding in shadows.

The outside balcony was a huge porch with marble floors and a guard rail made of rare woods from each of the moons. The wedding crowd included lunar governors, important generals from the armies, famous artists and entertainers, and all the lunar princesses. The dignitaries from the circus were there, too. Toberomi, Bucklebiter, most of the Hawken family—but not Braden—and Largent Farthing, the Q&D Circus owner. Johnny Hurricane hid in the crowd.

Marz floated high up in the air, above the bay, on the orca airship. Elizabelle spoke to him by QM. "Marz, the castle police are looking for SunKing. They will find him. How's the view up there?"

"I like high up sky," Marz answered through his QM. "See everything. Big."

Cameras placed around the balcony sent their signals up to the orca airship. The royal wedding would be projected into the matrix hanging from the airship, and from there, throughout the empire.

The backdrop for the ceremony was the celestial sight they had all been waiting for. All seven moons aligned perfectly, each reflecting its distinctive colored light onto the glistening waters of the bay. It was nature's symbol for the union of New Roma with all seven moons. And the union of king with queen.

Tancreido, supported by a guard at each arm, slowly approached the wedding altar. He gazed first at the moons, and then at their light glistening on the water. "The time is right, at last," he mumbled. In addition to his usual maroon robe, he also wore a metal mesh on his forehead. The mesh, and his firstlight scepter, were the ancient symbols of the power to bind a royal marriage, reserved for those destined to join the Fellowship of the Eternals. Once he was positioned at the altar, Rod Lightning's Thunder Drummers, arrayed on the meadow just below, counted out a soft beat while the Carillons hummed the wedding prelude.

Elizabelle stood nervously at attention in the front row of the Carillons, chin up, eyes forward, fake smile. When the prelude ended, she whispered to the choir leader. "I can't stand this. I must get out of here."

"You stay where you are," the leader said. "You begged to join us, and you know the rule: exactly fifty-six voices in the choir at any royal wedding. Seven singers from each of the eight worlds, seven moons and a home planet." The choir conductor raised her baton to signal the next song.

When the Carillons' song ended, Donovan appeared in the doorway leading from the castle ballroom to the balcony. He was dressed in his royal military uniform, but he was not wearing his crown. At his side marched his life-long friend, Braden Hawken. Together they walked to the wedding altar.

Donovan stood at attention before Tancreido. Braden stood back. The crowd fell silent. The airship cameras zoomed in on the king and his advisor.

His eyes watery, Tancreido barely croaked the opening words of the ceremony. "I see a king before me. Why do you approach your lowly servant, oh king of all Empire Luna?"

Following the script, Donovan said, "Esteemed advisor to my grandfather and my father, I present myself to be joined as husband to a woman, who shall be wife to me."

"It is not enough that you are the king of eight worlds?" Tancreido asked. "What more could a man want?"

"No, it is not enough. I seek a bride. I am a man before I am a king. Like any man, I need a woman to be my companion, and to give me sons and daughters."

Elizabelle wanted to scream, *'Then you've chosen the wrong woman!'* but held her tongue.

"And where is the woman who would be . . . be your . . ." Tancreido began to sway unsteadily. His guards caught and held him. "Be your . . . wife."

A single trumpet played the queen's fanfare. After the first chorus, seven more joined in.

The ballroom doors opened again and Mai-Kellina strode out, resplendent in her deep blue wedding gown, covered with royal jewels. She took her position beside Donovan, and stood proudly at attention. Her maids lined up behind her, holding the wedding train off the floor.

Tancreido continued the ritual. "I see a woman before me. What brings you here today?"

Mai-Kellina held her head high. "I am here to wed Donovan. He is king to all, but he shall be husband to me alone."

"The man and the . . . wom . . ." Tancreido's voice trailed off; he started wheezing. His eyes drooped; his hands shook. The crowd stood in dumbstruck silence.

One of the guards grabbed Tancreido's hand and wrapped it around the walking staff. Donovan pulled a pony bottle of oxygen from the belt of one of the guards, knelt down and held the mouthpiece over Tancreido's mouth and nose. After a few moments, Tancreido started breathing again, and regained his composure.

Tancreido's guards helped steady him. He turned to the crowd. "Excuse me, ladies and gentlemen. This is my last royal wedding, I assure you." Then he looked to the couple before him. "The man and the woman agree. Do the people agree?"

The Carillons broke into their gentle chant, "Let it be, let it be." Soon the audience joined in with them. Before long, the crowd in the meadow below, and even the people assembled at the Ardemia Shrine, joined in.

Even with the crowd's chants nearly drowning out her own thoughts, Elizabelle still managed to chant quietly to herself. *Let it not be.*

Tancreido held up his staff to call for silence. "Donovan and Mai-Kellina, my only power is to mark the beginning of your marriage. The two of you will create your family, and your home." From his robe he removed the firstlight scepter. He touched the scepter first on Donovan's forehead, and then on Mai-Kellina's. "You two agree. The seven moons agree. The people agree." He then waved his scepter down the line of moons in the sky; in a moment, the end of the scepter glowed. "My scepter agrees. That makes it so. You are now a new royal family."

The Carillons broke into the royal wedding song, as they had rehearsed inside the tambour at Tambora. But at this performance, it was not just a few taiko drums pounding out the beat, but Rod Lightning and his Thunder Drummers. Elizabelle tried to sing the words, but tears flooded her eyes and dread filled her heart; she mouthed the words but no sounds escaped.

As the Carillons finished their song, the bells pealed in each of the seven towers of Castle Tulamarine. The crowd broke into applause and hurrahs. The bride and groom hugged and bowed to Tancreido, then to the crowd, then to the cameras on the airship.

Tears filled Elizabelle's eyes. Mai-Kellina had won. Everything. Soon Mai-Kellina would begin to sap the king's power, and in secret cahoots with Proco, control all of Empire Luna.

Elizabelle broke from the ranks of the Carillons, and ran up the stairs to be with her mother. The sounds of the crowd applause and the bells ringing made her feel sick. She struggled to get a breath, but could not. Her face blanched.

She felt inside her pocket and found the crimson gem she had stolen from the bride.

Chapter 8 ♪ ♪ ♪ ♪ ♪ ♪

ORACLE

Dead kings and queens stared down at them. The royal eyes seemed to glow, whether the portraits were photographs, view-gem images, or the work of skilled painters.

The "Claire de Lune" song played softly on a piano. A faint whiff of gabania smoke, from the fireplace at the back of the room, drifted in the air.

Elizabelle had heard many stories about the Ancestor's Chamber in the castle, but never expected to visit it. In normal times, only members of the royal family could enter. But Donovan had invited a few personal friends and important guests to join him and his new bride. He wanted several witnesses to see the Oracle deliver the approval of the dead kings and queens, allowing the new royal bride to be crowned queen. The guests included the other six lunar governors, Tancreido, and the entire Hawken family. But not Marz, who was still up in the airship.

The small room was crowded. The guests all squeezed together in the center, to clear a walking path for the king and his bride, as they rounded the room.

Mai-Kellina, the new bride, strode triumphantly into the room with her husband, King Donovan. They took the seats of honor.

Elizabelle thought the king seemed stiff, showing no emotion. *His body is here, but where is his heart?*, she wondered.

"Ladies and gentlemen, your quiet attention please." Jura-Moraine sounded solemn. "We are here to continue the tradition begun by our First Queen. Since we have no living queen . . ."

The king closed his eyes and bowed his head.

Jura-Moraine continued. "Under Aldebaran's law, all the royal ancestors must approve the new bride to be crowned queen."

The piano music stopped. The room lights dimmed. The eyes in the royal portraits lit up.

At the front of the room, purple curtains opened. A single spotlight shone a soft light on the marble table and the pierce-light mounted upon it. Only the hands of the Oracle were visible. The Oracle rose and, while still hidden from sight, announced in a sturdy male voice: "The king and his bride will present themselves to the royal ancestors."

Donovan and Mai-Kellina rose from their seats of honor, held hands and rounded the room. As they came to each royal family portrait hanging on the wall above, they respectfully bowed. While they were busy appeasing the ancestors, the Oracle slipped into the light. Elizabelle saw the profile and gasped. Even with only a fleeting glance, hidden in shadow, she was instantly certain: the half-face of the Oracle in the dim light was . . . Lady Patrizia.

Then Elizabelle remembered her mother's words. "The Oracle must be able to receive messages from both the former kings and the departed queens. Very few people can do that." *Did my mother know that Tricka is the Oracle?*

Elizabelle tried to read her mother's expression, but her face was blank. The solemn tradition was made almost unbearable by Donovan's mood. No man, king or commoner, could mourn the death of his beloved first wife and in the same day be joyous in marrying his second. Especially when the second marriage was mostly about duty and power, and setting an example.

Patrizia winked at Elizabelle, then touched a blue gem on one of her rings. Elizabelle nodded, and quickly passed to Patrizia the crimson red view-gem she had stolen from Mai-Kellina. Elizabelle wondered if Patrizia would place the stolen view-gem into the light machine.

But it was not to be. It was already too late. The wedding was done. Thousands of people personally witnessed the marriage.

Patrizia chose a blue gem and cradled it in the projector.

The king and his new bride finished paying their respects to the portraits of his ancestors. King and bride stood at attention before the Oracle. Donovan seemed pale, even in the dim light.

"New wife of the king," Patrizia intoned, "why do you approach the Oracle?"

The voice of Mai-Kellina was full of confidence and pride. "I seek the approval of all the Arkenstone queens who were crowned before me. I ask them to admit me into their circle, and consent to me taking the throne that each of them once held, wearing the crown of our beloved First Mother, First Queen Aldebaran. In this way the royal family may continue, and peace will prevail throughout all eight worlds of Empire Luna."

Elizabelle closed her eyes and shook her head in disbelief at Mai-Kellina's words.

"King Donovan, Lady Mai-Kellina . . ." Patrizia paused, milking the silence. "The royal ancestors are pleased that you present yourself to them." She touched the view-gem projector on the desk. "First, let us confirm that they are all here with us today." Brief little movies of the marriages of each of the Arkenstone kings and all their queens flashed into the mist above the machine. Then it flashed to Donovan's marriage to Galena, and showed her playing the harp. Again, the king bowed his head.

A frown crawled across Mai-Kellina's face, but she kept silent.

"Let us now hear from our most recent queen," the Oracle said.

Elizabelle wondered. By "our most recent queen" did Patrizia mean Galena Selena, or Donovan's mother, Queen Rubicania?

The light frame showed Galena's face. But it was not a scene from her wedding with Donovan. She looked disheveled, her face dirty, her eyes red. Staring straight into the QM camera, she implored, "Proco, why do you treat me so badly? Let me go home to Donovan."

Hearing these shocking words, inside the Chamber of Ancestors, with his new bride at his side, the king jerked back in disbelief. His appearance changed in an instant, from a man dutifully going through the motions, to a man suddenly stunned. This was not part of the ceremony. At long last he knew what had become of his beloved first bride. She had become a prisoner of Proco.

A rustle of whispers filtered through the room. From his seat off to the side, Tancreido stared suspiciously at Mai-Kellina.

Eyes wide, the king stared into the view-gem. "What is this?" he demanded.

"Yes, indeed, what is this?" Mai-Kellina's eyes seemed aflame as she glared at Patrizia, the Oracle. "How have you created this . . . illusion? How dare you deceive us right here in this holy place, the Chamber of Ancestors?"

Patrizia answered calmly. "All the deceased queens have a right to be heard at this time. You reported seeing the dead body of Queen Selena. Just yesterday."

Silence settled on the room like a chilly fog.

Mai-Kellina took a deep breath. "If Queen Selena ever made such a recording, it was many years ago, long, long before I saw her body."

Like a lightning bolt firing her memory, Elizabelle recalled her father's words from the Cloud Forest. *"We will never get another chance like this."* And Tricka's words: *"Sometimes the dangerous chance is the only chance."* And even Mai-Kellina's words: *"Sometimes a woman must be a warrior!"* A flash of courage surged through her entire body.

Elizabelle stepped forward and confronted Mai-Kellina. "How would you know when Galena made this recording?" All eyes in the room turned to Elizabelle. Althea reached out to pull her back, but she stood firm. She would not let a ceremonial duty hide a lie.

Mai-Kellina's eyes glared. "Miss Elizabelle, in this room, children are to remain silent—"

"That line won't work on me anymore. I am no longer a child. I am a full-fledged Sister of Ardemia. I will not be silenced."

"I am the wife of the king. I have a right to the throne," Mai-Kellina declared, "to wear the crown of Aldebaran. You are an impudent servant, a silly circus girl. You're in my way. You'll pay for this."

Most of the audience pulled back, in case of blows between the flaming anger of the new queen and the determination of the circus girl who would not back down. Not even from royalty.

The king's body shook as he confronted Mai-Kellina. "Answer Miss Elizabelle's question. How would you know when that recording was made?"

Mai-Kellina moved closer to the king, and looked softly into his eyes. She tried to take his hand, but he pulled away. Her voice was almost a whisper. "I told you already. I saw Galena's lifeless body myself, only a few days ago. With my own eyes. I swear it."

Tricka moved completely into the light, revealing the full face, black and white, male and female. Making a show for all to see, Patrizia removed the first view-gem and, flourishing the hand like a magician, replaced it with the crimson red veegee that Elizabelle had stolen.

Mai-Kellina locked her gaze onto the crimson view-gem, her eyes wide. She grasped her bracelet, and rubbed her fingers on the crimson gem. The fake gem that Elizabelle had planted there. Then she glared at Elizabelle, her eyes burning with suspicion.

At first there was no picture, and the sound sputtered and squawked. But soon the crimson gem played the unmistakable voice of Mai-Kellina. "Oh, Proco, my love, how I miss you."

The new bride's whole body shook uncontrollably. "Give me that thing!" she shrieked.

"What is the truth of this?" Donovan demanded.

As Mai-Kellina fumbled, trying to collect her composure, her recorded voice continued to play. "You will be there, in case we must go to the backup plan. You promised me." And then her voice mixed with Proco's: "All the powers will be ours."

Donovan's jaw line tightened; he gritted his teeth. His face went rigid, turning the color of a red hot stone. "Mai-Kellina, I demand the truth. Answer me this second. What does this mean? What is your backup plan? Why are you calling Proco your love?"

"It's all a lie!" Mai-Kellina closed her eyes for a moment, breathed deeply, and then pointed at Tricka. "It's all brewed up by this . . . evil conjuror. She has taken recorded bits of my speech, chopped them up and stirred them into this ugly lie. *I never said such things.*"

Elizabelle stood up and shouted, "Yes you did!"

The king bent down slightly so he could look Elizabelle directly in the eye. "Elizabelle, we are in grave danger here. I am your king and your friend. Tell me the truth."

Elizabelle went down on one knee, bowed her head, placed her hand upon her heart, and looked up into the eyes of Donovan. "Oh, my beloved king, I swear upon the revered name of First Queen Aldebaran herself. I swear upon the memory of your mother Rubicania. I swear upon the memory of all the Arkenstone queens. I swear upon my own life. I heard Mai-Kellina pledge her love to Proco at Tambora, just a couple of days ago. It was after the Carillon ceremony, when the chamber seemed empty. Her words are burned into my memory. She said, 'Proco, oh how I miss you. You will be there, you promised me.'"

"Anything else?" the king asked.

"Yes, my king. She chanted with him, 'All the powers will be ours.'"

Mai-Kellina turned to Tricka, and switched into her lioness voice. "What poison have you fed to this girl child to make her lie like this? Have you hypnotized her? Planted false memories in her brain? You are not an oracle. You don't tell fortunes, you tell lies! Everything about you is fake. You are not a woman! You are not a man! You are lower than a mangy circus dog. You are a lying witch! I curse you for all eternity!"

Mai-Kellina grabbed the small dagger hanging from her necklace. She lunged at Tricka, growling like a desperate animal, screaming, "Liar! You kill my dream, you die!"

At the sight of the dagger, Braden and Althea pulled Elizabelle and Ripley away.

Mai-Kellina wrestled with Tricka, trying to sink the dagger into Tricka's neck. Donovan jumped out and pulled her back. Soon the royal guards joined in and forced her to the floor. All the while she kept screaming, "Liar! You kill my dream, you die!"

Donovan grabbed her dagger arm, twisted it behind her back, and forced the dagger from her hand. The knife clattered as it bounced across the floor.

The audience stood back in stunned silence. Even with her face pushed to the floor, Mai-Kellina kept ranting and screaming, "You kill my dream, you die." Her eyes rolled back, and her head wobbled.

An armed guard stood at the door, his stunner aimed at Mai-Kellina. King Donovan held up his hand. "Hold off. Just restrain her." The guard drew wrist and ankle ties from his belt. He strapped Mai-Kellina's hands behind her back, and tied her ankles.

Tancreido whispered something in the king's ear. The king nodded and ordered the royal guards, "Take her to the guard house. Hold her there, under constant watch. She must not escape."

ORACLE ☽ ☽ ☽ ☽ ☽ ☽

Once Mai-Kellina was out of the room, Jura-Moraine turned to the king. "What now?"

"We'll assemble in the ballroom. My first duty is to tell the people the truth."

☽ ☽ ☽ ☽ ☽ ☽ ☽

Donovan and Tancreido emerged from the Chamber of Ancestors first, looking pale, exhausted and solemn. The other members of the Oracle audience followed. They assembled on the interior walkway, above the ballroom. Red flames raged inside the giant fireplace.

The audience below eagerly awaited the coronation of the new queen. When they saw that the royal bride was not in the royal group, whispered questions flitted through the crowd. "Where's Mai-Kellina?" "What's wrong?"

Jura-Moraine addressed the audience first. "Ladies and gentlemen, honored guests of the royal family, we have sad news to report. We have received a message, through the Oracle, from one of the Arkenstone queens who is no longer with us. Because of this message, there will be no coronation today." A hush blanketed the crowd. "Now, hear your king."

The king's face looked gaunt, white as a chalk cliff. "Loyal citizens. Today I have learned that my wife Galena, your Queen Selena, has been held as a captive by the traitor Proco Haruma. I have also learned that Mai-Kellina has been plotting with Proco. Her deceit is deeper than any ocean, hotter than the mines on the Blood Moon. Queen Selena's death may be just another lie. Mai-Kellina tried to enter into a fake marriage with me, simply to gain power and to steal the throne of Aldebaran. Master Tancreido, please tell us what this means."

Tancreido hobbled to the giant fireplace. He withdrew his first-light scepter from its case and held it up to the crowd. His voice cracked as he announced: "This ancient scepter has bound the marriages of every Arkenstone king and queen. But today, it has been defiled by lies of the most treasonous order. Because of that, this scepter shall never again mark the first day of a royal marriage. Its time as a symbol of the binding power of the Fellowship of Eternals is done. All its ritual authority must be destroyed." He handed the scepter to King Donovan.

The king held the scepter in both hands, facing the fire. He lobbed the scepter into the flames. At first the gabania fire choked and sputtered, as if the scepter were a soggy log, determined to drown the fire. But gradually wisps of steam arose. Then little sputtering flames found a way around it, and released swirls of smoke. A little pit of dried pitch popped. Soon eager flames devoured the ancient scepter.

"As the scepter turns to smoke," Tancreido said, "so too does the marriage of Donovan and Mai-Kellina. It is turned to ashes, as if it never happened at all."

Jura-Moraine nudged Elizabelle and whispered, "You have one more duty to perform."

Elizabelle stepped forward, holding the crown of Aldebaran on its velvet cushion. She curtsied to Donovan, then presented the crown to him. He took the crown, placed it on the queen's throne, and announced, "This crown shall rest on the throne of Aldebaran until its only rightful wearer, Queen Selena, returns to us. Or we know for certain that she has joined the Ancestors."

Chapter 9 ♪ ♪ ♪ ♪ ♪ ♪

PROCO

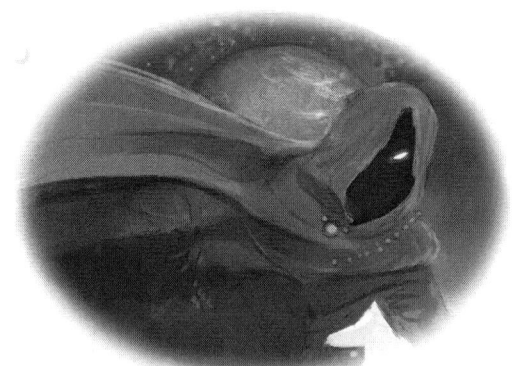

The royal guards hauled Mai-Kellina out through Donovan's private passageway at the rear of Castle Tulamarine. Once they were outside, she stopped her chanting curses, fell silent, and went limp. They carried her to the guardhouse and locked her in a jail cell, a tiny, dark room with solid iron bars from floor to ceiling.

Mai-Kellina sat on the bed, silently staring at the floor, trembling, sniffling and wiping her eyes. After a few minutes, she called to a guard. "I need water."

Soon the guard approached and offered her a cup of water. She drank deeply. "Thank you," she said. "Would be so kind has to help me out of all this jewelry?"

She backed up to the bars. "Kindly release the clips." While the guard fiddled with the clips, she reached down, furtively pulled the QM from his tool belt, and cupped it in her hand. When the last necklace fell loose, she handed it to the guard. "Return all this royal jewelry to Jura-Moraine."

"Yes, ma'm." The guard then returned to his post.

Mai-Kellina lay down on the bed and pretended to sleep, with her back to the guard. She took a gem from her bracelet and inserted it into the guard's QM. Once she had reset the QM, she whispered into it. "Oh, Proco! Our beautiful plan has failed."

"Where are you?"

"They have me locked in the guardhouse. I should've seen it coming." She kept looking over her shoulder to see if the guard was paying attention. He was nodding off. "Even at Tambora I knew that Tricka was a fake. She—or he, or they, or it—had no right to be on that island. Neither did the circus girl—she wasn't really fourteen yet. We were done in by a conspiracy of impostors."

"Don't give up. We will not be defeated by a dizzy girl and a circus freak."

"What now?"

"They have forced us into the hard choice."

It was just past sunset, and the seven moons still hung in the sky, glowing. Only the Blood Moon had begun to wander away from its key position in the Crestival alignment.

The news that there would be no crowning of a new queen today spread through the ballroom crowd. "So hard to believe." "A crisis for the Sisterhood." Slowly the ballroom people drifted out onto the castle balcony. On the meadow below, the visitors from various moons began packing up for their long journey.

Elizabelle waited on the castle balcony, with King Donovan and Tancreido. Giant images of the three of them, and the entire balcony scene, were projected in the matrix hanging beneath the orca airship, high above the bay. Elizabelle realized that everyone in the empire was watching them. She looked up to the orca airship and saw Marz climbing around on the undercarriage and placing protectors over his ears.

A gravelly voice blasted out from the orca airship. "Attention Donovan, you spawn of the usurper house of Arkenstone! You, on the ground. You, pretender king!" The voice blared over the sound system, echoing throughout Tulamarine. "I am Proco Haruma, the reincarnation and only rightful heir of the Crimson King. Today I shall restore the Ancient Order."

Donovan strode to the front of the balcony. "Proco!" he shouted, gripping the railing and glaring up to the airship. "Show your face, traitor. If you still have one."

Proco's voice bellowed above it all. "I see you Donovan, but you'll never see me. I have the wild boy. I have the quagga. The airship is under my command. From a distance."

"Of course," Donovan sneered. "Remote control. The way of cowards. Fits you."

"Insult me all you wish. In the end, it will make no difference. Look across the bay."

From a box beneath the control car of the airship, four long rods extended. They rotated for a moment, and then aimed at the Ardemia Shrine. Beams of intense light shot out. When they tightened to a perfect focus point the spire exploded in a blinding flash, scattering shards of mirror in all directions.

Elizabelle looked up to Marz, stranded atop the matrix. He was climbing toward the long rods beneath the airship control car. The same rods that had just shot deadly light beams.

People gathered around the castle panicked. Frantic parents grabbed their children; old men and women stumbled and fell. Everywhere people ran wildly in any direction leading away from the castle.

"Guards!" King Donovan shouted. "Call out the royal airstrikers. Destroy that airship!"

Elizabelle cried out to the king. "No! Marz is still up there!" She aimed her QM to the underbelly of the airship, and zoomed the camera lens to 10x, and showed the scene to the king. Marz was on one of the long rods, trying to take it apart. "He's wearing ear protectors that block out all sounds except my QM messages. He doesn't know the coronation is off. He's waiting for my signal."

"Get him down from there," the king said, "before the strikers arrive. They're going to blow that airship out of the sky."

Proco's voice droned on, blasting down from the airship. "You will release Mai-Kellina immediately. You will surrender your crown to me."

"Or what?" the king shouted.

"I will destroy you and your family and your castle."

"I have no family to destroy." The king conferred with Tancreido.

"I have your Galena," Proco's voice called out. "I've had her for fourteen years."

"Prove it."

The castle balcony scene faded from the matrix. In its place appeared a moving image of Galena working in a garden, looking young as on her wedding day. Suddenly she turned and looked up. "Who are you? What do you want?" Then the image suddenly went dark.

The king clenched his fists and widened his stance. With a defiant look on his face, he stared up into the airship cameras. "That's an old recording. Prove you have her today."

"I have proved my power. I have shown you that Galena lives."

Six royal airstrikers broke over the horizon, heading straight for the airship.

Proco's demands continued to blare out from the airship. "Donovan, you will surrender to me by placing the crown of Aldebaran on the floor. Then you will then lie down flat on the ground to show your unconditional surrender to the me as the reincarnation of the one and only Crimson King. Everyone in the empire shall witness it."

King Donovan turned to Elizabelle. "Time to join your family."

"I have to help Marz get down from there!"

"I'll try to buy you a bit of time, then." Turning his face back to the airship cameras, Donovan demanded: "If you want my crown, come down here in person and take it from me."

"Your crown for your wife. You made that choice once before. Make it again, and save her life, and yours."

Donovan conferred for a moment with Tancreido. Then, speaking up to the airship, "You have kidnaped the queen. That's high treason. The punishment is death or ejection into outer space, where you shall drift forever in cold, empty darkness."

The droning sound of the approaching royal airstrikers kept growing louder. Their shining wings glistened on the horizon.

An old image of Proco, from his days as a general in the army of Donovan's father, appeared on the matrix. But his voice did not change. "Oh, Donovan, you are indeed the fool Mai-Kellina told me about." The rods on the airship swiveled away from the Ardemia shrine. Elizabelle expected them to take aim at the airstrikers.

But they did not. They aimed directly at the castle. Right where the king, and Tancreido, and Elizabelle stood together.

The airstrikers were within shooting distance of the airship.

Proco's thundering voice continued. "You would attack my airship? Stupid fool. Here's your last chance. Send your strikers away. Surrender and live, or defend and die."

To his guards, Donovan ordered, "Tell the strikers to hold fire. We must get the circus boy down first." Then he turned and shouted to the airship, his fist defiantly in the air: "I will not betray my ancestors. Or my people."

"Your choice seals your fate."

"Marz!" Elizabelle screamed into her QM. "Forget the cowboy rescue. Rescue yourself. Climb back down the rope." Marz waved to her as he scrambled toward the connection point for the tether line.

But just as he approached, the tether disconnected from the airship, and dropped straight down. Twisting and turning, it fell into the bay, curled like a dead snake. The airship propellers sped up. The flaps twisted. The airship groaned under the sudden pressure. At first it turned slowly. Then it turned nose down.

The royal airstrikers zoomed into the Tulamarine sky, passed over the castle, and buzzed the airship. Elizabelle overheard their messages on the king's QM. "Ready on your order, king. That whale in the sky is the biggest, easiest target we've ever seen."

"No!" Elizabelle screamed. "They'll kill Marz!" She grabbed her QM. "Marz, forget the plan. Just get off that thing, right now. It's gonna crash!"

PROCO ☽ ☽ ☽ ☽ ☽

"We must leave now," Tancreido said to the king. "Come with us. Your life is far more important than the castle."

"I will join you," the king replied. "Soon." Elizabelle could not believe her eyes when she saw the king turn and run into the castle, leaving her and everyone else dazed and confused on the balcony.

Tancreido tried his best to rush down the balcony stairs, but he soon fell. His guards clasped their hands together, to make a chair for the old advisor, grunting together as they lifted him and bore him down the stairs.

Elizabelle could see Marz, still at the top of the matrix, scrambling around in the fibers. As the matrix twisted upon itself, the image inside it faded. Soon the whole matrix was a field of sparks, flashing. Quickly, the sparks grew into flames; the flames leaped up the matrix, growing like a forest fire whipping up a dry mountain side.

The castle's fire siren wailed.

For just a moment, Elizabelle recalled the time her imagination had created a whale cloud, as they approached the Cloud Forest. But now the floating whale was real. And on fire. And careening for Castle Tulamarine.

Elizabelle grabbed her QM and yelled. "Marz, jump now!"

☽ ☽ ☽ ☽ ☽ ☽

Marz grabbed his ear protectors and heard Elizabelle's scream. "Marz, jump now!"

He looked down. The ground was rushing up toward him. Hot flames licked his feet.

The flames from the matrix reached the control car of the airship, immediately above him, setting it afire.

Marz pulled a few fibers loose from the matrix. He donned the royal cape, and then used the fibers to tie the corners of the cape to his wrists and ankles, so the cape would work like Capitano Zucchini's bat wings. He took a deep breath, steadied himself . . . and jumped.

He leaped straight out into the open air, with the bay waters below.

As he jumped free of the flaming airship, the matrix dropped away from the underbelly, and fell straight down to the bay below. When it hit the surface, the water erupted like a geyser, sending stinking smoke and fumes into the air.

Marz spread his arms and legs, opening the cape wide, to give him air resistance and lift in the updraft of the hot air currents. Summoning all his strength, he flapped the cape wings until he gained a little height. As he soared above the bay, the cape fluttering wildly behind him, he looked down to the scene below. And shuddered at the sight.

The flaming airship crashed into the castle. Nose first. As it hit, a huge explosion shattered the giant stones forming the walls of the castle. The main body of the airship smashed through the doors to the grand ballroom, setting the wooden panels of the walls on fire. Smoke spewed and flames erupted.

The sound beans in Marz's ear protectors delivered a message from Elizabelle. "King Donovan just ran back into the castle. Get down here!"

Marz pulled out his cowboy rescue whistle and blew it as loudly as he could. Could SunKing hear it? He scanned the meadow again. Finally, he spotted SunKing locked behind a false wall inside an animal car in the Q&D circus train. Twisting the cape wings, he soared over the train and blew the rescue whistle again. This time SunKing heard him.

PROCO ♪ ♪ ♪ ♪ ♪ ♪

With one mighty blast of his powerful hind legs, SunKing smashed the door of his cage, turned and leaped out into the meadow. He wandered around for a few steps, confused. Finally, he looked up, directly at Marz, gliding and soaring high above him, his colorful cape outstretched like wings on a bat.

Marz adjusted his flight to head straight for the castle, and blew the rescue whistle again. Soon SunKing was directly below Marz, moving in perfect time with him. Marz adjusted his cape wings to slow for a landing. The quagga matched him, as they had rehearsed so many times. The boy fluttered the cape, pushing hard to slow his descent. He aimed to drop out of the sky and land directly on the saddle of the galloping quagga.

It worked. All their practicing had paid off.

Marz settled into the saddle and leaned forward. He released the fibers holding the cape to his wrists and ankles. The cape flapped in the breeze, shifting colors rapidly.

Reunited once again, the boy and his beast friend tore for the castle. They rode straight up the balcony staircase, navigating around the burning pieces of the airship.

Marz still wore his ear protectors. "Marz, save the king!" Elizabelle shrieked.

Clicking his heels into SunKing's flank, Marz urged him into the burning castle.

♪ ♪ ♪ ♪ ♪ ♪ ♪

The walls of the ballroom blazed. Leaping flames devoured tall velvet curtains. Painted portraits, hung in positions of honor, dripped paint as their frames went up in smoke. Acrid smoke from burning carpets filled the air.

Marz called out. "King Donovan, Marz humble servant!"

The smoke was so thick that Marz could barely breathe. SunKing began coughing, making a hacking sound, and leaned down low, where the smoke was less dense.

King Donovan stumbled out of the hallway, the crown of Aldebaran clutched tightly in one hand. In the other hand, his fist clenched some small object. Flames shot from the sleeves and back of the king's royal robe, and his face and hands were covered with ash and soot. The pants on his bad leg were torn, and the skin burned.

Directly above the king, a large ceiling beam had nearly burned through.

"King Donvan!" Marz called out again. He urged SunKing toward the king.

"Marz!" King Donovan stepped forward as the ceiling beam, just behind him, cracked, then collapsed. Shooting flames, it crashed to the floor, barely missing the king's head.

SunKing tried to turn and run, but Marz pulled the reins tight, and guided him. Marz and King Donovan met in the middle of the ballroom. The boy dismounted, and offered the stirrup. When the king placed his left foot in the stirrup, SunKing chuffed and backed away.

Whispering to the quagga, Marz said, "King Donovan, fren zokay." He stroked the beast's neck, and then remounted. Releasing his left foot from the stirrup, he again invited the king to mount, seated behind him. This time SunKing allowed it.

PROCO ☽ ☽ ☽ ☽ ☽ ☽

The king held one arm around Marz; his other hand tightly gripped the queen's crown and his secret treasure.

When King Donovan and Marz rode out of the burning castle astride SunKing, people in the meadow below broke into wild applause, shouting and whistling. The three of them made their way around the burning rubble of the airship, down the balcony stairs, and rode out into the meadow.

"Put out that fire!" shouted one of the king's guards. Many men, and some women too, gathered around him, ready for instructions.

"No!" shouted the king. "It's too dangerous in there. Let it burn."

Elizabelle thought the worst was over. The king was safely out of the castle, only slightly burned. Tancreido, Marz, SunKing, and all the members of her family were all out, and gathered together. Her mother attended to the king's burned leg. The crown of Aldebaran had not melted in the fire.

The flames of the castle slowly died down. The damage could have been much worse. Only the central portion of the castle—the grand entrance and the huge ballroom—had been severely damaged. The seven towers had some smoke damage, and broken windows, but were still standing. The madness of the crowd, with adults screaming and children crying, was over. Proco's voice was heard no more.

But there was a rumbling sound. Up high. Far away. Approaching, getting louder. Elizabelle thought she recognized it. They all looked up and scanned the skies. No balloons. No airship. No strikers.

And then . . . the Buzzard buzzed over them.

"Hurricane!" Marz and Ripley shouted together. They jumped and waved wildly.

But Elizabelle stopped in mid-wave. She had caught a glimpse of the long-neck cockpit as the space bus flew away. The sight shocked her, for it was not Johnny Hurricane at the controls. She couldn't be sure, but it looked like the pilot . . . was Mai-Kellina.

EPILOG

The grand ballroom of Castle Tulamarine, the pride of Empire Luna, lay in ruin. Ashes, smoke, and rubble. The central palace had collapsed and burned, leaving the seven lunar towers standing like wounded, lonely sentries.

When the airship attacked, its metal framework had worked like a huge battering ram. Stone walls, once thought impenetrable, had cracked under the impact. Windows made of shatter-proof glass had fractured and collapsed in a jumble of shards.

King Donovan, the whole Hawken family, and the king's scribe walked together, slowly and silently. Four bodyguards carried Tancreido on a stretcher. Marz led SunKing by his halter.

The king, limping on his burned leg, slowly made his way into the area that had been set up for a queen's coronation. The others followed him. At the sight of the devastation, everyone remained speechless.

Every part of the grand ballroom that could burn was now in ashes. Hand-carved furniture—gifts from the craft guilds on each moon—had been reduced to cinders. Luxurious curtains, four stories tall, were transformed into piles of blackened powder. Portraits of four generations of the royal family lay curled on the floor, scarred and smeared. On the inside balcony, the king's piano was nothing but a metal frame, sprung wires, and tangled keys. Queen Selena's harp had somehow survived, twisted in metal agony. Strangely, the throne of Aldebaran stood defiantly in the center of the ballroom, as if the coronation were only minutes away.

The king surveyed the mess, and slowly shook his head. Finally he broke the sad silence. "I could expect this of Proco. But how could Mai-Kellina become involved in such evil?"

Tancreido raised up from his stretcher, his eyes watery. "The lust for power knows no limit. Once the heart has been corrupted, every evil is excused as . . . necessary."

The king walked to the throne of Aldebaran and brushed the ashes from the cushion. "Were any bodies found inside the wreckage of the airship?"

Elizabelle's dad answered. "None. The entire attack was by remote control."

The king signaled to his scribe. "Are you ready?"

"Yes, my king. Just speak. Your words shall be our law."

Standing in the ruins of the grand ballroom, and surrounded by his scribe, his advisor, his friends the Hawkens, and Marz and SunKing, for the first time in his reign, King Donovan announced royal decrees.

"One. Proco Haruma is enemy number one throughout Empire Luna. A king's warrant for his arrest and capture shall go out to all the moons. The bounty of twenty-one gold bricks, a reward for his capture, shall be doubled. It will be paid to anyone who brings him to me. Dead or alive.

EPILOG

"Two. Mai-Kellina is enemy number two throughout Empire Luna. The bounty on her head is the same as Proco, since she is his equal conspirator. She will never again serve as a governor of any moon, or hold any position of power, so long as I am king. When captured, she will face charges of high treason before a jury of all the other lunar governors.

"Three. I award the Hawken family fifty bricks of gold, from the royal treasury, to be used to pay Hurricane's fee for delivering the quagga, and to purchase all the animals of the Quattro and Diamond Circus. I will hold the Hawken family responsible for the care of all the circus animals. They are to make sure that all the animals are treated humanely, fed properly, and given enough space. The animals must be allowed to choose their own mates, and to make their babies whenever they wish. The rule is the same for all animals, whether they are performing ring stock, show animals, or beasts of burden. No training by pain, punishment, or starvation.

"Number Four. I award Seven Moon Circus an all-moon travel license. 7MC may tour every moon, and perform anywhere there is an audience for them. They are to give at least one free performance for all poor families and orphans, on each moon, and at least one performance per year on New Roma. And during their travels, they are to keep their eyes and ears out for anyone who might have information about whether Galena is still alive, and if so, where she is and how she can be saved.

"Five. Jonathan Hertzicona—Johnny Hurricane—" The king paused. "Don't write this one. We will leave the Hurricane matter open for now. We must find out if he is somehow tangled up with Mai-Kellina and Proco. Or if she has just stolen his space bus. He might be in cahoots with her, or he might be her victim. With those two, it's hard to tell what's going on.

"Six. The royal architects are to begin work designing a new central palace of Castle Tulamarine. The destruction wrought by Proco and Mai-Kellina must be turned into something magnificent, much more grand than the original design. The New Castle Tulamarine must be the most impressive structure in the empire. Its very existence must defy Proco, and everyone working with him.

"Seven. To thank Marz, known as the Wild Boy, and his animal friend SunKing the quagga, for saving my life, ten bricks of gold, from the royal treasury. This gift shall be reserved for him until next Crestival. During that time, Miss Elizabelle Hawken will continue to tutor him, help him learn to become a civilized young man. He is to learn with the other circus children. If we cannot discover his true date of birth by next Crestival, we will assign him an official birth date the same as Crestival alignment day. By next Crestival, Marz will be a full adult, and entitled to claim his fortune. For his part in saving my life, SunKing deserves a reward too. So I order the labs at Yerkoza, and all other bio-labs in the realm, to make their most important project the creation of a mare, a mate for SunKing."

At this news, the Hawkens applauded.

"Is that all?" the scribe asked.

"Not quite. We still have the question of where Marz will live, and who will be his family. Marz, where do you want to live?"

"I circus boy. Hawkens circus family." He opened his palm and pointed to each of them. "Braden, Althea, Elizabelle, Ripley." And finally to himself. "Happy Marz."

"You shall have your wish. Until his natural parents may be

EPILOG

found, I award permanent custody of Marz to the Hawken family." Elizabelle and her family gathered around Marz, hugging him.

"Happy. Bang on drum all day!" Marz beamed.

"Yeah, and we need to go home to Baraboo," Ripley added. "Maybe even back to the Cloud Forest some day."

GLOSSARY

7MC—Seven Moon Circus
Aldebaran—the first queen in the Arkenstone Dynasty
Althea—mother in the Hawken circus family
Amarna—Lunar princess from the Blood Moon
Ardemia—Empire Luna name for the Greek Goddess Artemis
Arkenstones—the royal family of Empire Luna
Baraboo—training camp for Seven Moon Circus
Big Hair Woman—another name for Maleeza
Bluemist—a type of dragonfly
Boyd "Bucky" Bucklebiter—Master of Spectacle in Seven Moon Circus
Braden—father in the Hawken circus family
Buzzard—a space bus that flies between moons
Carillons—an all-female singing group
Castle Tulamarine—the home of the royal family of Empire Luna
Claire deLuna Taroona—a high-wire performer
Cloud Forest—a tropical rain forest and nature preserve
Converticopter—a helicopter that converts into an airplane
Crestival—The Grand Festival of the Seven Crescent Moons

GLOSSARY

Crimson King—an ancient king of Empire Luna

Dane Steele—animal trainer in the Quattro & Diamond Circus

DB—Decoy Bird

Dokon—a mountain-climbing animal that lives only on Luna Verdanta

Donovan—King of Empire Luna; official name title: Arkenstone IV

drakkar—a Viking longship with a dragon masthead

Duke—a young male lion

Eefanannies—a "singing" group of clowns

Elizabelle—a circus girl, age 13 when the story begins

Empire Luna—the new human world system, consisting of:
> **New Roma**—the home planet
> **Silver Moon**—Halcyon
> **Golden Moon**—Electra
> **Green Moon**—Verdanta
> **Gray Lady**—Moon of Clouds (ancient name: Merope)
> **Blue Moon**—Kayleno
> **Lavender Moon**—Azura
> **Blood Moon**

Gabania—a tree that grows only on the Blood Moon

Galena—the name of King Donovan's wife before she became queen (see: Selena)

Gliderbirds—a group of high-wire performers

Gun Man—an animal trainer working for Mai-Kellina

GV—Governor's Vehicle

Hawken Family—a family of animal experts from Seven Moon Circus
> father: Braden; mother: Althea; daughter: Elizabelle; son: Ripley

Hurricane—see Johnny Hurricane

ICC—Intralunar Custom Charter—a space bus company

GLOSSARY

Idonya—a guard on Mai-Kellina's GV

Jefferson Spitfire—a hot air balloon

Jerry Cherry—a clown

Johnny Hurricane—pilot of the Buzzard space bus (real name: Jonathan Hertzicona)

JoJo Brightfeather—leader of the Gliderbirds, high-wire performers

Jorona Maasai—a lady lawyer

Jura-Moraine—aunt to King Donovan, half-sister to his mother

Karianta—Lunar princess from the Silver Moon

Karoo, Sea of—the deepest ocean on Luna Verdanta

Keeli—a mother bonobo

Kiko's Guild—highly skilled weavers of "chameleon cloth"

kitanza—an animal native to Empire Luna

Kokomo—a bonobo

Lady Patrizia—the female half of Tricka; fortune teller and oracle

Largent Farthing—owner of the Quattro & Diamond circus

Lataan—Commander General of the Army of the Golden Moon

Lunar Council—the group of all governors of the various moons

Mai-Kellina—Lady Governor of the Green Moon

Maleeza—a tutor at Yerkoza

Manjaro—a young male bonobo, first born son of Keeli

Marz—the Wild Boy

New Roma—the home planet in Empire Luna

Norzah—space ship captain who led the exodus from Earth to Empire Luna

Ol'Terra—planet Earth

Oracle—a ghost talker

Orfala—Lunar princess from the Golden Moon

GLOSSARY

Patrizia—the female half of Tricka

Patrick KirPatrick—the male half of Tricka

Peg Leg Meg—a clown

Pincher—a three-fingered mechanical claw

Pippa-Luka—Lunar princess from the Moon of Clouds

Proco Haruma—a former general in the royal army

Q&D—the Quattro and Diamond circus

QM or **Quicksilver Messenger**—a long distance communication device

quagga—a type of Plains Zebra, with tan and brown stripes, that went extinct on Earth

RCU—remote control unit

relay looper—a system for moving passenger and freight cars between moons

Rexor—an old male lion

Ripley—a circus boy, younger brother of Elizabelle

Rod Lightning—leader of the Thunder Drummers

Rope Man—one of Mai-Kellina's animal trainers at Yerkoza

Rubicania—mother of King Donovan

Saba—a mother lion

Sammy Stutterfingers—a clown

Sea of Karoo—the deepest ocean on Verdanta

Segonko—a mother skunk

Selena—the name of King Donovan's wife after she became queen (see: Galena)

Seven Moon Circus—a space traveling circus

Shyama—Lunar princess from the Blue Moon

Sparky—a dwarf clown

Spitfire—see Jefferson Spitfire

GLOSSARY

Steele—Dane Steele, animal trainer in the Quattro & Diamond Circus
SunKing—a quagga zebra (see: quagga)
Tambora—a hollow volcano
tambour—the chamber inside the Tambora volcano
Tancreido—counselor to the Arkenstone Kings
Tanji-Moa—worker at Yerkoza
Taroona—see Claire deLuna Taroona
Terry Tripple—a clown
Toberomi ("Big Tee")—owner of Seven Moon Circus
Toolachie—a meadow-dwelling animal that exists only in Empire Luna
Tricka—a half man / half woman circus freak
Tulamarine—the castle where the royal family lives and the Lunar Council meets
V-1—Mai-Kellina's converticopter
Veegee—see view gem
Verdanta—the Green Moon
Vertijet—a backpack that allows its wearer to fly
View-gem—a jewel that can hold recorded information
Yerkoza—a biological research and animal training center; also a reformatory
Zina Zucchini—daughter in the "human cannonball" circus act
Zorino Zucchini—father in the "human cannonball" circus act

FURTHER READING AND EXPLORING

Can the quagga be revived? www.quaggaproject.org

The real Tambora volcano: http://en.wikipedia.org/wiki/Mount_Tambora

Read about circus history & performers:

Circus—Noel Daniel, Editor; contributors: Linda Granfield, Dominique Jando, Fred Dahlinger (original large edition Taschen 2008, condensed edition Barnes & Noble 2009)
Two Hundred Years of the American Circus—Tom Ogden (Facts on File, 1993)
Clown Alley—Bill Ballantine—Little Brown 1982
http://www.flying-trapeze.com/

Circus and carnival slang:

http://www.goodmagic.com/carny/c_a.htm (American circus lingo)
http://www.hobonickels.org/circus.htm
http://circushof.com/glossary.html (International circus hall of fame)

FURTHER READING AND EXPLORING

Circus museums:

http://www.ringling.org/circusmuseums.aspx

http://www.sarasotacircushistory.com/

http://www.barnum-museum.org

http://www.circushistory.org/

http://www.circusworldmuseum.com (Baraboo Wisconsin)

http://www.circusmusic.org

Hot air balloons:

The Joy of Ballooning—George Dennison—Courage 1999

http://www.hotairballoon.com/ (info on balloon festivals)

SPECIAL THANKS

Idea seed: Alexander Patrick
Model for E.H.: Katrina Emily
Editor: Deborah Halverson (deareditor.com)
Story consultants: Mrs. Karen Dee, Gigi Orlowski
Proofreader: Cathy Nanz (nanzscience.com)
Circus logo designer: Bill McCloskey (thewondershop.com)
Illustrator, cover designer: SC Watson (oreganoproductions.com)
Interior text designer: Greg Smith (gsmithdesign.com)
Teacher's Resource Guide developer: Grace Nall
    (www.teachingseasons.com)

This book's text was set in Adobe Garamond, named for French type designer Claude Garamond, though most modern Garamonds are actually more closely based on the designs of Jean Jannon. The display font is Trajan, a typeface based on the chiseled typography found at the base of Trajan's Column, in Rome, Italy.

ABOUT THE AUTHOR
& THE ILLUSTRATOR

Randal R. Morrison, known to friends and young readers as Randy Morrison, was formerly a radio broadcaster. He is now a lawyer and author of books for young readers. A native of Utah who spent part of his childhood in Australia, he now lives in Southern California. He is a member of SCBWI, the Society of Childrens' Book Writers and Illustrators.

S.C. Watson is a freelance illustrator who's been drawing in one form or another since he could pick up a pencil. His interests range from figurative art, science, science fiction, macabre, ancient history, fantasy, fairy tales, philosophy, religion, myth and children's picture books. He lives and works on an island in Washington State's beautiful Salish Sea, surrounded by wild life, hippies and ferries. www.oreganoproductions.com

Made in the USA
San Bernardino, CA
05 January 2014